Morbid Habit

Annie Hauxwell was born in London. She abandoned the law to work as an investigator and now combines this with writing. She lives in a small country town in Australia when not in London. Her career includes prize-winning short crime fiction and professionally produced theatre and film, and her feature screenplays have been optioned in the U.S. and Australia. Her working life has also included stints as a psychiatric nurse, cleaner, sociologist and taxi driver. She is the author of the Catherine Berlin series which includes *In Her Blood* and *A Bitter Taste*.

ALSO BY ANNIE HAUXWELL

In Her Blood
A Bitter Taste

ANNIE HAUXWELL

A Morbid Habit

Penguin Random House is committed to a sustainable future for our business, our readers and our planet. This book is made from Forest Stewardship Council® certified paper.

arrow books

1 3 5 7 9 10 8 6 4 2

Arrow Books
20 Vauxhall Bridge Road
London SW1V 2SA

Arrow Books is part of the Penguin Random House group of companies whose
addresses can be found at global.penguinrandomhouse.com.

Penguin
Random House
UK

Copyright © Annie Hauxwell 2014

Annie Hauxwell has asserted her right to be identified as the author of this Work in
accordance with the Copyright, Designs and Patents Act 1988.

First published by William Heinemann in 2014
First published im paperback by Arrow Books in 2015

www.randomhouse.co.uk

A CIP catalogue record for this book is available from the British Library.

ISBN 9780099590989

Typeset in Adobe Garamond 12.5/16 pt by Palimpsest Book Production Limited,
Falkirk, Stirlingshire

Printed and bound by Clays Ltd, St Ives plc

For Peta

Your own prison you shall not make.

The Thieves' Code

The hands were warm. Soft fingers, but flesh imbued with iron. Squeezing. The small hyoid bone cracked and the tongue, to which it was connected, lolled and protruded from the mouth.

Vertebrae fragmented: one, two, three. Finally the hands relaxed and the limp body slid from their embrace.

The crackle of cellophane was followed by greedy sucking and a fruity scent, which hung in the still air. The sweet wrapper lay where it had been dropped on snow that gleamed blue in the moonlight.

Blood turned to ice and sealed the nostrils.

'Let's go home,' came a whisper.

The victim

Catherine Berlin sat alone gazing at a bank of monitors that each captured a slice of a vast industrial estate in north-west London. Park Royal. Nothing moved except the occasional rat or fox, eyes jaundiced in the floodlights. The earth's frigid crust was cracked, seamed with frost.

Four days until Christmas.

It was the season to be jolly.

Berlin unscrewed the flask of tepid coffee to which she had added a drop of something stronger in a Yuletide gesture. A flicker at one end of the array caught her eye and she watched a white van cruise the perimeter fence, disappearing momentarily from one screen to appear on the next.

When it turned onto a slip road and backed up close to the roller door of warehouse 5B she took the clipboard off the hook to check the delivery and pickup schedule at the warehouse. Nothing listed.

Berlin jiggled the joystick and brought the camera into sharper focus. A thickset man with a pudding-basin haircut and stubble jumped out of the van: white Ford Transit, long wheelbase, high roof, dirty. He strode to the roller door and raised it.

The van backed up and its rear doors opened. Another

man got out. He was also stocky and unshaven, with thick, dark hair that appeared curiously flat on the monochrome screen. They could have been brothers.

The list must be wrong. The computer schedule would be more up to date. Keeping one eye on the screen, Berlin tapped the keyboard and woke up the machine.

With the rear doors of the van open she could see only the men's legs as they moved back and forth between the van and the warehouse. Then the van reversed right into the warehouse and the roller door came down.

The system was slow. The yellow Post-it note with the guest password scrawled on it was crumpled. It took Berlin a couple of tries before she managed to log on. The online schedule finally opened.

By this time the roller door had gone up again, the van had emerged and the brothers were leaning against it, lighting cigarettes. A mixture of dragon's breath and smoke hung over them; a cloud of nonchalance.

Berlin clicked through the complicated spreadsheet. Nothing in it about a pickup or delivery at warehouse 5B.

She reached for the two-way radio but before she could pick it up the door of the control room swung open. Bright light spilled across the console.

She blinked.

A hulking shape filled the doorway. It stepped inside and, as the door swung closed, it resolved into the shape of a man in a heavy-duty weatherproof jacket. Like hers, it was emblazoned with a globe encircled by the words 'Hirst Corporation'. Hirst had the world sewn up. A badge clipped to the lapel of his jacket read 'Supervisor'.

'Where's Raj?' growled the supervisor.

'Sick,' said Berlin. 'I'm the relief.'

The supervisor didn't look relieved. He took a mobile from his pocket. 'No-one fucking told me,' he said.

Berlin glanced back at the monitor.

The supervisor followed her gaze. She indicated the radio.

'I was just going to call it in,' she said.

'Consider it done,' said the supervisor, dialling a number on his mobile. 'What the fuck's going on?' he demanded of whoever answered his call. He turned away from Berlin, listened for a moment, then turned back.

'Are you Catherine Berlin?' he asked.

She nodded.

The supervisor hung up and flicked on the two-way radio clipped to his pocket. 'Get rolling,' he said. 'Now.'

Berlin glanced at the monitor. The two men had dropped their cigarettes and were scrambling to get into the van.

'Listen, Catherine,' said the supervisor.

'Berlin will do,' said Berlin.

'Listen,' said the supervisor, 'whatever you think you might have just seen . . .'

'What I *saw*,' she corrected.

The supervisor regarded her for a moment. He shrugged.

'Look, Berlin,' he said. 'This is just a couple of casuals, like you, knocking off surplus stock to flog down the market. Storemen who'll be out of work after the Christmas rush. Their kids want the latest bloody computer games in their stockings but the bank still expects the mortgage to be paid. Understand?'

Berlin knew all about zero-hours contracts. You had to be available and on call at all hours, without any guarantee of work. When you did work, the pay was strictly by the hour. By the minute. No holiday or sick pay. No other benefits.

The supervisor took a few steps across the tiny room and loomed over her; he had the face and gait of a heavy-weight boxer.

She glanced back at the screens. The van was already disappearing off the last one.

The supervisor gripped the arm of her chair and turned it away from the console. An odd smell of hot tar hung around him, and something else: the rancid scent of a threat. He reached into his pocket.

Berlin stood up.

The supervisor lay fifty quid on the console.

'Have a bit of compassion,' he said.

Berlin walked along the Grand Union Canal towpath. The canal was an historic legacy that ran through the twelve-hundred-acre site. The landscape was a patchwork of abandoned Victorian engineering works and sterile modern units.

Strings of lights sparkled against the black sky, marking the outline of lorries arriving from Eastern Europe. The turbulence as they thundered past rattled her.

The whole place was ringed with mountains of unstable rubble. Cranes swayed in the wind. It was difficult to tell if construction or demolition was in progress.

Berlin made her way to the night-bus stop. The people

mover that had dropped her off at the start of her shift wouldn't be back to collect her, or the Hirst guards from all the other sites, until dawn. She had knocked off early.

A noise behind her made her jump. She tightened her grip on the bag slung across her body and picked up her pace, ignoring the finger of pain that ran up her calf. Her torn Achilles tendon had healed short and left her with a slight limp. It was the least of her problems.

She patted the laptop in her bag. After the fourth burglary she took her computer everywhere. The insurance premiums in her postcode were off the chart.

The bus was approaching. There was only one every hour. She started to run, but lost her footing in a puddle of toxic run-off that had formed black ice. She staggered on and ran into the road in front of the bus. It screeched to a halt. The doors wheezed open.

'Got a death wish?' shouted the driver.

Berlin made her way slowly up the worn stone steps that led to her flat and thought about the supervisor's fifty quid and compassion. The milk of human kindness didn't run freely in her veins – it had some competition there – but she tried not to judge.

It was five in the morning and the occupants of the flats were still sound asleep.

Bar one.

When Berlin reached her landing the door opposite hers opened. Insomnia was a curse she shared with her neighbour Bella, a former dancer in her eighties who fitted the description of a 'theatrical type'.

At any time of the day or night Bella was to be found in full make-up. A willowy beauty when high-kicking at the Windmill Theatre during the war, she remained an imposing sight, even when encased in a woolly hat, fingerless gloves and two tracksuits. Her vanity was legendary. So was her drinking.

Bella had been absent for long periods over the years, 'convalescing', which meant drying out. The cure didn't always take, but after decades of practice Bella had reached an accommodation with her tipple in which they were now on good terms, rather than locked in a doomed passion.

Bella took the carton of milk Berlin had picked up from the twenty-four-hour shop and offered a dazzling smile in return.

'I'll fix you up later,' said Bella.

Berlin nodded. How many times had she heard that?

Bella peered at her. 'Rough night?' she enquired.

'It had its moments,' said Berlin, as she worked her way through the three locks that now secured her front door.

'Come in for a hot toddy,' said Bella. 'A Scotch is what the doctor ordered.'

Bella's doctor invariably prescribed strong spirits.

'Thanks, but not this morning, Bella,' said Berlin. 'I'm knackered.'

Bella waved cheerio and retreated.

Berlin's Christmas decorations rustled in the draught as she closed the door. The streamers and paper bells were a riot of colour in defiance of contemporary minimalism.

The small flat, a studio in modern parlance, was freezing. She turned on the central heating and went straight to the bathroom. The cabinet held something that would deliver a little more than whisky.

Addicted to heroin since the eighties, Berlin was now on a programme that provided her with a month's supply of an opioid replacement, buprenorphine. Before the regime change she'd been on the old Home Office register, which meant her doctor could give her a pure daily maintenance dose of the real thing.

But the register had long been archived, and with it people like Berlin – remnants of a discredited past. At the age of fifty-seven she sometimes felt that she was a living embodiment of the history of drug policy.

It was this, a sense that she was dependent on the whims of a capricious state, that fired her recent determination to shatter the confines of addiction. That, and her encounter with the vicious nature of those controlling the illegal trade.

When it came to drugs, the only thing that never changed was the street. She was grateful she wasn't out there.

She slipped the bupe under her tongue and lay down on the sofa. It would take a few minutes to dissolve and then be absorbed straight into her bloodstream.

The taste was bitter.

Just before the miserable dawn broke over Park Royal the supervisor made his way back to the control room. He cursed when he saw the fifty quid still lying on the console. It was just his luck.

2

Major Alexander Sergeevich Utkin of the Moscow Criminal Investigation Department stood just beyond the arc of illumination provided by the floodlights. He watched the listless *militsya* mill around; he corrected himself: the *politsya*.

The name may have changed, but the smoking, ball-scratching dullards trampling his crime scene remained the same. The generator sputtered and the lights flickered. The officers appeared to be moving like puppets.

It was no trick of the light. Utkin wished he could shake off the impression that the workforce of the entire Russian state behaved in the same fashion: no-one made a move without an order. He corrected himself: nobody made an *official* move without an order. There was plenty of action behind the scenes.

A female officer gave the generator a practised kick and it resumed normal operation. Utkin trudged into the pool of light. He was barely acknowledged. The new name had brought with it a new structure to law enforcement: redundancies and a 'Stop Corruption' helpline.

The consequent changes had been profound: instead of an over-manned, lazy and corrupt political tool, they had become an under-manned, lazy and corrupt political tool.

The body of a man – middle-aged, apparently of Russian ethnicity, nice suit – lay in a rubbish-strewn alley in an area of dubious reputation. What had he been doing there? Pissing? Buying drugs or a woman? There were a number of nightclubs nearby. Wallet, watch, rings: long gone. The corpse could have been there for hours or days. It would have to be thawed out slowly for the autopsy.

Nothing special, except he had been strangled.

This type of homicide was surprisingly rare in a city of twelve million: women were the usual victims of strangulation, by their partners, their pimps or their customers. Men were stabbed, shot or bludgeoned.

Why did the dead wait until dark to reveal themselves? Perhaps they were too embarrassed to be found in the cold light of day.

A police car was parked across one end of the alley.

'Sergeant,' called Utkin.

The sergeant extracted himself from the warmth of the vehicle.

'I want a sweep. Everything collected and bagged.'

The sergeant glanced meaningfully at the litter strewn from one end of the alley to the other.

'Everything,' said Utkin.

Yuri swung his legs out of bed and reached for his cigarettes. He lit one for himself, and one for Maryna. She propped herself up on an elbow and took it. He was sweating like a pig. All Moscow buildings were over-heated in winter. Everyone was soft now. He was a case in point.

Yuri was aware of Maryna watching his back. It was the only time she did. He lived with the expectation that one day she would plunge a knife into it. He realised that, despite the heat, now he was shivering.

'There was no other way, Yuri,' said Maryna.

She could read his mind.

Yuri gazed down at his thin, hairy legs. His skin was grey, the sheets were grey; outside, the sky would be leaden. He took a deep drag on his cigarette.

Maryna touched his shoulder. He turned to her, but he was too late. She was already getting out of bed. He closed his eyes and listened to her dress, brush her hair and snap the little grips that held it in place. All with such resolve.

Maryna had lost her beloved older brother to Chechen separatists during the siege of Grozny; they had dragged him from the tank he commanded and cut off his head. Then her father had drunk himself to death, mourning his only son.

Grief drove Maryna's calculated, murderous rage. And she had driven Yuri too, to murder. They hadn't used their own hands, of course. Yuri had arranged it, making sure he minimised the risks associated with using a third party. The important thing was never to make yourself vulnerable. He had lived by this principle. Until he met Maryna.

Her devotion to the motherland was real; she believed in the new Russia. It was the only Russia she knew. Yuri had a longer memory. Maryna's allegiance was to the ideal of a powerful, respected nation, secure in the integrity of its lands and traditions.

Yuri's allegiance was to himself. He was motivated not by the interests of his country, but by desire.

Maryna came over and kissed the top of his head. 'It had to be done, Yuri,' she said.

'We broke the law,' he said.

'It wasn't illegal,' said Maryna. 'The operation was authorised at the highest level.'

'I'm not talking about that,' said Yuri. 'Misha was different. That wasn't authorised at any level.'

Maryna stepped back abruptly. 'Why is it so different?' she said. 'He was a threat. It's not a crime to liquidate an enemy.'

She had taken her husband's betrayal personally; at first she had wanted to expose him, to hand him over to the authorities. But these things always carried a taint: guilt by association. Questions would be asked. Her authority would be undermined. She was ambitious, not just for herself, but for her country. This devotion would be wasted.

They had decided to deal with it themselves.

Yuri was nearly fifty. Perhaps it was a sense of his own mortality that had given rise to these qualms; life expectancy for Russian men was sixty-four. For women it was seventy-six. Maryna could look forward to a good forty years. But how long was he going to last? He had been raised an atheist in the Soviet Union, but belief was making a comeback. Perhaps he should go to church.

He stubbed out his cigarette. 'I have to go,' he said. 'I'm expected at home.'

'You promised me there would be no loose ends,' said Maryna.

'A promise I intend to keep,' said Yuri. He had a bad feeling that there would be other loose ends to deal with; he'd been a policeman too long not to recognise the pattern. When it came to murder, there was always a problem. Dispose of it and you were safe. Until the next time.

He reached for her, but she shrugged him off. The thought of losing her made him feel giddy, nauseous.

Yuri retrieved his crumpled uniform from the floor.

3

Berlin was woken by the insistent drone of her mobile. She checked the display and picked up.

'Hello,' she said.

'Ms Berlin, I'm calling to confirm your shift at the Park Royal site tonight,' said the woman, her tone brisk.

Berlin didn't respond.

'Ms Berlin, may I remind you that Hirst is the world's leading international security solutions group. They control many important contracts.'

It was true. Hirst liked to boast they ran global 'end-to-end' operations. They delivered payrolls, prisoners and close protection; they guarded everything from nuclear installations to borders, provided logistics in war zones, deployed surveillance systems. They also managed compliance, regulatory and fraud investigations.

Hirst had nearly a million employees in one hundred and twenty-five countries and she would never work for them again.

'Are you reading from the brochure?' said Berlin.

'Are you refusing a shift?' said the woman. 'Because if you are, we'll have no choice but to take you off our books.'

'Merry Christmas,' said Berlin. She hung up.

She rolled off the couch and put the kettle on. Christmas was looming and she was out of a job.

Summer had been torrid; her one and only foray into matrimonial work had just about finished her as an investigator, let alone nearly ended her life. Her response since had been to work night shifts, guarding empty office buildings and deserted industrial estates. The pay was poor, but the absence of other human beings was a bonus.

Now it looked like it was going to be a long, hard winter. She had bills that were overdue, and more to come. *Well done, Berlin*, she thought as she poured a huge mug of coffee.

It wouldn't be so bad if she could take comfort in the thought that she had the moral high ground. That option wasn't available. She had walked away because she had been treated like a fool.

The one thing she couldn't stand was someone telling her fairy stories. The supervisor had lied.

4

Donald Fagan scratched at his stubble. He'd been up all night and now he was going to be working all day. At the end of it he could look forward to a long drive home and a frigid glare from his wife. She said she didn't know who he was any more. Which was lucky for her, really.

He barely had the energy to clasp his phone to his ear. He laid it on the dashboard of the old Audi, in which he spent most of his time, one way or another. It was reliable, unexceptional and fast when it had to be. Qualities he emulated.

'What does she know?' said his boss through the phone's distorting speaker.

'She doesn't *know* anything. She saw something,' said Fagan. 'She's casual night shift. It was bad luck, that's all. Raj was sick and—'

'No.' His boss cut him off. 'It was bad management. So who's she working for?'

'Er, Hirst,' said Fagan.

'Really, Fagan,' said his boss. The disdain was palpable.

Fagan imagined his boss sitting somewhere warm. Neat and clean. Manicured. It didn't matter what Fagan did, he was aware that he always looked as if he needed a good wash. His mum used to say he had been born with dirt under his fingernails.

He cleared his throat to suppress a snarl. 'There's nothing to indicate she's involved with another outfit,' he said.

'Look at her background,' said his boss, in the tone you would use with an errant child. 'Why would someone like that work as a security guard?'

Fagan knew he was going to take the fall if this operation went south. 'If that was the case she would have kept the money,' he argued. 'So we wouldn't catch on.'

'Perhaps,' said his boss. 'This relationship is important, Fagan. No mistakes. So find out.'

The line went dead.

5

Berlin hesitated to get in touch with old clients. If she put out feelers and made herself available there might be work after the New Year, but it wasn't great timing: she was struggling to break the habit of a lifetime. It was amazing how much energy it took *not* to do something. On the other hand, it might do her good to get back into the fray.

Festive occasions often resulted in sexual harassment complaints; frauds came to light when employees failed to return from Christmas holidays; and in the fallout from seasonal family punch-ups, pissed-off spouses suddenly felt compelled, in the public interest, to expose the scams and rip-offs their partners were running.

Management, or their insurers, or their lawyers, would call on Berlin to investigate, anticipating hefty claims, litigation or bad publicity – or all three. She would conduct an impartial enquiry and then lay out their risks and the options available to manage them: settle, sack or sanction.

Other people's fuck-ups had been her bread and butter for more than twenty years. But she was sick of becoming embroiled in messy lives while her own turned to shit.

There was all that, and then there was the cupboard, which was bare.

At five o'clock it was dark again. She'd been pondering her options most of the day and was sick of it. In the absence of a job to go to, the pub seemed the best bet. She grabbed her coat and was about to leave when someone knocked at the door.

She opened it to a courier, cradling a beautiful Yule log wrapped in cellophane.

'Catherine Berlin?' asked the courier.

She nodded. He thrust a digital tablet and a stylus at her.

'Sign here,' he said. She did as she was told and handed it back. The courier thrust the snowy log, resplendent with robins, holly and ribbon, into her arms and turned to leave. There was no card.

'Hang on!' called Berlin. 'Who's it from?'

He stopped, checked the tablet and shrugged.

'Must be a secret admirer,' he said, and kept going.

The Approach Tavern was heaving with Christmas shoppers unable to face the crush and the relentless jingle of sleigh bells for a moment longer.

The barmaid placed a double Scotch on the bar in front of Berlin.

'Put it on my slate,' Berlin said.

The barmaid glanced at her guv'nor, who frowned and nodded. Berlin raised her glass to him; he owed her a lot more than a few bloody drinks – she had tracked down his business partner, who was also his father-in-law, after he absconded with the previous, much younger, barmaid and a month's takings.

The police had decided it was a civil dispute and wouldn't get involved. Berlin had seen a once-in-a-lifetime opportunity to bank a pub landlord.

'Cheers.' She glanced around, looking for a seat, and saw Magnus Nkonde waggling his empty glass at her. She returned to the bar.

Berlin slid into the booth opposite Magnus and put a Scotch on the table in front of him.

'How are you, Magnus?' she said.

'Still fighting the good fight, old darling,' he said. 'Merry fucking Christmas.' He raised his glass and downed the double. Berlin did likewise.

Magnus Nkonde was a journalist who preferred the title 'investigative reporter' to 'scum-sucking bottom-feeder', which was how he had once been described in Parliament. Foreign correspondent for a left-leaning newspaper during the eighties, he was fortuitously on the spot when the Berlin Wall came down.

Rumour had it that he had been given a heads-up by a cleaner in the household of Erich Honecker, the GDR chief. When asked if this was true, Magnus had darkly observed that 'good help is hard to find.'

He did everything possible to conform to the caricature of the boozy old-school muckraker, but his contacts were second to none and his bulbous, vein-flecked nose could smell a political rat a mile away.

In London, they were usually much closer.

Magnus claimed Maasai warrior blood, on his mother's side. It was well hidden by his upbringing in St Albans, where his father had been Dean of the cathedral. Magnus had certainly once had the looks; he retained the height, but the muscle had turned to flab and gone south.

Berlin and Magnus lived at different ends of the manor – he in a gentrified terrace, she in a former council flat – but were united in appreciation of their local, the Approach.

The din around them rose a notch as the patrons took up the refrain of 'Silent Night'. Berlin relaxed in the warm fug of Christmas cheer. Magnus joined in with the carol singers. His sonorous bass creaked, but remained in tune. His stint in the choir had paid off.

Magnus's druncle performance didn't fool Berlin. 'How's business?' she asked.

'And ye shall know the truth, and the truth shall make you free,' declared Magnus. 'But unfortunately, my dear, the Fourth Estate has been routed – hijacked by a bunch of touchy B-list celebs and nervous politicians who don't want their dirty habits and scurrilous ways exposed to public scrutiny.'

Magnus was now a 'stringer'. Sacked six months ago by his newspaper, *The Sentinel*, following his conviction for paying a public official for information, he was now forced to prowl the corridors of power, looking for stories to sell. Accordingly, he spent most of his time cadging drinks.

Berlin was sympathetic. Her own profession often relied on buying information. It was a commodity, like any other, and sources were not always motivated simply by cash. Going up against powerful interests often involved a catastrophic loss of income, broken legs – or worse.

Berlin recalled one salutary case of a private investigator who had tried to expose police corruption and ended up with an axe buried in his head. Given the risk to one's personal well-being, an individual could hardly be blamed for trying to maintain a healthy bank balance.

'Things are quiet, then?' she asked.

'Not a fucking dicky bird,' he said, rueful. 'Anything come your way?'

Berlin took pity on him. At a more pragmatic level, she also respected the old adage 'one good turn deserves another'. Magnus had proved handy in the past, and might do so again one of these days. That, and she was curious.

'I may have something,' she said. 'Although it could be nothing.'

Magnus perked up. 'My round,' he said.

Magnus listened attentively to her tale about the unscheduled appearance of the van at warehouse 5B. She described the vehicle and the men in it, and the subsequent attempt to bribe her.

'This bloke wasn't happy to see me. He was big,' she said. 'So I wasn't inclined to ask a lot of questions.'

Magnus was unimpressed. 'Why would I be interested in a bit of seasonal pilfering?' he said. 'It's hardly front-page stuff.'

'Because they weren't nicking anything,' said Berlin.

'What were they doing?'

'They were unloading something.'

'How do you know?' asked Magnus. 'You said the van backed into the warehouse.'

Berlin knocked back the dregs of her Scotch. 'Because when it drove away, it was sitting much higher on its axles.'

'Lighter,' said Magnus.

'Exactly,' said Berlin. 'They weren't taking stuff out, they were putting stuff in. So what was it? More to the point, why lie about it?'

The pub door swung shut behind Berlin, abruptly cutting off the warmth, light and good cheer. She confronted the black evening and biting wind. At least she had left Magnus happy. It was a Christmas gift. Something to distract him during the long, lonely hours of the holiday. And it hadn't cost her a penny. Just her job.

Tugging her black woolly hat down over her straggly blonde locks and turning up her coat collar, she set off towards Roman Road. Her Peacekeeper boots gave her an extra couple of inches. An Armament Systems and Procedures telescopic baton in her pocket gave her extra confidence.

Lenny, her father, had always said you can't fatten thoroughbreds. Her mother had lived in hope that she would 'fill out'. Berlin had disappointed her in so many ways.

But her grandfather Zayde, Lenny's father, never judged. When he stood beside her, she was defiant. When he taught her to swear in Yiddish, her mother despaired. When she mimicked his surly silences, Lenny warned her that Zayde wasn't playing: he mourned for what he had lost. But he never told her what it was.

Berlin would run to find Zayde's things; she would bring his braces, his shaving mug, his watch, and drop them in his lap. Then he'd smile. That was it. His smile. She had brought it back.

Crossing the road, Berlin took the steps down to the canal. The path was deserted, which was how she liked it; no dog walkers or cyclists to disrupt the rhythm of her stride or the flow of her thoughts. Which inevitably turned to one thing.

Addiction was as dark and menacing as the dirty water beside her. Its grip was as cold. But the promise of heroin was relief. It offered respite from the self. Berlin feared that if she truly abandoned it she would be embarking on a life of regret and longing that would be just as onerous.

She wasn't sure that she was ready to look grief in the eye.

6

Magnus sat in the cabmen's shelter in Russell Square, munching on a sausage sandwich. He wasn't a cab driver but he was tolerated, and at this time of night, if he required a good, hot, strong cup of tea and a bit of peace and quiet, this was the place for it. The green timber shelter with its shingle roof was no bigger than a garden shed, which it resembled. It was a Victorian monument to philanthropy.

Magnus wasn't one for mourning the good old days, which struck him as invariably awful, but there was no doubt the nineteenth century had been a golden age for newspapers: London alone had had fifty-two.

Chagrined by the government's vendetta against journalists, Magnus had been forced to implement sordid cloak-and-dagger methods to allay the fears of potential sources.

These days it was increasingly difficult to get the cooperation of people with access to information that in Magnus's opinion should be in the public domain. The owner of a vehicle, for example. It had to be done in writing, on a special form, and you had to have 'reasonable cause'.

Being a nosy bastard wasn't regarded as reasonable any more. It all took bloody ages.

A quick phone call would no longer suffice; middlemen had to be involved, so-called 'cut-outs'. Meetings had to be held in places where there were no cameras, and there were fewer and fewer of those. The biggest impact of course had been on price, which – unsurprisingly – had shot up. Berlin had provided the van's number. Now it was up to him.

A bleary-eyed cabbie wandered into the shelter and ordered a bacon sandwich with brown sauce.

Magnus wiped the grease from his chin with his less-than-snowy-white handkerchief and vacated his place.

The cabbie sat down in it, opened his newspaper and moved Magnus's plate. Beneath it was a fifty-quid note and a piece of paper with a vehicle registration number on it.

The cabbie slipped them both into his pocket.

Magnus left the shelter with a spring in his step. Game on.

Fagan was finally on his way home. But instead of turning off to Chigwell, he kept going around the Fulwell Cross roundabout and took the road to Fairlop Waters. It was as if the car had a will of its own.

The transition from suburb to green belt was abrupt. Fields opened up on either side of the road, expanses of darkness blurred at the edges by the glow of the city.

He pulled into the deserted car park beside the lake and switched off the motor. The moonless night was still. A thin mist drifted across the water, the frost on the jetty iridescent in the sulphur glow of security lights.

Fagan reached into the glovebox and retrieved his kit from beneath the false bottom he'd installed.

The ritual of preparing a pipe filled him with sweet anticipation. He would limit himself to a small toke, using just a thumbnail of the sticky resin so he could get a decent night's sleep when he got home. On empty roads it was an easy ten-minute drive and would pose no problems.

Opium was a habit he'd picked up when serving in Afghanistan, where it was cheaper and more readily available than a pint of bitter or a bar of chocolate.

The small bowl glowed, and he inhaled deeply.

If this business went pear-shaped, he wouldn't be able to shoot his way out of trouble. That was the problem with being a civilian. No-one had your back.

Hirst had brought him into this operation for his size, he knew that. A bit of muscle was always handy. But he'd been kept on for his connections and his other more esoteric skills.

Smoke seeped into his lungs and stress slipped away.

Once again he shed a skin that was too tight.

7

Berlin arrived home just before dawn, harbouring the hope that she'd tired herself out enough to be able to sleep. She dropped her bag as soon as she was through the front door and made straight for the Advent calendar on the wall. It wasn't really her sort of thing, but Bella had given it to her and she didn't like to offend. She popped open the little flap marked '22' and devoured the chocolate behind it.

The grins of the elves that guarded each of the three remaining doors seemed to taunt her, so after a moment's consideration she opened those marked '23' and '24'. The illicit chocolate was all the more delicious.

Now I'm two days ahead of myself, she thought. It was a relief, as she had no idea how she was going to fill them.

The Yule log in the middle of the table glowed when she turned on the standard lamp. It was a nice thought on the part of whoever had sent it, even if it had been one of dozens dispatched by an erstwhile corporate client, an insurance company or a big legal firm – someone she'd worked for in what seemed like an increasingly remote past.

A noise outside drew her back to the front door. She

glanced through the spyhole at the gloomy landing; it was too early for the postman and Bella didn't seem to be around. The sound of scuffling came from the stairwell, which was beyond the spyhole's range.

Berlin opened her front door and peered out. She had only the merest impression of a man, and then a forehead coming towards her before it connected with a sharp crack.

A few seconds later she came round on the floor, aware of an intense pain in her ribs. Someone was kicking her. Her weak grunts of protest were drowned by a blood-curdling cry as Bella scuttled across the landing, brandishing a carving knife.

Berlin's startled assailant ran for it. Another man came running out of the flat, ducked Bella's knife and took off down the stairs. He was clutching Berlin's bag. The one she always carefully stowed her computer in, in case she was burgled.

Bella poured Berlin a Scotch. She sipped it, wincing.

'Want me to call the police, love?' asked Bella.

Berlin shook her head. Both men were wearing hoodies and bandanas. She wasn't the local station's favourite person, either.

Bella frowned at the state of Berlin's face. 'Better do something about that,' she said. 'It will definitely ruin your good looks.'

Before Berlin could protest she placed her fingers either side of the broken nose and shoved. There was a bone-crunching sound. Berlin yelped, her eyes watering with the shock.

'There,' said Bella, stepping back to admire her handiwork. 'It's straighter than it was before.'

'Jesus,' mumbled Berlin. 'Those shits were up and about early.'

'Maybe they thought you were a dealer, love,' said Bella.

Berlin got to her feet and handed Bella her glass.

'Thanks, Bella,' she said. 'I owe you.'

Berlin crossed the landing, went inside and kicked the door shut behind her. She grabbed a packet of frozen peas from the fridge, lay down on the sofa and plonked them on her nose, ignoring the smirking elves.

They hadn't got much, thanks to Bella. Not that there was much left to get. Her computer had been in the bag, but everything was backed up online. It was just the bloody inconvenience of it.

Her head was throbbing. She was tempted to pop a couple of extra bupes. But that would leave her short at the end of the month, and the prospect of two days without pharmaceutical support wasn't appealing.

Which led her to wonder how realistic it was to aspire to being drug-free for the rest of her life.

She could practically hear the elves cracking up: who was she kidding? She couldn't even resist chocolate.

8

Berlin was woken by a dribble of cold water running down her neck: the peas had defrosted. Late afternoon, but it was already dark again.

She switched on the radio and put the kettle on. There were wars in all the usual places; pensioners were choosing between eating and heating; gay-rights activists had stormed the prime minister's lunch for the Russian president and his delegation. Five arrests and disruption to traffic.

Berlin shuffled into the bathroom: the creature that stared back from the cabinet mirror would have won a prize at Halloween, but the look just didn't work for Christmas. Too bad. Cinders was determined to go to the ball.

The one email invitation she had gladly accepted was from Del. She had promised him she would put in an appearance at his firm's Christmas party, although this wasn't quite the appearance she had intended.

Delroy Jacobs had stepped up for her more than once over the years. They had worked together, chasing loan sharks for a notoriously inept government agency. The agency's incompetence hadn't made the job any less dangerous. They rarely managed to get together these days. Del was now a family man and out of the operational side, but Berlin knew he missed the street. And she missed him.

The circulating waiter offered caviar on black bread, which Berlin gratefully accepted. Del had recently been promoted to a senior management position at Burghley & Associates, a boutique intelligence firm that was flourishing.

Apart from servicing the pressing needs of private clients for information about their competitors, the public sector market for intelligence services was booming. Outsourcing had become the rule, rather than the exception, as the government relentlessly pursued 'value for money'.

Not that Burghley was cheap. They worked at the opposite end of the market from Hirst; they were very discreet, and entirely focused on intelligence.

Berlin scanned the room. It was all very cosy. Experienced government workers who had been made redundant, or who had quit because of continual budget cuts, set up their own outfit, such as this one. They took their business knowledge and their contacts with them, and won the contracts that were necessary to fill the gaps they'd left.

Surveillance, covert operations, analysis: trade craft had succumbed to market forces. Rendition appeared on invoices as 'transport and logistics'. The dissolution of the boundary between national security and enterprise was so well advanced as to be invisible.

Del handed Berlin a glass of champagne. 'You look like you could use a drink,' he said.

'Can you remember a time when I didn't?' said Berlin.

Del gently lifted the dark glasses from the bridge of her nose. 'Ouch,' he sympathised. 'Anything I can do?'

'Get me something stronger,' she said.

Del returned with a single malt. Berlin took the glass and raised it in a toast. 'Here's to capitalism,' she said.

Del ignored the jibe. 'So are you really working for Hirst?' he asked.

'Touché.'

'You spend your nights staring at screens?' said Del.

'Needs must, Delroy,' she said.

'Bullshit,' he retorted. 'What are you really up to?'

Del was her oldest – some would say her only – friend. She let him get away with it.

'May I remind you,' she said, 'That Hirst is the world's leading international security solutions group. They control many important contracts.'

Del laughed. 'You mean, you can creep around in the dark and not have to deal with the duplicitous, fucked-up human race.'

'Present company excepted,' she said. 'How are Linda and baby Emma?'

'They're fine, thanks. We keep telling Emma that her fairy godmother really does exist and one of these days she'll appear.'

'I've been meaning to come over, Del, but you know how it is . . . Anyway, I'm not working for Hirst any more. I'm joining the dole queue.' She held out her glass for a refill. 'So don't hold back.'

*

Fagan stood at the bottom of his garden, smoking. He speed-dialled a number on his mobile and waited, glancing up at his sons' bedroom windows. A flickering glow played across both of them. Computer games. Finally, his call was answered.

'She's not working for anyone else,' he said.

'Why are you so sure?' said his boss.

'It looks like she's handing it off,' said Fagan.

'Don't tell me she's gone to the police,' came the response.

'Worse,' said Fagan. 'She met with a reporter.'

There was a silence. Fagan took a drag on his cigarette and waited.

'This could compromise the business,' said his boss.

'Ours or theirs?' said Fagan. 'I mean, we're just keeping an eye on things, doing them a favour.'

'We're building a strategic relationship,' said his boss.

If that's what you want to call it, thought Fagan. Protecting the warehouse would give Hirst a lot of leverage: big government contracts were up for grabs and the company would have the inside running in future if they, meaning the subcontractor, meaning him, got this right.

'There's a job scheduled, to move the commercial partnership forward. In a useful location.'

'That's up to the legal eagles. It's not my end.'

'I want you to make it your end,' said his boss. 'We can deal with this risk by removing it temporarily. But in the worst case scenario it's better suited to a permanent solution.'

The mention of a permanent solution made Fagan uneasy. He preferred containment. Escalation often led to more problems than it solved. These people were always ready to embrace the quick and dirty solution, because they weren't at the pointy end. Which could get messy.

'Fagan?' said his boss. 'The reporter?'

'Yeah. I'll sort it.'

Fagan looked up. Both his sons were at their windows, staring down at him. Even at this distance and in the dark he could see their pale, impassive faces watching him, as if he were something feral that had wandered in, unbidden. A fox fouling the neat lawn.

The Swiss Re building, known universally as the Gherkin, shimmered against the orange glow of London's night sky. Del and Berlin weaved their way through the knots of well-oiled City types in Santa Claus hats who were clustered around its base, suffering the cold for a smoke. Cigars and Eastern European accents were in evidence.

The Underground was closed and the competition for cabs was fierce, but a taxi drew up beside them as if on cue. They leapt in, ignoring the cries of protest from a bunch of traders wearing reindeer antlers.

'Bethnal Green, then Plaistow, mate,' Del directed the driver. The cab did an illegal U-turn and headed east.

'Do you have to work tomorrow?' said Berlin. She was anticipating the sore head that would complement her aching face. When would she learn?

'Yeah,' said Del. 'Although it's reasonably quiet this time of year.'

'Anything interesting on?' said Berlin.

'Nah. Not really,' said Del, yawning. 'We're doing an audit on the export of licensable goods for a parliamentary subcommittee.'

'What's that all about?' said Berlin.

'The usual,' said Del. 'Lawyers, guns and money.' He yawned again. Berlin chuckled.

'I'm going to Hamleys tomorrow to do some shopping,' said Del, showing more enthusiasm.

'Hamleys?' said Berlin. 'And I see you're buying your bespoke suits in Savile Row these days, too.'

Del looked sheepish. 'Needs must,' he said. 'What are you doing this year?'

'Spending it with the ghost of Christmas past,' said Berlin.

The cab dropped Berlin outside her flats and took off again for Plaistow. Del waved a cheery goodbye through the back window. She waved back, but felt uneasy. Something wasn't right.

She glanced around. The road was deserted. There were no shadows hovering, no-one had been dogging her footsteps. Her paranoia was going into overdrive. Being mugged on your own doorstep can do that to you.

Halfway up the stairs to her flat she realised that the cabbie hadn't switched his meter on. It was unusual, but explained her anxiety. Just a driver on the dodge.

One day she would rein in her suspicious nature.

One day.

9

Berlin woke to the sound of a door slamming and an argument somewhere in the flats. Her mobile flashed: she had slept through a call. Her head throbbed, but a night out with Del had done her good. The headache was worth it.

The missed call was from Magnus.

First, she needed coffee. She put the phone down again.

She wanted to ring Del, too, and find out what had happened with the cabbie. And she'd forgotten to ask him if he sent the Yule log. He tried to keep his sentimental side hidden, but you only had to see him with his daughter to know he was a pushover.

Just as the kettle boiled her phone rang. It was Del.

'I was about to call you,' she said. 'What happened—'

'Berlin, listen,' Del interrupted. 'I've got a job for you. It just came in.'

'Wait, what?' said Berlin.

'Wake up,' said Del. 'The rest of us have been at work for hours. I'm trying to get out of here and down to Hamleys. So are you interested or not?'

He sounded a bit short, but then he hadn't had the benefit of sleeping off his hangover.

'Why isn't one of your people doing it?' she asked.

'Your particular talents are required,' Del replied.

It wasn't unusual for a firm like Del's to use trusted subcontractors, but it was the first time they'd called on her.

'You mean everyone with a life has already gone for the holidays,' said Berlin. 'You're desperate.'

'Come on, Berlin,' said Del. 'The arrangements have all been made. Apparently the investigator the client had booked cancelled on them at the last minute.'

'So who's the client?' she said.

'I can't tell you. It's commercial-in-confidence.'

Berlin sighed. Del was so damn straight.

'Look,' he said. 'It's someone you've worked with before. Okay?'

Berlin knew Del wouldn't lie to her. 'Okay. What is it?' she asked. It would probably be a petty meltdown at a Christmas party: a blow-up sex doll at the office lunch or a sex toy sneaked into someone's bag for their spouse to find. Stress, bullying, harassment. Jolly japes.

'It's due diligence,' said Del.

Berlin was surprised. She poured boiling water onto the last of the Kenyan Arabica.

'When?' she asked.

'Tomorrow,' said Del.

She paused. The aroma of the coffee soothed her sore nose; with a decent corporate job she would be able to stock up on more. And on ten-year-old Talisker.

'What's the rush?' she said. 'Tomorrow is Christmas Eve.'

'Not where you're going,' said Del.

10

Moscow. Candy-striped cathedrals with gold cupolas, sinister men in fur hats drinking vodka, Gorky Park, nesting dolls and spies. Berlin recalled her grandfather's muttered 'Cossacks', and added this to the impressionistic list.

The flood of Russian money into London had become a tsunami since the late nineties. The oligarchs were beloved by estate agents flogging mansions in Mayfair, commercial lawyers flogging writs in the Royal Courts of Justice, and the Square Mile flogging complex revenue shelters.

The émigrés loved the tax regime, the public schools and the police. London was safe. Unless your name was Litvinenko, Perepilichny or Gorbuntsov.

A clerk from Burghley arrived a couple of hours later with a new tablet-style computer and a standard forty-eight-page confidentiality agreement, which she signed without reading; it would just insist she kept her mouth shut.

The clerk took a photo of Berlin for her Russian visa application, which would be accompanied by a letter of invitation, an essential visa support document. The visa would be lodged in her British passport, which she had always kept up to date as it was useful for ID. She handed it over. The clerk was very apologetic about the fact that she would have to collect it herself at the Russian visa centre in the morning.

Anything was possible if you had the budget.

Berlin fired up the tablet and downloaded her online backup. She hadn't used a tablet before, but this one had a singular advantage: it would fit into one of her voluminous coat pockets. No bag to be snatched.

While her backup was coming she stared at the single folder already displayed on the tablet's home screen. It contained her instructions, details about the subject of the due diligence, and the arrangements: flights, hotel and interpreter.

Her fingers hesitated. She hadn't ventured abroad since roaming the hippy trail in the eighties. Her memory of those trips, and that's exactly what they were, was murky.

Travelling with heroin, or just using abroad, had become difficult and dangerous once the 'war on drugs' kicked off, and so travel had dropped off her agenda. It wasn't the only sacrifice she had made in order to manage her addiction.

The cursor blinked beside the folder icon. Berlin reminded herself there was no good reason to refuse this assignment. Her withdrawal was controlled by a perfectly legal pharmaceutical, of which she had an ample supply. She had undertaken dozens of similar enquiries over the years; it was good, clean, straightforward commercial work. It was just that this time it was in Moscow.

A ping alerted her to an email. It advised that an

advance for expenses had already been paid into her bank account. The fee for service would be paid promptly on delivery of her final report.

She tapped the folder icon.

Instructions

To interview, obtain and collate information in relation to MIKHAIL PETROVICH GERASIMOV in order to perform effective due diligence on Mr Gerasimov as a potential business partner, with particular reference to Section 7 of the Bribery Act 2010, whereby a commercial organisation may be committing an offence if it fails to prevent persons associated with it from bribing another person on their behalf.

The Act provides a defence to Section 7 if it can prove it had adequate procedures in place to prevent persons associated with it from engaging in bribery.

The conduct of due diligence on those persons will assist in meeting that standard.

It was an arse-covering exercise. A UK firm wanted to do business with a Russian, or in Russia, where business was synonymous with bribes. No doubt Del couldn't disclose the identity of the firm because of the potential for insider trading: it was a listed company. News of potential deals in Russia could affect the share price.

When Berlin had asked Del why they hadn't instructed a Russian investigator to do the job he'd laughed and said that they would have had to do due diligence on them first. It made sense.

Del had pulled an analyst's briefing off the Burghley

database and included it for Berlin's edification. It covered the current political, diplomatic and economic relationship between Russia and the United Kingdom. She was interested in how they would characterise the murders, attempted murders and unresolved deaths of various Russian businessmen that had occurred on British soil.

The language was typically neutral.

Executive Summary

Concern has been expressed in relation to the transparency of commercial operations and standards of governance in the Commonwealth of Independent States, and, in particular, Russia's reach beyond its borders.

The Chancellor of the Exchequer welcomes investment from non-EU citizens at a minimum of one million pounds, committed for no less than three years. Such investment brings certain entitlements.

Russian citizens represent about a quarter of all those obtaining UK residency visas by this route. There is usually no enquiry into the source of the capital funds. Russians, and citizens of other members of the CIS, have also been granted political asylum in the UK.

The apparent tension between these positions is symptomatic of tension in the bilateral relationship.

Russia is the UK's fastest-growing export market.

The upshot was that the relationship between Whitehall and the Kremlin was fraught. Something that Berlin understood. There was a lot of money to be made, and money was the lifeblood of the City of London.

The Executive Summary went on to refer to the current session of the Intergovernmental Steering Committee on Trade and Investment in the UK and Russia. Talks were being held in London, involving various levels of both governments. They were complex, and deals potentially worth hundreds of millions of pounds were at stake. Discussions were expected to last into the New Year.

Bars and clubs all over the capital would be celebrating a truly festive season.

Berlin had a strong track record in financial investigations and good cognitive interviewing skills. She knew how to deal with snotty bankers and captains of industry. Unlike most lawyers, she understood the difference between taking a statement and conducting an interview. Unlike most coppers, and former coppers, she didn't approach everyone as if they were a suspect.

Although the interpreter might stand between her and the subject, the techniques of forensic linguistics would still offer an insight. She was well qualified for the job, but the Russian angle made her nervous. She went to the wardrobe and dragged out her business suit to see if it needed cleaning.

On the top shelf was an old shoebox she hadn't touched for years.

The grainy black-and-white photos still bore scorch marks where her mum had tried to burn them. Berlin, a teenager at the time, had had an adolescent's skill at detecting parental lies. When she had asked what her mother was doing, Peggy had told her it was none of her concern. A red rag to a bull.

The minute her mother turned away, Berlin had rescued the shoebox, which also contained Zayde's old watch. It didn't work, but that had never seemed to bother him, so it didn't bother her. It was sheer juvenile defiance: if her mother wanted to destroy it, suddenly it was worth saving.

There were only a few pictures in the box, including a couple of Zayde: one with her father and one with them both when she was maybe eight or nine. Zayde was a very old man then, but he could still make his biceps jump, wiggle his eyebrows and twirl his moustache – all at the same time. He was never frail. He seemed to come and go from their lives, but she remembered that when she and her mother had moved to Leyton, he moved into the flat above the shop with her father, Lenny.

Peggy blamed Zayde for everything in general and, in particular, Berlin's failings, which were many and which had all apparently come from her 'father's side'.

Berlin gazed at the photo of Zayde. Her father had told her he had been beaten first by the Cossacks, then by the Reds. What had this persecuted old man done to attract her mother's opprobrium?

The phone was answered with a friendly 'Hello'.

'Hello, Peggy,' said Berlin.

It was astonishing the way a copper cable could convey a sudden chill in the atmosphere.

'Catherine,' said Peggy. 'What's wrong?'

'Nothing,' said Berlin. 'How are you?'

'Fine. Thank you for asking.'

Berlin was inured to this type of expansive hyperbole.

Almost. She knew it was her mother's pre-emptive strike: Berlin wouldn't be calling unless there was a problem.

'Look, Peggy, there's a problem,' said Berlin. She faltered.

Peggy's response was a long-suffering sigh, honed to perfection. They had only recently reached a rapprochement. The peace was tenuous, and would be tested by her failure to appear on Christmas Day.

'I can't make it, Peggy,' said Berlin. 'It's work.'

'I've got everything in,' said Peggy. 'The fridge is full.'

'I'm sorry, Mum. It can't be helped. I need this job.'

'What could you possibly be doing on Christmas Day?' snapped Peggy. 'It's not as if you're a nurse or an ambulance driver . . .' She sighed. '. . . or something useful.'

'I have to go to Moscow,' said Berlin. 'It's not Christmas there until the seventh of January.'

'Heathens,' said Peggy.

'Orthodox Christians, actually,' said Berlin. 'And I'm only going for a couple of days. It's a chance to get in touch with my roots. My paternal roots, that is.'

There was a long silence on the other end. This was provocation of the highest order.

'Do you mean like in that television programme, *Who Do You Think You Are?*' said Peggy. Icy sarcasm was her forte. The conversation had taken its usual turn.

Berlin came back in kind. 'It would be more like *Who the Hell Do You Think You Are?* if it involved our family,' she said.

Peggy hung up.

II

Berlin's nocturnal promenade took her further than usual that night. She set off to walk in a straight line from Bethnal Green to the river. She knew it wasn't possible, but it meant she paid more attention than usual to her choice of route.

It was as if she were saying goodbye to London. It had always been enough for her: cantankerous, difficult, unpredictable – a place of buried treasure and opaque charms. But it was more than that. It was who she was; the collective memory, however false, was a conduit into her own history.

It wasn't the past; it was an invocation, more real to her than God. She had never known her grandmother, but in her fingertips she felt the shape of the calluses on her knees, the mark of a lifetime in service as a scullery maid.

She hadn't been born then, but she had heard the whistle of a doodlebug, the VI rockets that had terrorised London.

She had skipped around a barrel of herring long after they came in jars, and recalled their sharp perfume, melded with the cloud of black dust as the coalman emptied his sack into the bunker.

Berlin mourned the loss of a world in which she hadn't existed. A moment of panic seized her at the prospect of leaving it.

She veered left when she reached the river and turned her back on the City, taking the Thames Path east, but skirting Limehouse Basin, which held disturbing memories of the sharks that had lurked there. They had had legs, not fins, but apart from that there wasn't much to tell them apart.

She still had the scars to prove it.

12

Lieutenant Colonel Yuri Lukov sat in his cramped office at Moscow Police Headquarters with his feet up on the desk. The door was closed, so his subordinates wouldn't be able to observe this lack of decorum. He pinched the bridge of his nose between his thumb and forefinger, in a bid to relieve the dull ache behind his eyes. He wasn't used to this pressure; his career had flourished by avoiding trouble, not courting it.

The mobile phone on the desk vibrated and he nearly jumped out of his skin. He glanced at the ID, then answered.

'Hello,' he said.

'Yuri,' said Maryna.

He swung his feet off his desk. 'What?' he said.

'Something's happened.'

Yuri strode down the corridor with his cap under his arm. Just ahead, he saw a familiar figure leaning in a doorway, talking to someone. Yuri swore, but he couldn't very well turn around now. He hurried past, hoping to go unnoticed.

'Yuri Leonidovich,' came a shout from behind him.

Yuri had no choice but to stop. He spun to face the voice. 'Alexander Sergeevich,' he said. 'How are you? I'm just on my way out.'

Utkin pursed his lips. 'No time for your old friend?' he said. 'I have a new case.' He flourished the file he clutched in one hand.

'Oh yes?' said Yuri. He made a show of putting on his cap: a man in a hurry.

'Let's have a drink some time.'

'Sure,' said Yuri.

'I've got an unusual cause of death here, for a healthy male,' said Utkin. He made a show of putting a hand to his throat and squeezing.

Yuri strode away. 'Call me.' He pushed through the security turnstile at the end of the corridor, but it got stuck halfway. He knew Utkin was still standing there. Yuri swore, backed up and shoved the turnstile again. Finally it gave way and let him pass. He practically ran out of the building, as his collar, soaked with sweat, chafed against the soft place beneath his Adam's apple.

Maryna was waiting for him in the lobby of her apartment building. It was a solid Soviet edifice originally built to house senior apparatchiks. It had been refurbished in the nineties and everything worked: the plumbing, the wiring, the lifts. It was not for the likes of Yuri.

The lift doors opened and an elderly couple with a poodle emerged. When they saw Yuri's uniform they averted their eyes and quickly passed by. He followed Maryna into the lift. The doors closed. He immediately wanted to touch her.

Maryna wasn't beautiful. She was too tall, her nose too big and her mouth too wide. It was her spirit that entranced him, and the way she moved: she had a poise that reflected the certainty at her very core. She was a woman without doubt. She was disgusted by the thoughtless plunder of their country by men who cared nothing for the national interest: everything was for sale, including, as it had turned out, her husband.

Yuri needed the fire of her idealism to keep his cold disillusion at bay. He found himself lacking in national fervour and indifferent to callow greed. He wanted only Maryna; and only her unwavering convictions and her sharp intelligence could save him from this emptiness. These days she sometimes wore a little too much make-up. But her passion for justice was undiminished.

They travelled up to Maryna's floor in silence.

'What's going on?' said Yuri once they were safely ensconced in her apartment.

'I was checking Misha's email,' she said. 'He received a message from a British firm, confirming a meeting.'

'What do you mean?' said Yuri.

'They're sending someone here, from London, to meet with him.'

Yuri stared at her. 'What for?'

'The company he's been negotiating with has hired someone to do a face-to-face interview. An independent third party. Apparently it's part of their process. They say it's routine in a proposed joint venture,' said Maryna.

'Do you believe them?' said Yuri.

Maryna raised her hands. Who knows?

'They've instructed an interpreter, too. A Vladimir Matvienko,' she said.

'Is it true, about the process?' asked Yuri.

'The explanation is plausible,' said Maryna. 'Their law requires they vet prospective business partners. Misha would have had a stake in the new concern and an executive position.'

'And, he hoped, British residency,' said Yuri.

'His value as a security asset would have been much greater than his value to British commerce,' she said. 'Misha always resented my success.'

Yuri had met her at a seminar on inter-agency cooperation; he had been there as an assistant to his boss, but he'd been able to hide this fact. For a while. She was a refreshing change from the bloated, self-serving men who ruled his life. He'd been at pains to give her the impression that he had excellent contacts and was more powerful than his rank implied. That had perhaps been a mistake. She expected a lot of him. It wasn't always easy to deliver.

'Why don't you just say you've changed your mind?' he said. 'I mean, Misha should say he's changed his mind. He's no longer interested in the deal.'

'And what if it is British intelligence?' she said. 'If he suddenly backs out, it would make them more suspicious. He gave this company information to pass on to the government. That's what started this mess. But we don't know exactly what he told them.'

'You think they might be sending someone to get more out of him?' said Yuri.

'Misha was cunning,' said Maryna. 'He would keep something back until safely in London with a British passport.'

'How do we play this?' asked Yuri.

'We play for time,' said Maryna. 'I have an idea.'

13

Berlin was surprised by the number of people waiting outside the Russian visa centre so early on Christmas Eve. She hadn't been home. When the doors finally opened and they all shuffled inside, she took a number from the machine and squeezed down a row until she found a seat.

The vistas of Moscow displayed on the wall confirmed her own iconic images of the city: St Basil's Cathedral; Red Square and the Kremlin at night; snow. But no revolutionaries or spies. Just Chekov, Tolstoy and Tchaikovsky.

While she was waiting she called Del on his personal mobile, not at the office. When he answered, she could hear the clank of the Underground barriers, which told her he was just entering a station.

'Hi, Del,' she said. 'I just wanted to say thanks for this gig.'

'Don't thank me,' said Del. 'They were after you.'

It seemed a funny way to put it. 'Well, they had me at expenses,' she said.

The signal was breaking up.

'Merry Christmas,' she said.

'Berlin,' said Del. There was a pause, a rush of wind. 'Take care.'

'Del?' she said. But the signal died. She hung up.

Berlin's number came up. She made her way to the counter and handed her ID to the smiling young woman behind it. She shuffled through a pile of plastic envelopes until she found the one with Berlin's name on it and checked the bundle of documents inside to ensure that each one bore a blood-red circle of Cyrillic script. The rubber stamp lived on in Russia.

One document named the hotel where Berlin would stay and the name of the company that had 'invited' her. This was the visa support letter.

Berlin leant over the counter to get a closer look at the letter, which might provide some idea of Burghley's client. But the name 'The All-Russia Travel Agency' gave nothing away.

'Please remove your glasses,' said the young woman.

Berlin dutifully removed her dark glasses. The young woman didn't react to her black eyes, just checked the photo against the one in her passport, which she then handed over.

'Enjoy your trip,' she said. She swept all the other documents back into the plastic envelope and dropped it into a slot in her desk.

On the way home Berlin bought a tough nylon overnight bag that she could carry slung across her body. The salesperson guaranteed the strap couldn't be slashed.

Berlin resisted the temptation to tell him that it didn't protect your throat, which the desperado might slash instead if they were frustrated by the strap.

The fairy lights and plastic streamers put up by the council in Bethnal Green Road also did service for Diwali and Eid al-Fitr. Berlin felt their warm glow touch her secular heart, as she threaded her way through clutches of girls wearing Father Christmas hats over their hijabs.

At home, she donned the business suit and put two shirts, two pairs of socks and two sets of thermal underwear in the overnight bag. It was minus five in Moscow, but her long black coat and woolly hat would suffice; she wouldn't be sightseeing. She didn't need much for two and a bit days, particularly in a four-and-a-half-star hotel. She had checked it out online. The toiletries provided were of a much better class than those in her bathroom.

She counted the tablets of buprenorphine in the two blister packs and read the instructions again, although she had been taking them for nearly five months.

Under the heading 'For opioid-dependent drug addicts who have not undergone withdrawal' the manufacturer stated:

When treatment starts the first dose of buprenorphine should be taken when signs of withdrawal appear, but not less than 6 hours after the patient last used opioids (e.g. heroin; short-acting opioids).

Berlin was well past that stage, stabilised on a daily dose of 8mg. Suppressing a frisson of concern at venturing beyond the reach of the National Health Service, she put one pack into the overnight bag and the other in her coat pocket. She was ready to go.

On the way out, she knocked on Bella's door. She had

stuck a red rosette from the newsagent on a bottle of Talisker. When the door opened, she thrust it at Bella.

'Merry Christmas, Bella,' she said.

'It will be a bleedin' sight merrier now,' said Bella. She hugged the bottle. 'Thanks ever so.'

She eyed Berlin's overnight bag.

'I'm going away,' said Berlin.

'Somewhere nice?' said Bella.

'For work,' said Berlin.

She set off down the stairs.

'Don't forget Twelfth Night,' called Bella. 'Your decorations have to come down before then or it's bad luck.'

'How would I know the difference?' Berlin called back.

The sound of Bella's laughter followed her down the stairs.

14

On the Tube to Heathrow Berlin concentrated on the reputational due diligence guidelines that had been loaded onto the tablet. The investigation had the complete cooperation of Mikhail Gerasimov, as you would expect.

He had provided a Letter of Authority to his prospective business partners, which entitled them to make all enquiries necessary pertaining to his 'background, qualifications, reputation and past performance'.

Del's colleagues had assembled the declared financials, bank statements, equities, and so on, and the criminal conviction checks. Berlin's folder also identified Gerasimov's current businesses: transport, logistics, security services.

The character references consisted of statements to the effect that Gerasimov loved his mother, was kind to animals and had never taken or offered a bribe in his life.

It was clear that the work done by Burghley was very last minute. In the rush, gaps had been left in her briefing. She had tried to fill these online, but there was nothing. Gerasimov was by no means an oligarch, more of a middle-ranking entrepreneur apparently trying to move up.

This job was window-dressing. No-one expected, or even wanted, her to find anything murky or untoward in Gerasimov's past or present. She was required to do a couple of interviews, enjoy the minibar at the hotel, then fly home.

It was all just for the record.

The soaring glass canopy that was Terminal 5 conferred a sense of space and tranquillity on the travellers beneath it. On the other hand, it was a late flight on Christmas Eve and the place was closing down.

There were only half-a-dozen flights left to depart. The last one went to somewhere called Abuja at 22.40. After that, the next flight wasn't until 07.25 on Christmas Day. The Heathrow curfew ensured a few precious hours of silence for those who dwelt below its flight path.

The flight to Moscow would take four hours. Moscow was four hours ahead of London, so she would arrive at five in the morning. Christmas morning.

She was held at the check-in desk until an authorised British Airways employee arrived to confirm her visa was genuine. He told her they were expensive and it was not unknown for people to forge them. To Berlin, it sounded like a cover story for yet another security check. He duly scrutinised her visa and marked her boarding pass with two stripes of his bright blue felt-tip pen. Very high tech.

Boarding the aircraft, Berlin was impressed by the attentive service, the roomy seats and the drink that was served as soon as she sat down. Things had certainly improved since her last flight – to Bangkok, in the eighties. That trip hadn't ended well.

This time it would be different. She had changed, and

so, it seemed, had the standards of international aviation. Then she peered back down the cabin and noticed a curtain across the gangway. She was in business class.

Beyond the curtain she could see the aircraft was packed with Russians milling in the aisles, engaged in animated discussion; the topic appeared to be the allocation of overhead locker space.

Elbows were being deployed as they attempted to cram into the lockers enormous shopping bags and parcels: Selfridges, Hamleys, Harrods and a number of bespoke Jermyn Street outfitters were over-represented among the labels.

Berlin sat back, relaxed and enjoyed the spectacle of brands jostling. It was only as the jet thundered down the runway and jerked its nose skyward that she realised she'd forgotten to call Magnus. She settled back in her seat. It would wait.

Nothing much would happen over Christmas.

15

Christmas was proving to be the usual trial for Magnus Nkonde. The Approach had closed early, it being Christmas Eve, as had public transport. He was forced to walk two miles in freezing drizzle to another pub that he knew would still be open, at least for a couple more hours.

Every now and then he would come upon a small knot of bemused tourists who'd found themselves stranded in a corner of this vast city.

The Magi had had an easier journey to Bethlehem; at Christmas wise men didn't travel across London.

Settling into a quiet corner of the Shakespeare's Head with a festive mulled wine, Magnus didn't pay much attention to the burly gent with a comb-over who sat down beside him. Just another lonely soul.

But when a much younger chap, all fresh face and pungent aftershave, sat down too close on his other side, he began to pay attention.

'Can I help you fellows?' he enquired, attempting to sound jocular.

'Fancy a breath of air, sir?' asked Comb-Over, briefly displaying his ID.

Magnus raised an eyebrow, indicating he was impressed,

but not overwhelmed. They were coppers, but not the common-or-garden variety: representatives of Counter Terrorism Command.

'I don't think so,' he said. 'I'm quite comfortable here, thanks all the same.'

Comb-Over and Aftershave exchanged a glance. Magnus could see the latter was raring to have a go. A wiser head prevailed.

'You've been making enquiries, sir,' said Comb-Over. 'About a vehicle.'

'Have I indeed?' said Magnus. He sipped his warm wine, poking an errant clove back into the glass with his tongue. He had to disguise his excitement. The game was really on.

'Could I ask you, sir, where you obtained that registration number?'

'You'll have to ask my editor about that,' said Magnus with relish. 'And my paper's legal eagles.'

They would have no idea that these days he was a stringer.

Comb-Over sighed and stood up. 'Very well, sir,' he said. 'We'll do that. Merry Christmas.'

His young colleague sprang to his feet, fists clenched. Magnus raised a glass to him.

'God bless us, everyone,' he intoned.

When Magnus finally staggered out of the Shakespeare's Head, steeling himself for the trek home through the frigid night, he found Bethnal Green Road utterly deserted. He was depressed to see that even the mixed businesses run by Hindus, Sikhs and Muslims were closed. Bloody Christmas.

Under the circumstances he decided a hymn might provide some comfort and, as there was no-one on the street to offend, he began a rousing rendition of 'Onward Christian Soldiers'.

He had barely reached the end of the first verse when a man appeared in front of him. Magnus blinked. It was Comb-Over. He sensed, or rather smelt, Aftershave behind him.

'Aha,' exclaimed Magnus. 'My drinking companions.'

They took an arm each and steered him towards a car.

Magnus tried to put up resistance. But he was flabby and drunk.

'Mind yourself there, sir,' said Aftershave, bouncing Magnus's head off the car.

'Ow! What the fuck is this?' protested Magnus. 'Bastards!' He felt sick.

Aftershave shoved him into the back seat, then got in after him. Magnus heard the motor start. Comb-Over was driving. As the car pulled away from the kerb Magnus turned to Aftershave and, with great deliberation, threw up into his lap. 'That'll teach you,' he slurred, and passed out.

16

The cold air in the Domodedovo terminal was already beginning to creep into Berlin's bones. She scanned the signs held by the platoon of silent, grim-faced men in black puffa jackets, their thick checked shirts buttoned up to the neck: the meeters and greeters at the barrier.

None clutched a sign bearing her name.

With only cabin baggage, perhaps she had emerged more quickly than her interpreter had anticipated. But she was not in the mood for cock-ups this early in the job. In a haze of Scotch and fatigue she scanned the arrivals hall for coffee. A candy-striped sign beckoned.

The Snack Time Café was a bright, modern kiosk. The young woman who served her wasn't happy when Berlin offered a credit card to pay for her coffee: she snatched it, swiped it and flung it back.

'Welcome to Moscow,' murmured Berlin.

Keeping her sunglasses on, she found a stool that gave her a view of the greeters at the barrier, sat down and sipped the tepid coffee. It tasted like the décor: saccharine and plastic.

A few minutes later a short, rotund woman with a helmet of iron-grey hair scurried into view, clutching a piece of cardboard. She pushed her way to the front of the greeters, peering anxiously at the arrivals board and the passengers emerging from customs.

The motley piece of cardboard she flourished read 'Katherine Berlin'.

Berlin put down her coffee and left the café. Keeping one eye on the woman at the barrier, she promptly collided with two men in midnight-blue camo uniforms. The German shepherd between them snarled and the men glared at her. The welcome wasn't getting any warmer.

When Berlin looked up, the woman with the sign had seen her and was beckoning her forward with an impatient gesture. But instead of waiting, the woman took off towards a door at one end of the hall that was propped open with a chair.

Above the door were stencilled words in Russian and English. The English read 'Emergency Exit'. The woman strode through it without a backward glance. Berlin had no choice but to follow.

The door led into a stairwell. Berlin saw the woman glance up from the next landing, to make sure she was following, and then continue her quick descent.

Berlin hurried to keep up.

At the bottom she found herself in a small cargo bay. Three men in dirty orange overalls sprawled on a wooden trolley, smoking. They looked exhausted, and didn't even glance at her as she passed.

The moment her so-called greeter cleared the loading dock she stopped, took a pack of cigarettes from her pocket and lit one. Inhaling deeply, she offered Berlin her hand as she finally caught up.

'Charlotte Inkpin,' she said. 'Call me Charlie.'

Berlin had expected an accent, but not this one. Charlie, who was seventy if she was a day, spoke English with an accent redolent of class and privilege.

'Catherine Berlin,' she said. 'With a "C", actually. Call me Berlin.'

They shook hands. Charlie took a fur-lined hat from her pocket and jammed it on her head, grabbed Berlin's bag, as if she had just remembered why she was there, and led the way to a gleaming black Range Rover parked beside a wall of snow.

'Sorry about the wait. Traffic,' said Charlie.

Traffic. At five in the morning? But before Berlin could comment, she became aware of icy fingers reaching down her throat to seize her lungs. The cold was literally breathtaking.

'The sooner we leave, the less we pay,' said Charlie, throwing the bag in the back as she got behind the wheel, panting from her exertions. Berlin took the seat beside her. The luxury interior exuded the acrid odour of stale tobacco.

'Duty-free?' asked Charlie as the motor purred into life. Berlin imagined it was a company car.

'What?' said Berlin.

'Did you bring any duty-free? Decent liquor or English cigarettes?' said Charlie, querulous.

'I don't smoke,' said Berlin.

She wasn't about to mention the litre of Talisker in her bag.

Charlie put her foot down and the car shot forward,

bucking and skidding across an expanse of broken concrete, up a small bank and on into a snowy wasteland.

Berlin hung on as they headed straight for a fence constructed from steel cable. As they got closer, she could see a gap, protected by a sheet of corrugated iron.

At the last minute a shabby woman swathed in scarves stepped out of a small wooden hut and stood beside it.

Charlie slammed on the brakes, wound down her window and dropped some cash into the woman's gloved hand. The woman slipped it in her apron pocket, then dragged the iron to one side.

Charlie gunned the motor and they shot through the gap.

Berlin's sense of a seamless, comfortable transition between sanitised airport terminals evaporated.

She had crossed a border.

On the other side of the airport two tired kitchen hands dragged a waste bin towards a skip. The roar of the jets overhead precluded conversation, but gestures sufficed: they stopped. One sat down on the bin and lit a cigarette, while the other lifted the lid of the skip to see if there was anything worth salvaging. He peered into its depths.

Unseeing eyes stared back at him.

17

Berlin was nauseous from the smell in the car and Charlie's erratic driving. Charlie smoked incessantly, despite her wheezy chest, but Berlin didn't want to get off to a bad start by asking her to stop. She was at the mercy of this woman for the next couple of days. It could be a very bumpy ride.

The road was wide and flanked on one side by a dense phalanx of slender birch trees; their frosted white trunks sparkled against the black sky, in pristine contrast to the banks of grubby snow piled high in the service lane.

If there was a speed limit on the highway, Charlie ignored it. As they entered a built-up area, the road remained wide but became congested. Russian roads had been built to accommodate tanks. One would have come in useful during this early-morning chaos.

Charlie was forced to slow down, although she continued to lurch from one lane to another without warning, cutting up ancient lorries with high wheelbases that looked as if they had been converted from military vehicles. They were no match for the Range Rover.

Korean pop music blared from the radio, making conversation impossible. Berlin sensed that this was deliberate.

She didn't feel much like chatting herself. Perhaps Charlie wasn't a morning person either.

Berlin took a sideways glance at her. How did this apparently very English pensioner wash up as an interpreter in Moscow? She looked as if she belonged in a bus shelter: her neck-to-knee quilted coat, flecked with mud, had seen better days; her boots were scuffed, lined with yellowing fur that matched her hat.

She must be reliable, or Burghley wouldn't use her. When she called Del she would ask him where on earth they had found Charlie Inkpin. But before she did anything she needed more coffee, a bath and a couple of hours' rest. She had to be on her toes for her first meeting with Gerasimov at midday.

'Katarina Berlin, yes?' asked the receptionist with an efficient smile.

'Yes,' said Berlin.

Charlie hovered near the revolving door, clearly anxious to be on her way.

The receptionist handed Berlin a key card. The clocks behind her showed the local time as 06.35. In London it was 02.35. 'Breakfast buffet seven to eleven,' she said.

'Can I change some sterling?' said Berlin.

The receptionist pointed to a cash machine. '*Bankomat*,' she said.

'Thanks,' said Berlin.

'Enjoy your stay,' said the receptionist.

Berlin crossed the lobby to the cash machine.

'All set?' asked Charlie.

Berlin nodded as she negotiated the instructions on the screen and withdrew what seemed like a reasonable quantity of cash for a couple of days.

When she looked up, Charlie was leaving.

'Hang on,' said Berlin. 'I'd like to review the schedule with you.'

'Plenty of time for that,' said Charlie, backing into the revolving door. 'I'll pick you up at eleven.'

And she was gone.

18

Utkin took off his thick gloves and pulled on a latex pair, then stepped onto a plastic crate that someone had thoughtfully placed beside the skip for the photographers. He hauled himself over the rim with a grunt, struggling to retain his balance as his feet sank into the rubbish.

The poor fellow hadn't crawled in here to stay warm. He wasn't a large man, but he was well fed and wore a smart suit. Not a bum. Bruising around the neck indicated strangulation. Foreboding quickened Utkin's heart. He had seen the same marks only recently.

From the look of his hands, the man had put up a fight, but his assailant had been undeterred by the blows. It took strength and persistence to choke a healthy adult male.

Utkin slipped a hand into the man's inside pocket. No wallet. The rest of his pockets were empty too.

'Where's your car?' said Utkin, addressing the corpse. Then, for the benefit of the sergeant, who was giving him a funny look, he added, 'Maybe the keys are in here somewhere.'

Utkin wondered momentarily if he could prevail on his subordinates to sort and bag the contents of the skip and to have them forensically examined.

It was a fanciful notion. Moscow was in the premier league when it came to homicide. The laboratories of the Russian Federal Centre of Forensic Science had a massive backlog.

He peered at the mounds of trash, which shifted as he moved about. A piece of white cardboard, stained brown and yellow, caught his eye. He picked it up gingerly, between his thumb and forefinger, and sniffed: urine and faeces, often evacuated during the death throes. His legs go from under him, he pisses and shits himself, it's over. The man hadn't been killed in the skip. Which meant the victim had dropped the piece of cardboard during the assault and it had been thoughtlessly tossed in after him.

Utkin turned the cardboard over and held it in both latex-encased hands, tilting it towards the light.

Printed in large black letters were two words in English: 'Catherine Berlin.'

He took the sign with him when he clambered out of the skip. 'Bag this,' he said to the sergeant. The sergeant took the sign, grimacing.

Utkin pulled off his latex gloves and scratched his scalp, sweaty beneath his sheepskin hat. The cold feeling in his gut grew. 'Lend me your torch,' he said.

The sergeant frowned. The place was lit up like the Kremlin. But he handed it over.

Utkin plodded to where the darkness began and walked the perimeter, sweeping the torch beam back and forth. He didn't have to go far.

The snow was packed hard. A small, bright jewel sparkled

on the crystal plane: a crumpled cellophane confectionery wrapper.

The beam fluttered over it, unsteady in Utkin's trembling hand.

The traitor

19

Berlin had taken her buprenorphine, soaked in a hot four-and-a-half-star bath and was on her way to breakfast. She would eat, then call Del and Magnus. And Peggy. The dining room was decorated in warm, primrose tones. It took Berlin a moment to realise that the birdsong she could hear was a soundtrack. That could become irritating.

She peered over her sunglasses. A clear blue sky was visible through a narrow, double-glazed window and she took a table beside it. When she sat down, she was surprised to see the bottom half of the window obscured by snow. She had almost forgotten she was in Moscow.

Which might have been because she was trying hard to ignore the fact that she was fifteen hundred miles from London. While the hotel was a bubble of familiarity in an alien landscape, she knew that the bubble would soon pop.

In here they spoke English, automatically smiled at you as you walked past, provided English-language news-papers and BBC World News on the television.

But out there, it would be different.

Her sense of dislocation was slight, but jarring. It was a lack of ease. It could be due to her sudden departure, the flight, dehydration. But she knew those weren't the reasons.

London was at the core of her existence, a way of life carefully constructed to smother the anxiety that always seemed about to overcome her. She could navigate London's streets, its codes and classes, its threats and unwritten rules, without thinking.

Here, she might not be able to find her way.

A waiter approached the table, clutching a coffee pot. She smiled and indicated her cup, but he didn't smile back.

'There's someone to see you, madam,' he said. 'In the lobby.'

Berlin glanced at the clock on the wall. Unless she was totally confused by the time zones, Charlie was an hour early.

But the person who rose to greet her in the lobby wasn't Charlie. It was a scruffy man with blue eyes and drooping jowls. His suit jacket was taut across his belly.

'Katarina Berlinskaya?' he asked. Then stuttered, 'My apologies. Katarina Berlin.'

Berlin nodded. Had she been palmed off on one of Charlie's colleagues?

'Major Alexander Utkin,' he said.

Berlin saw the seams of his jacket gape as he reached into his pocket. He produced a shiny red-and-gold badge. The inscription, in Cyrillic, meant nothing to her.

'I am *operativiny rabotnik*. Detective of Moscow Criminal Investigation Department,' said the major. 'Police use military ranks here. You enjoyed breakfast?'

Berlin wondered momentarily if Charlie had been in an accident. The way she drove, it wouldn't be surprising.

But Berlin immediately dismissed this explanation. Someone would have called; they wouldn't send a detective. She wasn't a relative.

'Sit?' Utkin gestured to the table he had been occupying, where a plate of small pancakes and tea in a glass cup was waiting. 'I missed breakfast. You don't mind?'

'What's this about?' said Berlin. She noticed that the receptionists at the front desk were studiously not watching them.

'Please,' said Utkin, indicating the chair opposite his own.

Berlin sat. 'How can I help you, Major?' she said, pushing her still-damp hair back behind her ears.

'Very likely I can help you,' said Utkin. He popped one of the small pancakes in his mouth and chewed it thoughtfully.

Berlin knew the technique. He would give nothing away. He would answer her questions with a question, or a response that was meaningless. In growing frustration, she would talk too much and tell him what he wanted to know. But what on earth could that be?

'This is your first visit to Russia?' asked Utkin.

'Yes,' she said.

Utkin paused, widened his eyes – a visual cue that she should go on, he was interested in whatever she had to say.

Berlin remained silent.

'You are here on business?' asked Utkin.

'Yes,' said Berlin.

'Of what nature?' said Utkin.

'I'm here to conduct due diligence interviews with a Russian businessman, on behalf of a British company.'

'His name?'

Berlin hesitated. 'Mikhail Gerasimov,' she said, finally. 'Is there a problem here, Major?'

'You very likely have an interpreter?' said Utkin.

'Yes,' said Berlin. 'She met me at the airport this morning.'

'I see,' said Utkin. He sipped his tea.

Berlin heard the elevator doors open.

A uniformed officer strode across the lobby, bent down to whisper something in Utkin's ear and put two transparent plastic bags on the table. Evidence bags.

One contained her blister packs of buprenorphine, the other her passport.

Berlin stood up.

'Please sit down, Miss Berlin,' said Utkin. 'And please remove your dark glasses.'

'What's going on here?' demanded Berlin.

She lunged for the evidence bags but in the process knocked over Utkin's tea, which flooded across the table.

Utkin quickly lifted the bags out of harm's way. He nodded at the officer, who very smartly put her in a headlock, knocking her glasses off in the process. Then he stood on them. The crunch echoed in the absolute silence of the lobby.

'What the fuck?' shouted Berlin.

The officer tightened his grip.

The sound of birdsong drifted from the dining room.

'I want to speak to the British embassy,' gasped Berlin.

'Very likely, Miss Berlin,' said Major Utkin. 'But for them it's Christmas Day.'

20

The hotel manager, whose nametag identified him as Artem, seemed more than happy to make his office available for Utkin. It was clear he just wanted them out of the lobby.

Berlin was surprised when a waiter brought two cups of tea and more pancakes, and set them on the manager's desk. Behind it sat the apparently imperturbable Utkin with the two evidence bags. Berlin noticed that they weren't sealed.

Utkin had taken her mobile and given it to his officer, who was already in possession of her new tablet. When the waiter had gone, Utkin offered her the plate.

'Blini?' he asked.

Berlin ignored the offer.

Utkin ignored her black eyes. He sat back and regarded her gravely.

'You understand, Miss Berlin, that I must be seen to uphold Russian Criminal Code.'

'Which I haven't broken,' said Berlin.

'Very likely you have,' said Utkin.

His English was excellent but somehow archaic, as if he had learnt it by reading Dickens. He took a pair of reading glasses from his pocket, put them on and picked up the bag containing her buprenorphine.

'The story of drug addiction, *narkomania*, in Russia is sad,' he said. 'Penalties for possession are even more sad.'

'It's buprenorphine,' said Berlin. 'A prescription medication approved for the treatment of opioid dependence. It's perfectly legal.'

'Not here,' said Utkin.

Berlin felt a flush rise in her chest and creep up her throat, infusing faded scars with the heat of fear and humiliation. She didn't belong here. She belonged in the shadows, in the CCTV control room, not in business class.

It had all been a terrible mistake.

'Your interpreter will arrive at what time?' asked Utkin.

'Eleven,' mumbled Berlin.

Utkin glanced at his watch, removed his glasses, stuffed the evidence bags in his pocket and rose.

'I must consult with superiors,' he said.

'I need a receipt,' said Berlin. 'For my confiscated property.'

Utkin tore a piece of paper off a pad lying on the manager's desk. He scrawled some numbers on it and thrust it at her.

'My phone number,' he said. 'I will be in touch.'

He left, taking her passport and buprenorphine with him.

Black spots danced before her eyes. She gulped for air.

When Berlin emerged from the office the manager, Artem, was waiting for her, leaning against the wall with his arms folded. She cleared her throat and tried to find a normal tone.

'I'm sorry,' she said. 'A misunderstanding.'

Artem didn't bother to deploy his professional smile. Then she noticed her bag behind the reception desk. Her overcoat and hat lay on top of it, along with her tablet and mobile.

'Your company will be fully reimbursed,' he said. 'With the exception of a small administrative charge.'

'What's the problem?' said Berlin.

'Your visa. There is problem with your visa,' said Artem.

'Just a moment,' said Berlin.

She grabbed her phone, selected Del's personal mobile from her contacts list and hit 'call'.

'My visa is in order,' she said as she waited for her call to connect. 'It was checked by your staff when I arrived.'

She kept her gaze fixed on Artem as she listened to a message in English telling her in a cheerful voice that normal service would be resumed as soon as she paid her phone bill. She hung up.

'Please show me your visa,' said Artem.

'The police have taken my passport,' said Berlin.

'Foreigners must carry their passports at all times. It's the law,' said Artem. 'We must ask you to leave. Now.'

'You know I can't check into another hotel without my visa,' said Berlin. 'Where do you suggest I go?'

Artem muttered something in Russian. The receptionists, gathered together at the far end of the desk to enjoy the spectacle, sniggered.

'Fuck you, too,' said Berlin.

'What's going on?' came a gruff voice from the other side of the lobby. It was Charlie. Berlin snatched up her things, pushed past the manager and marched across the lobby.

'Come on,' she said to Charlie as she reached the revolving door. 'And don't look at me like that.'

From a discreet position alone in his unmarked Ford, Utkin watched the two women emerge from the hotel and hurry to a black Range Rover. As was his habit, he made a mental note of its number. The women appeared to be arguing.

He wasn't surprised.

'You've been engaged to interpret,' insisted Berlin. 'Call Gerasimov and reschedule.'

'You aren't listening,' protested Charlie. 'It's out of the question.'

Berlin was struggling into her coat and hat. 'Okay,' she said. 'Lend me your mobile. I have to talk to Delroy. How far is the British embassy?'

'I don't own a mobile,' said Charlie. 'Why do you want to go to the embassy? It will be closed, anyway.'

'Surely there's a night bell or an emergency number or something?'

'You haven't been abroad much, have you?' said Charlie.

'They've taken my passport,' said Berlin.

'Who's they?' said Charlie.

'The police,' said Berlin. 'Who do you think?'

Charlie went white. She glanced around, clearly alarmed, then got in the car, slammed the door and started the motor.

It looked very much as if she was just going to drive off.

Berlin grabbed the door handle, yanked it open and threw herself inside just as the car began to move. This woman was her lifeline. She wasn't about to let her disappear.

They drove in silence. Charlie smoked furiously and kept looking at Berlin as if she were a bomb that might go off at any moment.

'How on earth did you manage to come to the attention of the police?' she snapped. 'You've only been here five minutes.'

'It's just some misunderstanding,' said Berlin.

'What about?' said Charlie.

'My visa,' said Berlin.

Charlie scowled, but didn't comment further. She drove like a lunatic, taking sharp corners, cutting in and out of lanes.

They passed the grand façade of a railway station. People were surging in and out, breaking like waves around a shuffling crone in a headscarf and ankle-length coat who stood in their midst selling mandarins from a battered carton tied to a luggage trolley.

Berlin realised it was the third time she had seen her.

They weren't going anywhere. Charlie was obviously just driving around, thinking about what she was going to do with her.

This suited Berlin for the time being. She also had a lot to think about – principally, what would prompt a police search of her room?

The only possibility she could come up with was that housekeeping had spotted the drugs while she was at break-fast. The cleaner might recognise buprenorphine if she was a snout. Perhaps the ingrained methods of a totalitarian state had been adapted to free enterprise.

Old habits die hard.

A network of informants in hotels frequented by foreigners could provide lucrative soft targets: gay couples and human-rights workers sprang to mind. In fact, anyone whom the authorities regarded as undesirable.

She relaxed a little. Utkin hadn't arrested her. He was there with one offsider, not a squad. The evidence bags weren't sealed, so presumably nothing had been officially recorded or logged, and the contents could simply be removed and the whole thing forgotten. The Russian police had a reputation for graft.

The more she thought about it, the more certain she was that it was a shakedown. She only had Utkin's word for it that bupe was illegal in Russia. He would let her stew for a while, then return to collect the 'fine'.

This was the price of doing business in Russia; hence the UK Bribery Act 2010 and her due diligence mission.

The only problem was she wouldn't be able to put her so-called fine on expenses without exposing her status to Del's firm. She didn't know how much he had shared with them, but she imagined he would be circumspect with information about her addiction.

She was determined not to risk embarrassing him, or queering her chances of further work from Burghley, especially as she'd now jeopardised her pitch with Hirst.

Which brought her back to Gerasimov.

'Right,' she said to Charlie. 'Let's go to work.'

21

The foyer of Mikhail Gerasimov's very modern building was pristine and anonymous. Charlie and Berlin got in the lift and travelled to the top floor.

When the lift doors opened they stepped out directly into an apartment. It was a dazzling melange of white marble, gilt and mirrors.

The many reflections provided no place to hide. Berlin dragged her fingers through her hair.

A short, bald, unprepossessing man greeted them in Russian with a warm smile. Introductions established that this was Mikhail Gerasimov. He was wearing a navy-blue blazer with gold buttons, a white polo-neck sweater and loafers with tassels. Berlin wanted to call him 'Commodore'.

The woman in the smart charcoal suit who stood beside the little commodore was a good deal taller. Lithe and assured in her movements, she could have played a mean game of basketball for the Soviet Union if she'd been a couple of years older, Berlin imagined.

There was a good ten years between her and her husband, who Berlin knew from her documents was forty-eight.

When she shook hands with Berlin her grip was firm. 'I'm very pleased to meet you,' she said. 'I'm Mrs Gerasimova.'

Berlin, puzzled, turned to Charlie, who told her that

Gerasimova was the feminine form of Gerasimov, according to Russian custom.

Gerasimova then shook hands with Charlie and spoke to her in Russian. Whatever she said surprised Charlie, who scowled and informed Berlin, rather gruffly, that Mrs Gerasimova was going to act as her husband's interpreter.

So that's how it was going to be: interpreters at twenty paces, sir.

The room into which they were shown glistened: glass-topped tables, life-size ceramic snow leopards, fabrics that crackled when you sat down. It smelt like the interior of a new car – a combination of warm vinyl and formaldehyde.

The cloying odour was banished as soon as Charlie and the Gerasimovs lit up.

Utkin strode into the chaotic evidence room. Six new boxes sat on a bench. He lifted the lid of the first one and tipped it out onto the bench.

Plastic evidence bags tumbled out, stuffed with crushed drink cans, cigarette butts, used condoms, syringes, the remains of Big Macs. All collected from the alley behind the nightclub, under the watchful eye of the sergeant. Or so Utkin hoped. He sighed.

He picked up each bag, peered at it and tossed it back into the box.

When he'd got through the pile, he put the lid back on the box and started on the next one.

*

Berlin powered down the tablet. The air was thick with blue smoke and confusion. A full complement of questions had been asked and answered, but she was no closer to any assessment of Gerasimov, who had nodded and smiled throughout the process.

Each question had been translated by both interpreters, then the same rigmarole had been repeated with the answers.

At times his wife and Charlie would bicker in Russian about a particular word. Berlin had to insist these lexical discussions were repeated in English.

And so it went on, Gerasimov smiling and smoking. Whenever he hesitated in his response to a question, Gerasimova would fill in the gap and Gerasimov would nod in agreement.

Berlin was relieved when the farce was over.

The couple escorted Berlin and Charlie to the lift, where Gerasimov shook hands with Berlin and said something in Russian.

Gerasimova translated: 'My husband trusts you are satisfied that his responses were full and frank. He looks forward to your next meeting.'

Charlie began to speak, but Berlin raised her hand to silence her. She didn't need to hear it twice.

'He wishes you a merry Christmas,' added Gerasimova quickly, making the most of her edge over Charlie. She pressed the button and the lift doors opened.

Charlie and Berlin got in and the doors closed.

'That went well,' said Berlin. 'Now I need a drink.'

*

Strings of onions, garlic and blood-red chillies hung from the branches of a sturdy oak tree, whose heavy green canopy formed the ceiling of the large octagonal room. A rustic cart leant against the trunk. More produce hung from the giant cartwheels.

None of it was real. Berlin couldn't read the specials board, but she knew a themed restaurant when she stumbled into one.

They were shown to their table by a Balkan maiden in a charming smocked outfit. Charlie plonked herself into her chair, reeled off instructions in Russian, and within a matter of moments a waiter brought a large carafe of rosy liquid.

'What's this?' asked Berlin, pouring them a glass each.

'Cranberry juice,' replied Charlie.

Berlin took a long drink. She gasped, blinking back the tears.

'. . . and vodka,' added Charlie. 'Down the hatch.'

Utkin held one of the evidence bags up to the light. It was the last from the fifth box. From his pocket he retrieved the cellophane sweet wrapper he had picked up at the airport crime scene. He compared them. It was a match.

Gently, he opened the evidence bag and peered closely at the small piece of crinkled cellophane. Using a thumb and finger he delicately withdrew it from the bag. He closed his eyes, brought it close to his nose and inhaled deeply.

He held his breath until he was dizzy, then put it in his pocket with the other one.

On his way out he tossed the empty bag into a bin.

By four in the afternoon it was already dark and Berlin had doused her panic at the loss of the buprenorphine with a significant quantity of cranberry vodka. She was on her second jug, and almost beginning to enjoy the place.

'What is all this, anyway?' she asked Charlie, indicating the timber-panelled walls festooned with bear skins and boars' heads, the chickens perched on wicker baskets and heavy stone jars.

Charlie mumbled, her mouth full of little dumplings. She had already made short work of two enormous platefuls.

'Balkan folksiness. Nostalgia for a time none of this lot can remember.' She indicated the mostly young patrons, all as drunk as she and Charlie. 'And which probably never existed.'

'Are there Soviet-style cafés with busts of Marx and Lenin hanging from the ceiling?' joked Berlin.

'What do you know about Marx and Lenin?' retorted Charlie.

Before Berlin could mention her degree in political science, the maiden appeared with the bill.

'Credit card,' said Charlie. It was a command, not a query.

Berlin put one on the table and the maiden went off to fetch the machine.

'I must call my mother and wish her a happy Christmas,' said Berlin.

'You can do it from the hotel,' said Charlie.

Berlin looked at her steadily. 'Do you know somewhere that will let me in without a passport?' she said.

'I have to go to the loo,' said Charlie.

Berlin waited until Charlie disappeared behind a barn-yard wall, then followed. Beyond the faux wall a long, narrow passage led to the toilets. At the end there was another door. It was just closing.

Berlin picked up her pace. The bloody woman had got her drunk and now she was going to do a runner. She pushed the door open. Beyond it was a strip of neon-lit concrete, divided from a car park by a shoulder-height fence. She could hear Charlie's voice on the other side of it.

It sounded as if she was pleading or complaining. But then, to Berlin's ears, Russian was a doleful language.

It went quiet, but no-one responded to Charlie.

She was on the phone. She *had* a bloody mobile phone.

A frigid draught of air cleared Berlin's head.

The one-sided argument, which meant nothing to Berlin, continued. Then she heard her name mentioned.

She backed away from the door, closing it quietly.

22

Fagan had just started to carve the turkey when his mobile rang. His wife gave him a look. Fagan put down the knife and took his phone out of his pocket. His sons took this as a signal to leave the table and lope back to their rooms.

His wife snatched up the knife and for a moment Fagan thought she was going to plunge it into his ribs, but instead she picked up the serving dish bearing the untouched bird, and carried it back to the kitchen.

The whole thing had been a pantomime anyway.

As if on some pre-arranged signal Fagan heard a TV talk show, rap music and the sound of a computer game all start up at once in different parts of the house.

'What?' he hissed to the caller. 'I was carving the fucking turkey.'

'There's a problem,' came the terse reply.

Fagan listened for a moment and then hung up. On the way down the hall he grabbed his wallet, keys and jacket. He wished he'd stayed in the army. He'd encountered less hostility from the bloody enemy than from his own family. There were no rules of engagement at home. His visits then had been brief and infrequent, which suited everybody.

He lit a cigarette as he backed the car out of the drive

onto Chigwell Road, which was very quiet. Hardly surprising at lunchtime on bloody Christmas Day.

People took the piss out of Essex – people like his boss. There had been a programme on the telly, some BBC thing, which said there were now seven classes in Britain. As far as Fagan was concerned there were only two.

Us and them.

23

Utkin waited patiently in the apartment block's lobby. The building dated from the fifties; it was solid, secure and very well appointed.

Twenty minutes later he heard the lift descend. The doors opened and a woman emerged. They shook hands.

'Colonel Gerasimova,' she said, by way of introduction. 'Foreign Intelligence Service.'

Utkin sighed inwardly. Really, that was all she needed to say.

'Major Utkin, Moscow CID,' said Utkin. 'Thank you very much for meeting with me.'

'My husband offers his apologies. Business, you know,' she said.

She opened a door onto a small anteroom, some sort of receptionist's cubicle, and invited Utkin to enter.

They stood awkwardly between a desk and shelves. There were no chairs.

'What's this about?' asked Gerasimova.

This time Utkin did not disguise his sigh. He had not been invited up to the residence, nor offered any tea.

He kept it brief. 'Your husband met with an English-woman called Catherine Berlin today?'

Utkin saw a flicker of concern in the Colonel's cold eyes.

'Yes,' she said.

'She attended with an interpreter?' said Utkin.

'Yes,' said Gerasimova. 'Is this woman in some sort of trouble?'

'When do you think your husband might be available? I can wait. It's no problem.'

'I'm sorry,' said Gerasimova. 'He has left Moscow, as I said, on business. If there is anything else, perhaps you could make an appointment.'

'It's very important I speak with him,' said Utkin, 'in person.'

Gerasimova folded her arms.

'He could come to the station at any time,' wheedled Utkin. 'I would be happy to accommodate him.'

She glanced at her watch. 'Major,' she said, 'perhaps you could ask your superior to submit any further requests in writing through my office.'

'Colonel, my apologies. Just one more thing. Do you know if any vehicles have been stolen from your husband's company?'

'Are you implying that I make his business affairs a matter of my professional interest?' said Gerasimova. 'That is a very serious accusation, Major.'

Utkin retreated, before he made things any worse.

Climbing the stairs to his apartment – the lift was out of service again – Utkin contemplated the prospect of asking his boss to write to the Foreign Intelligence Service to request a meeting between the spouse of a colonel and one of his grubby little homicide detectives.

He didn't contemplate it for long.

The padded front door closed behind Utkin with a soft sigh. The hooks that lined the tiny vestibule were crowded with bulky coats and jackets, although he lived alone.

He sat down on a low wooden bench and leant in among the winter garments as he dragged off his boots. The coats still held faint traces of his wife and son, preserved in the stuffy airlock. He buried himself beneath them, pressed the coarse fabric to his face and inhaled deeply.

Utkin enjoyed eating, so he'd learnt to cook. The kitchen was tidy and well equipped. His younger colleagues ate out at restaurants with décor that evoked an era they couldn't remember and which offered poor approximations of dishes their grandmothers had once served.

Expensive food and wasted sentiment – he could do better at home.

He put a pot of water on the stove to boil, then went into the living room and sat down at his desk.

The small apartment had come with the job. Promotion brought with it bigger apartments in nicer locations, but his wife had liked this estate, her friends were here and she knew the best stalls at the nearby market.

He had wanted to move. She hadn't. They had argued about it endlessly – that, and everything else – but now she was gone he was glad they had stayed.

He opened one of the desk drawers and pushed aside the coiled lengths of string he kept there. His wife used to laugh at the way he carefully unpicked the knots on a parcel to reuse the string, but it always came in handy.

He reached into the back of the drawer and found a small sandalwood box that had once held his son's crayons. He took it out and lifted its lid.

He took the two cellophane sweet wrappers from his pocket; one from the alley, the other he had found at the airport.

What one sought was never in plain sight.

He picked them both up and laid them carefully beside the one that was already in the box.

24

When Charlie returned from the loo Berlin was finishing the dregs of her cranberry vodka.

'I can offer you accommodation,' said Charlie. 'And you can complete the final interview with Gerasimov tomorrow and return to London the following day. Business as usual.'

Someone had given Charlie her orders. It wasn't Del, or anyone else at Burghley, or she'd have spoken to them on the phone in English. Perhaps she was talking directly to the company in London – the company that was paying both of them – who might employ Russians, or Russian-speakers.

In theory, she and Charlie were on the same side. But Charlie had lied to her. Berlin didn't like being treated like a numpty. Perhaps the old bag was just mean, but she didn't think so.

'You're forgetting something,' Berlin said. 'I haven't got a passport.'

'We'll get on to the British embassy after you've finished with Gerasimov,' said Charlie.

Berlin thought her other problem might present rather more of a difficulty. She paused and leant forward.

'Do you know a good doctor?'

*

Berlin's impression of Moscow was fragmentary, but there was a grim, determined grandeur about the place that overwhelmed her. The architecture was alien, apart from a sprinkling of bland shopping centres that wouldn't have been out of place in Swindon.

Charlie drove down an elegant boulevard, then turned into a potholed street that wound through block after block of buildings under construction. Cranes reared up on massive sites guarded by roaming dogs the size of wolves. It was seven in the evening and had been dark for hours.

Unable to read the signs or identify the symbols on buildings, Berlin had no idea of their purpose. Nor of their period. History had deserted her.

Charlie sped down a narrow road that ran parallel with a waterway.

'Is that the Moskva?' said Berlin.

'Hardly. It's the Vodootvodny Canal,' said Charlie. 'It loops off the river and meets up with it again at a bloody great statue of Peter the Great. You can't miss it.'

In the distance Berlin could see a tiered tower of russet masonry.

'And what's that? The building with the star on top?' she asked.

'One of Stalin's Seven Sisters,' said Charlie. '*Stalinskie Vysotki*. They say he was embarrassed that Moscow had no skyscrapers.'

'Strange. He usually kept his sensitive side well hidden,' observed Berlin.

Charlie snorted, lowered her window and threw out

her cigarette butt. The blast of freezing air didn't diminish the flush of anger that coloured her cheeks.

'That's absolutely typical,' she said. 'Passing casual judgement. Based on what? Cold War propaganda. You've not even been in the country twenty-four hours. Bloody cheek.'

Wrenching the steering wheel to one side, she swerved in front of a minibus caked with dry mud. In the side mirror, Berlin saw it brake hard to avoid a collision. A hundred yards further on, Charlie was forced to stop at traffic lights.

Berlin could see the vehicle nosing its way through the columns of cars. It pulled alongside them. It was packed with men who were as mud-spattered as the bus. They leant out of the windows and screamed at Charlie. She shouted back in Russian.

The lights turned green and Charlie put her foot down. The Range Rover surged forward.

'Tajiks!' she cried. 'They should deport the lot of them. Drug dealers!'

Berlin thought it best not to engage in further political debate.

Charlie had driven up onto the footpath and squeezed into a line of cars hugging the low wall that bordered the canal, ensuring that any pedestrians would be forced onto the road.

It was clear the population had no fear of parking wardens. The traffic might have been brutal, but the parking was chaotic: vehicles crammed into any available space, at all angles.

Once Charlie had managed to squeeze herself out of the car door, they walked along the canal, until finally Charlie crossed the road and stopped in front of a dilapidated four-storey pink-stuccoed mansion consisting of two wings, separated by a once-elegant portico.

The derelict pile was flanked on one side by rubbish-strewn wasteland and on the other by a collection of ramshackle sheds. The broad front garden, a tangle of snow-laden shrubbery and bare, black trees, was protected by high cast-iron railings.

The street was poorly lit and, as far as Berlin could see, not a single window glowed in any of the buildings that lined this block.

'Up for redevelopment,' was Charlie's only comment.

A pair of rusty gates appeared to be secured by a heavy chain and padlock. Charlie jiggled the chain. The padlock fell open. She gave one of the gates a shove and pushed through the gap that opened up.

She beckoned Berlin to follow.

The prospect of sleeping on a park bench suddenly seemed inviting.

25

Berlin was astonished when Charlie switched on the lights. The overgrown garden and the bare, decrepit entrance hall on the ground floor had not prepared her for the 'accommodation'.

She was reminded of nothing so much as Miss Havisham's decaying mansion, except here the clocks had stopped at *perestroika*. The last gasp of communism.

They ascended a wide marble staircase that led to a long gallery running the length of the building. Charlie unlocked a set of imposing double doors and showed Berlin through a vestibule into what appeared to have once been a grandiose reception room. But the crumbling plaster walls were hung with yellowing posters from the era of socialist realism: heroes of the revolution, proletarians and agrarian workers united in forging a new order.

Busts of Marx, Lenin and Stalin cluttered rococo marble-topped chiffoniers. Dusty glass-fronted bookcases were crammed with leather-bound sets of their complete works, in English and Russian, it looked like.

The naked windows, floor to ceiling, were rectangles of darkness.

'It was the residence of a Tsarist functionary,' said Charlie. 'Then the Party took it over and installed some apparatchik, who left most of this stuff behind when he was . . .' She hesitated. 'When he moved on.'

To which Berlin could only nod.

Monstrous walnut dressers, chaises longues, armchairs upholstered in faded gold velvet and a dining table meant to seat the Tsar's entire court barely occupied the immense space.

The furniture was dwarfed by the high ceilings and three sets of massive double doors. Berlin looked up. The pools of yellow light from the electric chandeliers enhanced the gloom, rather than illuminated it.

'Impossible to heat the whole place,' said Charlie. 'I stick to this room. Make yourself at home. I'll put the kettle on.'

The grimy stainless-steel sink on one wall was clearly a late addition to the establishment, as was the gas ring and a rickety pot-bellied wood stove in one corner. A hole in the wall, roughly plastered, accommodated its chimney.

'Won't be a tick,' said Charlie as she opened a set of the double doors. Berlin caught a glimpse of a long corridor and another set of doors before she closed them again behind her.

The weak pendant lights created deep pockets of shadow, but Berlin was able to discern the pattern of threadbare rugs, littered with tiny turds.

The surreal effect intensified as Berlin's eyes adjusted to the half-light: the Soviet memorabilia was complimented by tawdry souvenirs of London and the English seaside.

A fly-specked reproduction of *The Hay Wain* hung between posters of peasants and workers arm-in-arm beneath the hammer and sickle. A collection of English seaside snowstorms sat among the flaking *matryoshka* nesting dolls.

A child's jewellery box, decorated with dusty seashells, lay open to reveal tarnished gilt medals, inscribed with Lenin's profile, lying on frayed damask.

Berlin heard a faint scratching sound, followed by whimpering and the double doors creaking as they opened again. A tiny piebald chihuahua came tearing through them and made straight for Berlin, barking furiously. The source of the turds.

Charlie reappeared, closing the doors behind her. 'That's Yorkie,' she said. 'I keep him in the other wing. Best not to venture down there. Floor's a bit dodgy.' She pointed at the pile of splintered floorboards beside the wood stove.

'Yorkie,' said Berlin.

The tiny dog imitated a growl.

'Named after the chocolate bar,' said Charlie. 'There's nothing like English confectionery, you know.'

Yorkie, who apparently suffered from a skin condition, bounced up and down in front of Berlin, yapping. She was seized by the sensation of having wandered into someone else's dream – or nightmare. But the insistent, plaintive whine in her blood was hers alone.

'I mentioned earlier that I needed to see a doctor,' said Berlin, cradling her tea. She had waited for an appropriate moment to bring the topic up again. Tea at the Tsar's table seemed about right.

'What's wrong with you?' asked Charlie, frowning.

'I've run out of medication,' said Berlin. She wavered. If Charlie was able to deal directly with Burghley's client she really didn't want her situation getting back to them. 'It's a long-standing endocrinal condition.'

'You're in trouble then,' said Charlie.

Berlin was beginning to realise that her surly manner did not disguise a warm heart.

'There must be a hospital with an emergency department somewhere in a city of this size,' said Berlin.

'Emergency?' said Charlie. 'You don't look like you've been run over to me. Although I'm sure it could be arranged.'

It was the way she said it. Impassive, inscrutable.

'Scotch?' said Berlin. 'I just remembered I've got a bottle in my bag.'

26

Fagan was tired and irritable. So much for fucking Christmas Day. He doubted Boxing Day would be any better. At least one problem had been tucked up for the night, so he could go home. The prospect didn't fill him with joy.

Why had he decided to spend Christmas in England? Because it was expected, and he had to maintain at least a semblance of normality. In Fagan's experience, once you let something slip, everything else soon followed. It was a juggling act, but he had had plenty of practice.

He drove onto the Fullwell Cross roundabout, but instead of taking the exit to Chigwell Road he drove around again. And again.

He kept going over and over the last few days; was there anything he should have done differently? A lot of things were outside his sphere of influence: he was just the subcontractor. Hirst paid him through a series of shell companies and offshore accounts that didn't just minimise tax – they eradicated accountability.

But not his. He had to answer not only to his boss, but to himself. Sometimes his answers came up a bit short.

The wife and kids had stopped asking questions long ago.

The fourth time he circled the roundabout he swore, and took the exit to Fairlop Waters.

He would go and feed the ducks, so their honking didn't keep him awake all night.

27

Berlin shivered under a set of dusty brocade curtains on one of the chaises. She imagined the drapes had once graced the windows, but were redundant now that the glass was painted black.

Charlie was snoring loudly on a couch beneath a pile of what appeared to be moth-eaten rabbit fur. Yorkie had been escorted back to his wing. Charlie had explained that her residency in the building was only 'semi-official', so she was obliged to black out the windows to disguise her presence.

Berlin's pleas to be taken to a doctor had got her nowhere. Her limbs were aching, but it was impossible to tell if this was withdrawal or the biting cold.

They had finished the Talisker. It had taken the edge off her ague, but her usual nocturnal restlessness was kicking in and wouldn't be appeased unless she could walk. Silence and darkness always conspired against her.

She was exhausted, but as soon as her head had hit the pillow – or in this case, the lumpy bolster – her mind raced.

Unable to stand it any longer, she flung off the curtains, tiptoed to the vestibule and put on her coat, hat, gloves and boots. She would walk beside the canal to avoid getting lost. Surely even Russian muggers and rapists wouldn't be out in these temperatures.

A thick layer of corrugated ice beneath six inches of fresh snow kept Berlin on her toes, literally. She was barely out of the gate when she began to consider turning back.

A sleepless night under the curtains was preferable to lying in a heap with a broken arm or sprained ankle. She guessed help would not come readily. The hum of traffic in the distance hinted at human habitation, but there was no-one in the street.

Agitation got the better of her, so she crossed the road and walked back the way she and Charlie had come earlier, between the parked cars and the canal wall.

A duck squawked and she leant over the parapet to take a look: it appeared to be complaining bitterly about the lack of swimmable water.

The opaque ice was a still life of modernity, a faded rainbow of polystyrene take-away cartons, disposable nappies, broken bottles and a solitary Nike, its tongue lolling.

She felt at home.

The clink of metal on metal echoed in the silence. She glanced in the direction of the noise. Fifty yards down the line of parked cars two figures were standing beside the door of a Range Rover. It was Charlie's Range Rover.

'Hey!' shouted Berlin.

One of the men detached himself from the shadows around the car just as the other opened the door. Berlin heard a distinct *pop-pop*. The man seemed to be pointing at her.

It was only when the concrete parapet beside her

exploded into shrapnel that she realised he *was* pointing at her. With a gun.

More *pops* were accompanied by the dull rending of metal as bullets hit nearby cars. Berlin flung herself to the ground between two of them. Her face struck ice. As she opened her mouth to scream, it filled with snow.

The sounds of squealing tyres and thrumming motors were suddenly all around her. A shadow fell across the space where she cowered. She looked up. A car door swung open.

'Quick!' came a command.

Berlin scrambled to her feet and flung herself into the car. It surged forward and the door slammed shut, catching her ankle.

'Christ,' Berlin exclaimed, then added in outrage, 'they shot at me.'

'Very likely,' said Major Utkin.

The tail lights of the Range Rover were about a hundred yards ahead, at a T-junction, one arm of which was a bridge over the canal. It turned right and sped across.

When Utkin reached the T-junction he turned left.

Berlin was astonished. 'What are you doing?' she shouted. 'Follow them!'

'Men with guns? Not very likely,' said Utkin.

The McDonald's was very busy. The long queues appeared to be composed entirely of clubbers: young men and women in designer clothes who, as far as Berlin could tell, did not feel the cold. She recognised with envy the warm glow conferred by the many substances that coursed through their veins.

Utkin put down a tray bearing two cardboard cups of black tea. 'First McDonald's in Russia,' he said. 'Pushkin Square. Six-hour wait on day it opened.' He chuckled. He smacked his hands together as if to emphasise the sudden nature of the cataclysmic change. 'Nineteen-ninety one! Freedom.'

Berlin took off her left boot and rubbed her sore ankle.

'Once was biggest McDonald's in all world.' Utkin sighed. 'Now Oklahoma. But still biggest in Europe.'

'What about the McDonald's at Olympic Park in London?' she said, amazed to find herself engaging in one-upmanship about anything, let alone McDonald's.

'Temporary!' cried Utkin.

That settled it.

'Not eating?' said Berlin, indicating the tray.

'Goodness me, no,' said Utkin. 'It is not eatable.'

From his inside pocket he produced a small flask and discreetly topped up their tea with a clear fluid.

'I assume that's antifreeze,' she said.

Utkin guffawed. 'Ah! English humour,' he said.

'I'm afraid I'm losing mine,' said Berlin. 'Are you stalking me, Major Utkin?'

Utkin's smile was benign. 'Very likely,' he said.

Berlin slurped her tea and burnt her mouth, which only added to her irritation.

'Why the hell didn't you go after them?' she demanded. 'You're a policeman, aren't you?'

Utkin sighed. 'I'm beyond retirement age,' he said.

'That's no excuse,' she said.

'No. But it explains how I lived this long,' said Utkin.

Berlin sipped her tea cautiously. 'Your English is very good,' she said. 'Is that common among Russian coppers?'

'*Coppers*,' said Utkin. He drew out the word, enjoying it. 'Few Russian *coppers* speak good Russian.'

Berlin noticed that although the restaurant was crowded and she and Utkin sat at a table for four, no-one sat at the empty places. The locals knew a policeman when they saw one, even in plainclothes.

A stocky, scowling man strolled past them. Berlin recognised him immediately. It was Joseph Stalin. Four more Stalins followed him, all carrying trays laden with burgers and fries.

'They hang about outside expensive stores, or in Red Square,' explained Utkin. 'For few roubles you have your picture taken with them. Stalins make more money than Lenins. Both do better than Brezhnevs.'

Berlin tried to focus on the issue at hand, rather than stare at the old tyrants.

'What are you going to do about the Range Rover?' she asked.

'Nothing,' said Utkin.

'Two blokes prepared to kill, just to steal a car, and you're going to let it slide?' she said.

'It was their car, after all,' said Utkin.

Berlin sat back and stared at him.

'That is, they collect it for owner,' said Utkin.

But before she could demand clarification, Utkin reached into his pocket and produced the photo of her grandfather.

She was so surprised she didn't know what to say. She

hadn't missed it, probably because she'd been so preoccupied by the seizure of her buprenorphine and passport.

Utkin laid it on the table between them.

In the flat, sterile light the scorched black-and-white snap seemed even more archaic: it was the photo of Zayde in his long johns, barrel chest exposed.

'Who is this?' Utkin asked her.

'My grandfather,' she said. 'Jacob Berlinsky. He was Russian.'

'Do you know what these are?' he said, pointing to the tattoos on Zayde's shoulders.

'Not really,' she replied.

She remembered tracing them with her finger when she sat in her grandfather's lap on rare hot summer days; he had a cat in a hat on one shoulder and five teardrops on the other.

'I think perhaps he had them done during the war,' said Berlin. 'Something to do with his regiment, perhaps?'

'His regiment?' Utkin echoed, rolling his eyes. 'Oh yes, his regiment: the *vor*. His war was fought against law, always and everywhere. They refused fight in Great Patriotic War, even in exchange for freedom.'

'I'm not with you,' said Berlin. 'What do you mean?'

Utkin pointed to the cat in the hat. 'This means your grandfather was *vory v zakone*. A thief-in-law. It's like Mafia. But worse.'

Utkin picked up the photo and offered it to her. She took it with both hands, stunned.

'And now I understand you a little better, Katarina Berlinskaya,' he said.

28

Berlin crept back into the apartment and sat in the vestibule. Charlie's stentorian snores were indication enough that she hadn't been missed.

Major Utkin hadn't returned her passport or buprenorphine, and he hadn't asked for money. He was keeping tabs on her, protecting his investment. He was dragging it out to soften her up. As her anxiety increased so would his price. The shakedown would come sooner or later. But she was angry that he had brought her grandfather into it.

Berlin was well acquainted with the major's type: pathetic. His job was his life, and it was deserting him. How much he would ask her for, and in what currency, was all that remained to be established.

She dragged off her boots and sat on the low wooden bench, rubbing life back into her toes.

Utkin's characterisation of Zayde as a criminal had dredged up memories that she thought had been long exorcised: her parents' fierce arguments when Zayde came home with shiny stuff: gold chains, thick rings with bright stones that Peggy would refuse to polish or sell in the shop.

Berlin padded across the room under the blank gaze

of the architects of communism. She crawled into her ersatz crib and drew the drapes over her head. She just wanted to do it and get the hell out of there.

29

Yuri was livid. He was surrounded by fools. Two of them stood in front of him, surly and unapologetic.

'You shot at someone,' he said. 'You think it could have been the woman?'

A sullen nod confirmed it.

'It was very dark,' said the other one.

Yuri turned to him. 'But not too dark for someone to intervene,' he said. 'And why shoot? I gave you the spare keys.'

'We were told to get the car,' the man mumbled. He glanced at Maryna, who was standing by the window, her back turned to them. 'No-one said anything about how.'

Yuri slapped him. He felt, rather than saw, Maryna flinch. It was a reaction he quite enjoyed. It was one of the few things he had over her. Correction. The only thing he had over her.

'It must have been this policeman, Utkin,' said Maryna. 'I told you. He came to see me about Misha and mentioned Katarina Berlin. Heroes are very thin on the ground in Moscow.'

Yuri's joy evaporated. He didn't like keeping things from Maryna, but he had failed to mention he knew Utkin, because it would only lead to more questions, and more pressure.

'But how did he connect them?' he said.

'Because he is investigating the death of the interpreter,' said Maryna, impatient. 'When they found the body at the airport this Utkin went looking for whoever he was supposed to meet. It would have been the first thing he asked her: "Why are you here?"'

And the second thing, thought Yuri, *would have been who actually met you.*

'She must have told him about her assignment,' said Maryna. 'He asked me about a car, too. Can't you do something?'

'You mean, like arrange to have him removed from the case? How, without arousing suspicion?'

'Well, you have to do something.'

Yuri stared at the floor. Maryna knew nothing of certain arrangements. She insisted on it. She said it was need to know, and she didn't need to know. It was an expression of her trust in him.

It also meant she couldn't be implicated.

'This British woman, Berlin, is what she seems,' said Yuri. 'I am assured she came to interview Misha to fulfil legal requirements, that's all.'

'What does Utkin know?' said Maryna.

'Nothing,' said Yuri. 'He's an old man pursuing a phantom. Don't be concerned.'

Maryna touched his cheek.

His heart soared with gratitude. She knew he was weak, but forgave him. What more could a man ask from a woman?

30

Charlie appeared dazed when she woke in the morning and saw Berlin sitting at one end of the imperial table, staring at her.

Berlin waited until the confusion cleared from her bloodshot eyes, then spoke. 'The car's gone,' she said.

'Oh,' said Charlie. 'Put the kettle on, would you?'

'How do you think they found it?' asked Berlin.

'Probably had one of those satellite thingies in it,' said Charlie.

When Berlin didn't move Charlie sighed and slid out from under the tatty furs, retaining one draped around her shoulders.

'So why did you steal it?' asked Berlin.

'You wouldn't happen to have an aspirin, would you?' asked Charlie. Berlin could hear the phlegm bubbling in Charlie's chest as she shuffled to the gas ring and put on the kettle.

'What happened to your own car?' Berlin persisted.

'It died at the airport,' said Charlie. 'I didn't want to lose this job. As you can see, I'm not exactly living high on the hog. So I pinched one.'

Berlin was astounded at the cheek of the woman.

'But you had the keys,' said Berlin.

Charlie hesitated a moment. She yawned in an exaggerated fashion.

'Oh, they always leave them behind the visor, like American gangsters in films,' she said. 'They can't believe anyone would have the nerve to steal from them.'

So Charlie, like Utkin, was well aware of who owned the car. It struck Berlin at that moment that Charlie was either desperate or deranged. Or both.

Wrapped against the cold in one of the brocade curtains, Berlin turned on her tablet and waited for it to pick up a Wi-Fi signal. Nothing happened. She got up and began wandering up and down the room, peering at the walls.

'What are you doing?' said Charlie.

'Looking for your modem.'

'I haven't got the Internet,' snapped Charlie.

Sure. Just like you haven't got a mobile.

'You couldn't work for Burghley without it,' said Berlin. She flung open the first set of doors, which led to Yorkie's wing.

Charlie seemed alarmed. 'All right, all right,' she said. She scuttled across the room to close the doors again, then reached behind a stack of ancient *Pravda* newspapers. Berlin heard a click. She went back to the tablet and saw five signal bars appear on the screen.

Charlie stomped off and set about preparing what looked like a large bowl of gruel to feed the scabrous chihuahua.

Berlin accessed the British embassy website, quickly scrolling through pages of cheerful information about building Britain's prosperity by increasing exports and investments, opening markets and ensuring access.

There were lists of contacts if you wanted to pursue trade opportunities, but she had to look long and hard to find consular services for British nationals 'in distress'. She found a pad and scribbled down a number.

She logged on to her mobile phone account and paid her bill. Now at least she could make calls. She went straight to Contacts and tapped one while waiting for her email to download.

Charlie shuffled towards Yorkie's wing with the gruel. The doors closed behind her.

Del's voice invited Berlin to leave a message.

'Hi, Del,' said Berlin. 'Hope you're having a good Christmas.' She paused and considered how to deliver the news, not wishing to alarm him. 'The job is fine,' she continued. 'I've just emailed you the first transcript. But some things have gone a bit pear-shaped. Call me as soon as you get this. I'm staying with Charlie Inkpin, so don't try the hotel.'

She hung up and quickly banged out another email to him saying the same thing, just in case his phone was switched off.

Meanwhile, spam had piled into her inbox. There was one message from Magnus sent late on Christmas Eve. It read, 'Where the fuck are you, old darling? Call me.'

Magnus didn't trust email, or voicemail for that matter, probably because he'd hacked into too many of other people's accounts. He wasn't even that keen on the phone, preferring face to face in a pub.

Berlin reflected that since communication had become so fast, so ubiquitous and so insecure, the old ways were making a comeback. No doubt everyone would go back to dead letterboxes sooner or later. She had read that one of the Russian security agencies had bought a load of typewriters, to avoid electronic surveillance.

She tapped Magnus's number on her Contacts list and listened to his phone ring. And ring. And ring. She knew he would either answer or it would ring out. No voicemail.

The sound of a series of doors slamming heralded Charlie's return. 'We should get this show on the road,' she announced.

Berlin hung up. She considered her crumpled, unwashed state. She hesitated, but decided it would have to do; she had used the toilet, an experience that had persuaded her not to enquire about a bath. She had changed her shirt. That would have to do.

She dumped the curtain that was draped around her shoulders, brushed off her suit, ran her fingers through her hair and trusted that the frigid air would kill any bacteria associated with unflattering odours.

Another interview and one more night in the House of Horrors.

Tomorrow she would be back in business class.

Charlie locked up behind them and followed Berlin down the broad marble staircase.

Berlin hadn't mentioned her encounter with Utkin. Her hostess's reaction when told that the police had taken Berlin's passport was ample evidence that she had a problem with law enforcement. Berlin wasn't going to take the risk of being dumped on the street.

'By the way, I checked the British embassy website,' said Berlin. 'It says that if the embassy here is closed you should call the Foreign and Commonwealth Office in London. But they're closed too.'

'There's a surprise,' said Charlie. 'It is Boxing Day, you know. The embassy here pretends it's really over there.'

They crossed the tiled marble lobby and stepped out onto the portico. Berlin blinked against the sudden glare from the snow. 'You'll have to take me first thing tomorrow,' she said. 'I've got the address.'

'I know where it is,' said Charlie. She stomped with practised ease through the thick snow that obscured the path through the garden to the front gates. Berlin slithered after her.

'They might be iffy about issuing a new passport when you tell them the police confiscated it,' said Charlie.

'What are you talking about?' said Berlin. 'I lost it.'

Berlin saw Charlie's face crinkle into a smile.

'You cheeky devil,' she said.

It took one to know one.

The battered, old-fashioned sedan parked in an alley at the rear of the mansion was certainly a better fit with Charlie than the Range Rover.

'What is it?' said Berlin.

'A Zaporozhets,' said Charlie. 'These cars can be fixed by anyone with a spanner. My mechanic collected it for me.'

The driver's door wasn't locked. But it was stuck.

Charlie yanked at the handle a couple of times and finally it creaked open.

'A marvel of Soviet engineering,' said Berlin.

'You can bloody well walk if you like,' said Charlie. Berlin got in and kept her mouth shut.

31

Gerasimov's get-up continued the jaunty nautical theme of his first outfit. The breast pocket of this blazer, which was a little large around the shoulders, boasted a ship's wheel embroidered in gold. Through his wife, he expressed his delight at seeing them again.

Berlin's delight, meanwhile, was reserved for the coffee and pastries.

'My husband trusts you slept well, Ms Berlin,' said Gerasimova, politely failing to notice the wrinkled condition of Berlin's suit.

Berlin nodded.

Charlie had produced a bottle of vodka from the car's glovebox on the way over. It had helped to quieten Berlin's jangled neurons, which were becoming restless as they waited for a pharmaceutical solution to their discomfort.

Charlie sat down beside Berlin. Gerasimova sat just behind her husband. The two interpreters glared at each other. Berlin flipped open the tablet.

'Mr Gerasimov, at the completion of this interview I have a document which I will ask you to read carefully and sign,' she said.

Charlie remained silent. She obviously wasn't in the mood to tag-team today, so Gerasimova took up the slack.

Gerasimov responded rapidly in Russian.

'Yes,' translated Gerasimova. 'I am familiar with the process.'

'Good,' said Berlin. 'It will ask you to confirm the truthfulness of the information you have provided and—'

'Yes, yes, he understands,' said his wife. 'There's no need.'

'Very well. Let's start,' said Berlin.

She double-clicked the due diligence interview template, part two. The template unfurled at the same time as her email program appeared on-screen. She heard a ping.

The tablet must have picked up a Wi-Fi signal.

The first line of Del's reply to her email popped up in a bubble. It read 'Who's Charlie Inkpin?'

Gerasimov was chatting in Russian, answering Berlin's first question. His wife, frowning, had not begun to translate. She spoke to her husband in Russian. He shrugged. He seemed offended.

Berlin had detected alcohol on his breath when they'd arrived. Now he and Gerasimova were engaged in a domestic. The commodore was acting up, which surprised Berlin.

But at least it gave her the opportunity to scan the rest of Del's email. He asked what things in particular had gone pear-shaped. He wanted to know if Charlie Inkpin was one of Gerasimov's people. He warned her against accepting hospitality, as it could create a conflict of interest.

Finally, he enquired about the performance of the accredited interpreter Burghley had engaged: Vladimir Matvienko.

Berlin conducted the rest of the interview on autopilot. She had a lot to think about. On top of everything else Gerasimov was not behaving like a businessman trying to impress. He kept getting up and strutting around the room, expansive and voluble, helping himself to vodka from a bottle that stood on a side table with four glasses.

If Charlie hadn't been engaged by Burghley, who was she working for? The interpreter they had instructed must have been paid off, or threatened, or both.

It was unlikely that Gerasimov himself would engage in such a stunt. If it were exposed, the pin would be pulled by his putative business partners in the UK. He had little to gain, as far as she could see. There were more efficient and less risky ways to mislead an investigator.

On the other hand, if you had something big to hide, you took risks. The interpreter, whom the investigator would treat as a colleague, might have an insight into her thinking, or be able to steer her away from enquiries that could prove problematic.

Berlin glanced at Charlie. There were two other possibilities: she could be working for Gerasimov's enemies, collecting intel from the interviews that would further their interests, or she was a criminal running a sophisticated scam that would result in a business visitor with a deep pocket buying their way out of trouble.

For which she would need a partner.

Utkin?

This could explain why he had been so conveniently on hand last night.

*

At the completion of the interview Gerasimov executed a squiggle on the tablet with a stylus, attempting to sign his declaration with a flourish. Four shots were poured from what remained of the vodka and they all toasted Russian–British cooperation and enterprise, once in Russian and once in English.

Gerasimova took Berlin's elbow and drew her aside. When Charlie attempted to follow, she waved her away. An interpreter was not required.

'We understand that you experienced some difficulties last night,' she said. 'Mr Gerasimov is very concerned.'

Berlin couldn't disguise her surprise.

'How do you know?' she said.

'We protect our business, Ms Berlin,' said Gerasimova. 'Which means protecting you.'

Was Utkin playing on Gerasimov's team?

The problem was that Berlin had no idea how many players there were in this game. But due diligence was at risk, whichever way you cut it.

'It was a minor incident,' said Berlin, as if she were shot at every day. 'I'm fine.'

'Thanks to the intervention of a champion,' said Gerasimova.

Berlin became aware of the pressure of the woman's hand on her arm. This was getting out of control. But the comment implied Gerasimova didn't know who had plucked Berlin from between the cars. So Utkin wasn't connected to them.

'A taxi driver,' said Berlin. 'I was lucky. A cab was passing.'

'Lucky indeed. You saw the little light illuminated and just flagged him down,' said Gerasimova. 'Remarkable.'

It suddenly struck Berlin as odd that Gerasimov spoke not one word of English, but his wife had a vocabulary worthy of the Bard. What was going on here?

'Oh no,' said Berlin. 'Not a taxi. I meant *chastniki*.'

Gerasimova frowned. 'You are a fast learner, Ms Berlin,' she said.

'In my business it's the quick and the dead,' said Berlin. 'But thank you for your concern.'

She extricated herself from Gerasimova's grip and thanked God for the city profile that Del had included with her briefing. *Chastniki* were unofficial taxis. Apparently Muscovites would simply stick their arm out and a car would pull over and give them a lift for a few roubles.

They were a resourceful and pragmatic people.

Which made them very good liars.

The Gerasimovs escorted Berlin and Charlie to the lift. The little commodore kissed them both twice. His wife offered a smile and a wave.

Goodbye and good luck.

32

Magnus had spent twenty-four hours drying out in a small room on a cot shoved into a corner. It wasn't a proper police station; the tea was proof of that. Weak as piss. They had also fed him McDonald's, instead of the bacon butty he had requested. He found it difficult to believe he was still living in a democracy.

The door wasn't locked, but a bruiser was stationed outside and it was pretty clear that if he tried to leave, things could get unpleasant.

But the truth was he was as weak as a baby; he was shaking like a leaf. He needed hair of the dog sooner rather than later in order to deal with this bloody mess he had got himself into.

Finally the door opened and Jolyon Carmichael, his erstwhile editor, walked in, accompanied by the bruiser.

'Christ, Magnus,' said Carmichael. 'It's Boxing Day.'

Magnus struggled upright on the cot. The bruiser stood beside the door. Carmichael sat down, moving the chair as far away as possible from Magnus.

Magnus imagined he was a bit whiffy. He remembered being sick. 'You took your time,' he said.

'You should be bloody grateful I turned up at all,' said

Carmichael. 'You're not even an employee, which means we can't help you on the legal front.'

'I don't need a fucking lawyer,' exploded Magnus. 'I haven't done anything wrong. Just make a call to one of your politician mates. Explain that a respected journalist has been illegally detained by a bunch of totalitarian nasties and it will be on your front page tomorrow if they don't sort it out.'

Carmichael sighed. 'I understand you've been up to your old tricks again.'

'Oh, for Christ's sake,' said Magnus. 'It's called investigative journalism.'

'It's called conspiring to commit misconduct in a public office,' said Carmichael. 'I believe the judge indicated another offence would attract a great deal more than a fine.'

Magnus contemplated a life without liquor. 'Perhaps we could get a decent cup of tea,' he muttered.

Carmichael heaped three sugars into his cup then dropped the spoon on the table. 'What I don't understand, Magnus,' he said, 'is why you want to pursue it – merely because this chap lied to your source about what was going on at the warehouse?'

'I suppose you haven't got a flask in your pocket?' said Magnus. 'Give this swill a bit of a lift.'

Carmichael frowned.

'That's a no, then,' said Magnus. He had to stall. He needed time to think. His head ached.

If the powers that be had managed to drag Carmichael

out early on Boxing Day, then it could only mean that the enquiries Magnus had made had stirred up a hornet's nest, beyond the miserably banal offence he had supposedly committed.

On the other hand, he had to offer Carmichael something more substantial if he was to persuade him to run the story, or at least support him in continuing to work his leads.

'Hirst are only the tip of the iceberg,' he said. 'A van that doesn't appear on any delivery schedule unloads into a Park Royal warehouse and a Hirst employee covers it up with a story about pilfering.'

'From which you infer what?' said Carmichael.

'It's the old one-two,' said Magnus. 'Confess to a small transgression to distract attention from the bigger one.'

Carmichael rubbed his face. 'I don't know, Magnus,' he said.

'Come on, Carmichael,' said Magnus. 'There's something going on. Let's just ask the question.'

'It's all based on what?' said Carmichael. 'Someone thinks they saw a van being unloaded.'

'My source doesn't make mistakes,' said Magnus.

Carmichael raised an eyebrow. It was a question: who was the source?

Magnus hesitated, uncomfortable. 'I'd rather not say, at this stage, if you don't mind, old darling. In the current circs.'

Carmichael nodded. 'You're going to have to let it lie, I'm afraid, Magnus,' he said. 'At least for the time being.'

'What?' said Magnus.

'Apart from your precarious legal situation, I've also

had a call from the Secretary of the Defence, Press and Broadcasting Advisory Committee drawing my attention to Standing Defence Advisory Notice Number Five,' said Carmichael.

Magnus stared at him. It meant there'd been an official request from the government not to publish anything about this subject.

'They've slapped a D-Notice on it?' said Magnus.

'You know that's not the way it works any more,' said Carmichael.

'Bollocks again,' said Magnus. 'So which one is Number Five, anyway?'

'It covers security, intelligence and special services,' said Carmichael.

'Christ Almighty,' said Magnus. He gazed around the room. Walls have ears. He dropped his voice to a whisper. 'You can ignore it,' he said. 'D-Notices, or DA-Notices, or whatever they call them these days, are only advisory.'

Carmichael ran his fingers through what little hair he had left. 'I don't like it any more than you do, Magnus. But there it is,' he said. 'In any event, there's no real story here.'

'Then why do they want to suppress it?' demanded Magnus. 'We can't find out what's going on if we can't tell anyone what we *do* know.'

'I'm sorry,' said Carmichael. 'It's a matter of national security.'

Magnus stared at him. 'Because of who owns the van.'

Carmichael nodded.

*

Fagan was parked in the lane behind the anonymous brick building in south London. It could have been a garage or a workshop, maybe a panel beaters or builder's merchant. But if you looked up at the roof you would think again: it sprouted a forest of satellite dishes and antennas.

It was a joke, really, because he was out here waiting for a signal. But this one would come via a nod and a wink. Something that didn't leave a trace in cyberspace.

If the bloke inside jumped the wrong way he was there as Plan B: biddable, expendable, unexceptional. With a reliable trigger finger. It was itching now.

He watched as two men emerged from the back door. One got into a dark blue Jag and sped off. The editor. The other bloke – tall, black, paunchy – looked the worse for wear. The reporter. He gazed about him as if unsure which way to turn.

Another unexceptional man strolled past the end of the lane. He stopped to light a cigarette and blew a thin spiral of white smoke into the still air.

Fagan started the motor.

33

The drive from the Gerasimovs' back to Charlie's was hair-raising. The car coughed and spluttered. The windscreen wipers struggled against the snowstorm. The ploughs couldn't keep pace with the growing drifts on the road.

They passed a team of men wielding long metal poles, chipping away at the ice, bent double against the bitter, driving wind. An overseer, standing close to a glowing brazier, watched them.

Berlin was disconcerted by the painterly scene. The outlines of the men, shrouded in long coats, were softened by the swirling flakes; their heavy-lidded eyes were blank, the sharp, smooth planes of their caramel faces impassive. It was a tableau that seemed to stand outside time.

She glanced at their ankles, almost expecting to see a chain half-buried in the snow. The traffic forced the car to a crawl.

One of the workers looked up. His deep brown almond eyes stared straight at Berlin. He raised his steel pole and for a moment she thought he was going to launch it at the car. The overseer barked something and instead he brought it crashing down. Splinters of ice flew through the air and struck her window.

She was relieved when they moved off.

Charlie drove in silence. Berlin had a lot of questions, but she wasn't going to distract her from the tricky task of keeping the car on the road. Instead, she tried to put the icemen out of her mind and think through the best approach to extracting information from her so-called interpreter.

She had very little to use in the way of leverage.

If Charlie wasn't working for Burghley, there was no point in threatening her with a bad report card. She obviously needed money, but if questioned she could say anything and Berlin would be none the wiser.

Charlie had been very nervous when Berlin had mentioned the police at the hotel. If she were working with Utkin, this would make sense: neither would want to risk their scam being exposed by Berlin approaching other members of the Moscow *politsya*.

Pressure in that direction was the most likely to yield results.

When they got back to the apartment, she would take a softly-softly approach.

Berlin kicked the front door shut behind them.

'Hand over your bloody phone,' she demanded.

Charlie backed up. 'I told you. I haven't got a phone.'

Berlin grabbed her and shoved her against the wall. She was about to rough up a pensioner. For a moment she was struck by how easy this could be when conscience was deadened by an overwhelming craving.

'I don't want to hurt you, Berlin,' said Charlie.

Berlin almost laughed, but then realised the dumpy woman was serious. She could have a weapon. Berlin thrust her forearm against Charlie's throat and pinioned her to the cracked plaster. With her other hand she searched Charlie's pockets.

'All right, all right,' gurgled Charlie.

Berlin removed her forearm.

Charlie unzipped her coat and reached inside.

Berlin stopped her. She reached into the deep pocket herself and found the mobile.

'Sit down,' commanded Berlin.

Charlie shuffled to the dining table and sat down, rubbing her throat. She reached for the vodka.

Berlin moved the bottle away.

'I want to know who you are,' said Berlin. 'If I don't get a satisfactory answer, I'm calling the authorities and reporting you for kidnapping, fraud, extortion. Whatever fits in nicely with the Russian Criminal Code.'

'I don't know what you're talking about,' said Charlie gruffly. She began to cough, clutching her chest, building to a hacking crescendo that culminated in her spitting into a square of grey cloth she dragged from her pocket.

Berlin saw a fleck of red. Charlie wasn't a well woman. The apartment was freezing. She thought of Bella, turning off heating she couldn't afford and donning two tracksuits to keep warm.

'Why are you so bloody difficult?' she said. She sat down at the table, poured Charlie a vodka and pushed it towards her.

Charlie drank it gratefully. Her wheezing subsided.

Berlin scrolled through the phone's log of recent calls. Only one had been made in the last twenty-four hours. She tapped the number and listened as it dialled.

'I wouldn't do that if I were you,' murmured Charlie, clearly exhausted by her coughing fit.

The unfamiliar burr of the Russian ringtone echoed down the line. Berlin didn't understand the phrase that greeted her, but she understood the pause and beep that followed: voicemail. It was enough. She hung up.

The interrogator's cardinal rule was *don't give anything away*. She had to avoid mentioning anything, or anyone, that Charlie might not already know about.

'You're not working for Burghley. You're working for someone here,' said Berlin. 'A Russian.'

Charlie pouted.

'Come on, Charlie,' said Berlin. 'Who are you?'

Charlie sighed. 'For God's sake, have a drink,' she said. 'You look as if you need one.'

Berlin had expected more resistance, but she could see Charlie was spent. She took the bottle and poured herself a drink. Charlie raised her own in an ironic toast, gulped it, then sucked in air.

'My name is Charlotte Svetlana Inkpin,' she announced. 'I am the so-called love child of Albert Inkpin and his mistress. He was the first General Secretary of the Communist Party of Great Britain. She was a Russian comrade. They met when he was running an organisation known as the Friends of the Soviet Union.'

Berlin wanted to laugh. But one look at Charlie told her she was deadly serious. Berlin was astounded.

'I was born in London during the war,' said Charlie. 'My father died when I was one.'

Berlin recovered enough to disguise her amazement. 'That doesn't explain anything.'

Charlie poured them both another drink. 'I came here as a sort of émigré,' she hedged. 'A refugee.'

'From what?' said Berlin.

'Capitalism,' said Charlie.

'What?' said Berlin. She considered what she did know about the woman: her class, her age, her choice of political memorabilia. 'You're joking.'

'Not at all,' said Charlie.

'You're telling me you were a spy, like Philby or Maclean?' said Berlin.

'Oh no,' said Charlie. 'Not in that league. I was a very minor defector.'

34

Berlin gripped Charlie's arm and steered her towards the front door. It had taken her a couple of shots of vodka to process Charlie's confession, but now she had to act.

'For Christ's sake,' said Charlie. 'Where are we going?'

'We're going back to see the Gerasimovs and find out what's going on. Do they know you're masquerading as my interpreter? Are they part of this set-up?'

'Bad idea,' grunted Charlie.

The recalcitrant woman dug in her heels; her round shape made it difficult to manoeuvre her through the apartment's imposing doorway, as wide as it was.

'Get off!' shouted Charlie, clinging to the architrave.

Berlin pushed and heaved.

A dull, repetitive thud started up somewhere in the apartment. Yorkie, no doubt disturbed by his mistress's cries, was using his little body as a battering ram. The noise seemed to have an effect on Charlie. Her resistance evaporated.

'You'll be sorry,' she said. She shrugged Berlin off, stalked out of the apartment and set off down the stairs.

Berlin slammed the door behind them and followed.

*

Charlie remained tight-lipped during the journey. She had flatly refused to discuss whom she was working for and denied all knowledge of the Gerasimovs, beyond their address and the purpose of Berlin's interviews. She insisted it was none of her business.

It was quite possible that the Gerasimovs were unaware that Charlie was not the interpreter assigned by Burghley. They were hardly likely to admit they were in on it, but their reaction would speak volumes.

If they weren't involved, Berlin could take it from there; she could let Del know that there was a problem and he could approach the client for new instructions.

Exposing Charlie's pretence, no matter what its purpose, could be a win for Berlin. The client would surely be relieved that their exercise in risk management, designed to protect them from the vagaries of the Bribery Act, hadn't fallen at the first hurdle.

The elevator doors slid open. For a moment Berlin thought they had the wrong floor. The walls were bare. No gilt mirrors, no chandeliers, no ornate side tables. No snow leopards. She strode to the double doors of the apartment and flung them open.

A vast white space lay before her.

Berlin hurried from room to empty room.

Charlie watched her. 'A Potemkin village,' she said. She muttered something in Russian that sounded very much like a curse.

'A what?' said Berlin.

'It's an expression,' said Charlie. 'Grigory Potemkin

built a fake village to impress Catherine II when she visited the Crimea.'

'It worked,' said Berlin.

'It's a popular ploy here these days,' said Charlie.

Berlin sat on the floor of the naked room, her back resting against the warm radiators. In a matter of a few hours they had cleaned the place out, but they'd forgotten to switch off the heating. Her luck was holding.

'You must have known,' she said.

Charlie turned on her. 'I told you. I'd never seen either of them before in my life until yesterday. I was engaged to meet you, ferry you back and forth to this address and interpret. That's all.'

'Whoever hired you didn't find you on Google,' insisted Berlin.

'This is Russia,' said Charlie. 'Nothing is what it seems.' She slid down the wall to the floor, stretched out her stubby legs and lit a cigarette.

'Don't give me that,' said Berlin. 'You know what this is all about. Tell me or we're going straight to the nearest police station.'

Charlie gripped her head, as if holding it together.

Berlin waited. If Charlie didn't cooperate she'd call Utkin. His mobile number was in her Contacts list. At this point she had no-one else to turn to.

Finally Charlie raised her hands in a sign of surrender. 'Somebody asked me to do them a favour,' she muttered. 'I couldn't say no.'

'Why not?' said Berlin.

'You wouldn't understand,' said Charlie.

'Try me,' said Berlin.

Charlie took a long drag on her cigarette. She squinted at Berlin through the smoke as she exhaled.

'He's my roof,' she said.

'Your what?' said Berlin. Even when they were speaking English she couldn't understand these people.

'Everyone here has someone they can turn to, someone further up the pecking order,' said Charlie. 'They look after you, they keep your secrets – but then you have to deliver, as and when required.'

'You mean, like a protection racket,' said Berlin.

Charlie shook her head. She put the tips of her pudgy fingers together and formed them into a peak. '*Krysha*,' she said. 'A roof.'

'A stand-over man,' said Berlin.

Charlie sighed. 'Oh, have it your own way,' she said. Her hands collapsed together, clasped in a gesture of supplication. 'There's no point in going to the police,' she added. 'It would just make things worse. Believe me.'

At this stage Berlin was inclined to think she was right. A pall of gloom had settled over Charlie, an air of resignation. Perhaps she *had* been kept in the dark.

'If someone has got something over you, you should deal with it,' said Berlin.

'Easy for you to say,' said Charlie. 'Never been in a tight spot, Berlin?'

'Of course,' said Berlin.

'Never had to do the wrong thing for the right reasons?' said Charlie.

It was a question Berlin would rather not answer. 'So who is it?' she said. 'This *krysha*.'

'Nobody you would know,' said Charlie. She lapsed into a glum, distracted silence.

Pressing the point was useless. Whoever the *krysha* was, and whatever it was that they had over Charlie, the eccentric Englishwoman was determined to keep to herself.

Berlin owed Charlie nothing. But she hated bullyboys and understood only too well the fear of exposure. She turned and gazed out of the window at the frozen Moskva River eight storeys below. Blank red battlements with twin keeps loomed on the riverbank. Gleaming onion domes floated above striped turrets. Backcloth for a fairy tale.

Berlin expected to see the Empress Catherine glide past on the ice, her retinue in tow.

A Potemkin village. The illusion that sustained her own life overwhelmed her. Dread swarmed through her veins.

'I have to see a doctor,' she said.

35

They had been sitting for hours among the coughs, sneezes and wailing children in the airless waiting room. The weak cries of a woman who seemed to be calling for help drifted to Berlin from beyond a flimsy partition. It seemed the Russian medical system was in as much disarray as the National Health Service.

'I've had enough of this,' said Charlie. She got up and marched over to the harassed receptionist behind the counter, addressing her in a low, intense tone.

The receptionist kept giving Berlin dark sideways looks, while Charlie harangued her sotto voce. Finally the receptionist shrugged. Charlie turned to Berlin.

'The doctor will see you now,' she said. 'If you've got the cash.'

Berlin followed her directions to a door at the end of a long corridor and knocked.

The door was opened by a woman in her forties wearing a threadbare white lab coat. She pointed at a chair. Berlin sat. Her consultation was to be private. No witnesses. Charlie remained in the waiting room. The receptionist had said the doctor spoke 'small English'.

A quick online search after her initial encounter with Utkin had not given Berlin any reason for optimism:

buprenorphine and methadone were both illegal in Russia, although the country consumed more heroin than any other in Europe.

The peculiar Russian discipline of *narkologija*, which had its roots in Soviet-era political correctness, forbade substitution therapy. Abstinence was the goal that drove policy and medical practice – and addicts into early graves.

'I'm in a considerable amount of pain,' said Berlin. 'A lot,' she added, in case 'considerable' wasn't clear.

The doctor, who was writing in a file, didn't look up. 'Yes?' she said. 'From where?'

Berlin removed her boot and sock, and rolled up her black thermal tights to display her scarred calf.

'A torn Achilles tendon, repaired badly,' she said.

The doctor glanced down, then returned to her file. 'And?' she said.

Berlin had encountered many abrupt medical practitioners in her time, but this one set a new standard in brusque bedside manners. She unwound her scarf and undid the buttons of her shirt to reveal the taut network of fading scars that rose up her neck and across her jaw. Those on her face were very pale now, their jagged pattern discernible only when traced from her throat.

The doctor put down her pen and reached out to touch the dead tissue. Berlin shrank back.

'How did this occur?' asked the doctor.

'It's a long story,' said Berlin.

The doctor held Berlin's gaze for a moment. 'You have cash?' she asked.

Berlin nodded.

'Codeine forte,' she said. 'The best I can do.' She picked up her pen as the phone on her desk rang. She listened, muttered something in Russian, replaced the phone in its cradle and put down her pen. 'I must ask you to leave,' she said.

Utkin watched as Berlin appeared outside the clinic and scanned the car park. Her mobile was in her hand. His vibrated. He slid down in his seat and answered.

'Ah!' he said, affecting surprise. 'Miss Berlinskaya. So nice to hear from you.'

'I know you're out there somewhere,' she said. She began to stride through the car park, peering into the vehicles. He noticed she had a limp. He slid lower.

'For God's sake, just name your price, Utkin,' she said. 'The embassy will be open tomorrow. I'll get the documents I need to fly out and you'll have missed your chance.'

Utkin tucked the phone under his chin, started the motor and drove away at a normal pace, so that his departure didn't attract any attention.

'Yes, yes,' he said. 'Very likely. Don't forget, negotiations are confidential. I'll be in touch soon.'

He hung up. He had underestimated this woman. She was tough, smart and resourceful. It was her Russian genes, no doubt.

36

Magnus glanced through the back window before he got out of the black cab. The car that had followed them since they left south London had pulled over and switched off its lights.

Carmichael had left him to fend for himself in the bloody back blocks of Bermondsey. He had nearly frozen to death, until the cab came to his rescue and delivered him to his bijou terrace in Victoria Park.

He had nearly lost the house in the third divorce, but luckily she had had more money than he did and the judge had taken a dim view of this spiteful attempt by some ball-breaker to wrest away an Englishman's castle.

Magnus got his keys out of his pocket, clambered out of the cab and hurried up the short concrete path to the front door, slamming the gate behind him. He cursed himself for not having a security light installed.

He fumbled, trying to get his key in the lock.

He heard the gate click open and spun around to face a man coming up the path.

'What do you want?' said Magnus. His hand was shaking so much he dropped his keys. 'Who the fuck are you?'

The man bent down and picked up the key ring. 'Peter Green, sir,' he replied. 'I'm the babysitter.'

In the kitchen, Magnus arranged the tea things on a tray. *Good Christ*, he thought, *there's a man with a gun in my living room who will only say he works for 'the government', and my response is to put the kettle on.*

'Earl Grey okay?' he called out.

'Fine, thank you,' came the response.

All so bloody English.

He carried the tray in and Peter Green jumped up to give him a hand. Magnus glimpsed the gun again, a big bugger, tucked into a shoulder holster. Then again, Green himself wasn't exactly slight.

'Are you authorised to carry that thing?' he asked.

'It depends what you mean by authorised,' replied Green. 'Shall I be Mother?'

Magnus nodded. He was shaking so much he didn't trust himself to pour. They sat down and Green did the honours.

'So, Peter,' Magnus said with as much confidence as he could muster. 'Why exactly are you here?'

'To protect you, sir,' he replied.

'From whom?' said Magnus. 'And why does it involve confiscating my mobile and unplugging my landline and modem?'

'Just sit tight for the time being,' said Green. 'Read a book. Watch the telly.'

'I need to check my email,' said Magnus.

'Your email's been taken care of,' he said.

'What on earth do you mean?' said Magnus. He stood up, knocking the table in the process. Tea slopped in all directions.

'An out-of-office message has been set up,' said Green, leaning over to mop up the tea with his hanky. 'Makes it easier all round.'

Magnus glanced at the door, but knew it was ludicrous to think he could take this goon on. He wouldn't get far. He wasn't being protected – he was being contained.

'You're here to prevent me following up this story,' said Magnus.

Green didn't respond.

Magnus was aware of a strange smell clinging to him – sort of smoky, but not tobacco.

'What was in the van?' said Magnus.

'Sorry, sir, I'm not with you,' said Green. He blew on his hot tea.

'Guns?' said Magnus. 'Drugs? Girls?'

Green sipped, looking at Magnus over the rim of his cup.

'How long will this so-called protection last?' said Magnus.

'Until it all blows over,' said Green.

Magnus caught more than a whiff of a cock-up. It was unusual for the secret-squirrel blokes to reveal themselves, and they'd done it three times: first by picking him up and letting him go without charging him, to keep the whole thing out of court; then by issuing a D-Notice; and finally by sending Peter Green around to keep an eye on him.

All in the space of twenty-four hours and over Christmas, what's more. Berlin had latched onto something big. The ship was sinking and these chaps were racing to plug the leaks. Now this.

Magnus decided it was time for bed.

Fagan stretched out on Magnus's sofa and tried to ignore the relentless tick tick tick of the grandfather clock in the corner.

The old boozer was tucked up in bed. He hadn't questioned Fagan's ID, which bore his *nom de guerre*, and he doubted Magnus was the type to try legging it down the drainpipe. He'd gone all wan and retired early.

Fagan was feeling a bit edgy himself. He got up and examined the hickory dickory dock, but couldn't see any way of shutting it up without smashing it. It bore a small brass plaque that recorded the gratitude of the congregation of St Albans for the service of their dean on the occasion of his retirement.

It struck one, but no mouse appeared. So much for poetry.

The shadows in the room flickered in the headlights of a passing car. His own vehicle was parked just down the road. It wouldn't take a minute to pop out for a quick toke or two.

A floorboard creaked overhead. He glanced up at the ceiling. There was the sound of the loo flushing.

Fagan locked the front door behind him. He had Magnus's keys and he could see the house from where he was parked. The residents of the gentrified premises up and down the street were asleep. They slept soundly, Fagan reflected, because they preferred to ignore the state of the world and what was happening on their own doorsteps.

He got into the Audi, closed the door quietly and turned on the wipers to scrape the icy windscreen. He needed to keep a clear view of the house.

A few moments later the sticky resin was glowing in the bowl of his pipe. Fagan sucked in its gentle vapour and relaxed.

The wipers slid back and forth in a hypnotic rhythm.

The garden path glistened, its soft crunch beneath Fagan's boots the only sound in the still night. He strolled back to the house, fishing the keys out of his pocket. As he inserted the key in the lock, the door swung open. The hallway beyond it was empty.

Fagan was stunned. He'd only been gone five minutes and had kept his eye on the place the whole time.

He glanced at his watch: ten past two. His heart skipped a beat. He'd lost an hour. Jesus Christ. The old bugger must have had a spare set of keys.

He had really fucked up this time.

The coward

37

In her fitful, vodka-induced sleep Berlin was again aware of the repetitive pounding of Yorkie, and the sounds of Charlie scurrying back and forth, hushing him.

A man stood over her, frowning. His face was obscure, but familiar. He closed his eyes and she saw that he had a word tattooed on each eyelid. She tried to move closer to read them, but she was paralysed. Panic choked her.

The man bent down. The words were formed by worm-like blue veins. The letters wriggled beneath the translucent skin, but the Cyrillic script meant nothing to her.

Berlin woke with a start. Her hands and face were clammy, her breathing ragged. She had failed to decipher the message, but she understood these signs only too well. They heralded the beginning of a short, slithery descent into hell.

Her teeth chattered, despite the weight of the drapes piled around her.

The dregs of the night would be spent in a tangle of intrusive thoughts she couldn't outrun. But there was no way she was walking the streets of Moscow in this state.

She slid deeper into her nest.

*

The next thing she knew Charlie was offering her tea. She must have finally dozed off.

The first time in years that she had ventured away from home, and everything had turned to shit. She should have stuck to guarding other people's property during the wee small hours and minding her own business.

Despite her best efforts to engage in a programmed withdrawal, now she had to endure the exact opposite: classic 'cold turkey'.

Her only support was an unpredictable former spy who was also a lying interloper engaged in God only knew what scam. And Berlin's assignment, the most straightforward job any investigator could undertake, was dead in the water.

Today she was supposed to return home, an efficient and professional operative who could look forward to a fruitful ongoing relationship with Burghley, and her old mate Del.

She could still be seduced by fairy stories.

Charlie bent over her and placed a cool hand on her fevered brow. 'You're a drug addict,' she said. She handed Berlin the mug of tea. 'What are you going to do?'

Berlin gratefully wrapped her hands around the mug. A tangy aroma wafted from the steaming black brew. She detected sympathy in Charlie's tone. There seemed little point in protesting that she had flu.

'If you could bring yourself to be more open with me,' said Berlin, 'perhaps we could do each other some good.'

It was obvious that Charlie's fear of the people she was working with trumped anything Berlin could use as a threat.

Charlie might be afraid of the authorities, but so was Berlin: the guardians of law and order were capricious and had their own agendas. Utkin, from whom she had not yet heard another word, was a case in point.

Charlie's recent observation about Berlin's status tended to indicate she wasn't in thrall to Utkin. But you couldn't be too careful in these circumstances. Every scrap of information could be useful in the right context.

More than anything else it was clear to Berlin that she and Charlie both had weaknesses that were now being exploited.

It made them strange bedfellows.

'What are you going to do?' asked Charlie again.

'What time does the embassy open?' she asked.

'Ten,' said Charlie. 'But you need to be there well before that to get in line.'

It would be a very British retreat.

One that began with a queue.

38

A fringe of icy droplets hanging from the eaves trembled as a fist hammered the front door. Marjorie Carmichael nudged her husband with her foot. 'One of the boys must have forgotten his key,' she murmured.

Carmichael swore. It was four in the bloody morning. The boys were drunken layabouts in their twenties – postgraduate students, and still costing him a fortune. He cursed higher education.

Carmichael had barely unlocked the door when Magnus pushed his way in and kicked it shut behind him. 'Jesus Christ, Magnus,' said Carmichael. 'What the hell's going on?'

Magnus grabbed a handful of Carmichael's pyjamas and dragged him close. 'You tell me, you bloody hypocrite!' he spluttered. 'You're in with all these people. Get the nod, did you?'

'What are you talking about?' said Carmichael. 'What people?'

'Spooks. I've been practically held at gunpoint under the guise of "protection". What happened to the fucking free press? Eh? Tell me that. Call yourself a bloody editor.'

Carmichael prised Magnus's fingers off his pyjama

jacket and turned away, unable to look him in the face. 'Not any more,' he muttered.

'What?' said Magnus.

'Over Christmas someone made our proprietor an offer for *The Sentinel* he couldn't refuse,' said Carmichael.

'They've flogged the paper?' said Magnus.

'Lock, stock and barrel,' said Carmichael. 'In fact, I'm told they've even changed the locks. Not to mention the editor.'

He led the way into the sitting room and poured two large Scotches. He handed one to Magnus. 'It's made me think, Magnus, I can tell you,' said Carmichael. He sipped his Scotch. 'On the back of this business with you, that is.'

Magnus drained his Scotch. They were all being done over, one way or another.

'Sleep on the sofa if you like,' said Carmichael. 'I hope we don't have the bloody police banging on the door, looking for you.'

'How would they know I was here?' said Magnus.

'Anyway, we'll talk in the morning,' said Carmichael. 'Feel free to use the facilities. There's a loo just off the hall. Marjorie likes to call it the powder room.' He put down his glass and shuffled to the door. Suddenly he was an old man.

'I'm sorry, Carmichael,' said Magnus. 'By the way, who's the new owner?'

'Someone called Kalandarishvili,' came the reply. 'One of these oligarch chaps.'

*

Magnus poured himself another Scotch. He knocked it back, then poured another. He dialled directory enquiries on Carmichael's landline. That bloody bastard Peter had taken his mobile. Magnus could barely recall his own number, let alone any of his contacts'.

The operator finally answered and asked for a name and address.

'Berlin,' said Magnus. 'Er . . . east London somewhere?'

Peggy was awake with the phone in her hand before the second ring. 'Hello,' she said, clearing her throat. It had to be an emergency, someone calling at this hour. She suppressed a frisson of anxiety.

'Hello,' said her caller. 'Sorry to disturb you at this hour. My name is Magnus Nkonde. You wouldn't happen to be a relative of Catherine Berlin's, by any chance?'

It was the call Peggy had been dreading for more than thirty years.

'I would,' said Peggy. 'I'm her mother.' The cold air nipped at her ankles. 'Is she . . . is she all right?' She held her breath.

'Yes, well, that's what I'm trying to find out,' said Magnus. 'I need to get in touch with her. Would you have her mobile number?'

Peggy closed her eyes and exhaled.

'I'm sorry,' she said. 'I just can't give out her number to anybody. I'm sure you understand.'

A barely muffled expletive indicated Mr Nkonde's understanding was limited.

'It's very important,' he said.

Peggy hesitated. 'I'll pass the message on and ask her to ring you,' she said. 'Just let me find a pen.' She opened the drawer in the bedside table and took out a pen and pad. 'Now, how do you spell your surname?'

'Oh, for God's sake,' said Magnus. 'Please, this is serious. Do you know where she is?'

'I believe she's in Moscow,' said Peggy.

The sudden silence disturbed her.

When Mr Nkonde spoke, his tone had changed.

'When did you last hear from her?' he asked quietly.

'It was the day before Christmas Eve,' said Peggy. 'Is something wrong?'

'Please tell her to call me as soon as she can.'

Peggy felt her chest tighten.

'Give her this message,' he said. 'It's very important. It's about a van. Are you writing this down?'

'Yes,' said Peggy.

'Stop,' said Magnus. 'Don't write this down and don't tell anyone except Catherine. Do you understand?'

'No, I don't,' said Peggy. 'What's this all about?'

'Listen carefully,' said Magnus. 'It could be a matter of life and death.'

After Mr Nkonde hung up she sat on the edge of the bed in the dark, her head bowed. The chill crept up her calves.

The second Magnus put down the phone he realised his mistake: Berlin would ring his mobile, which was still in the possession of Peter Green. He cursed, and pressed redial, but was greeted by voicemail.

No doubt Mrs Berlin was already on the phone to her elusive daughter.

Invoking life and death in that sepulchral tone Magnus's father employed in the pulpit usually galvanised people into action.

39

The clerk at the British embassy exuded a passive indifference that had clearly been perfected over a number of years. He scanned yet again the form that Berlin had diligently completed.

'You haven't provided a Police Report Number,' he said. 'You did report the loss of your passport to the local police?'

'Yes. No,' said Berlin. 'Not formally. I approached someone I took to be a policeman when I first noticed it had gone.'

The clerk frowned. 'In Red Square?' he asked.

Berlin nodded.

'Just a moment,' said the clerk. He left the counter and disappeared through a door.

The seated rows of supplicants sweated, sighed and muttered. The air was thick with tension and impatience. Security was tight and the guards twitchy. Any sudden movement attracted their attention.

The clerk reappeared. 'I'm afraid there's a problem,' he said.

Before Berlin could call on her rapidly diminishing reserves of patience, her mobile rang.

She glanced at the display. Mum. Shit. She had

forgotten to call and wish her a merry Christmas. Now she was going to hear all about it. She declined the call.

Stretching full length across the counter, she grabbed the clerk.

The sudden silence was broken only by the clanking of the security guards' tactical utility belts as they moved in behind her. Berlin released the clerk and turned to confront them.

'Take me to your leader.'

The forearm lock was expertly executed.

A sombre middle-aged woman entered the windowless room where Berlin had sat for nearly two hours. A guard stood in one corner. A small black plastic bubble set into the ceiling indicated that he wasn't the only person watching her.

The woman, who was clutching a manila file in one hand and a cup of tea in the other, gave Berlin a shrewd look. She didn't introduce herself as she sat down on the other side of the table.

'Now that you've attracted our attention,' she said, 'perhaps you'd care to explain.'

'I simply lost my passport and want it replaced,' said Berlin. 'It's very important that I leave Moscow as soon as possible. I have a flight booked later today.'

'I'm afraid you're not going to be on it.'

'And who the hell are you?' said Berlin.

'Mrs Muir,' replied the woman.

Berlin glanced at Mrs Muir's left hand. No ring. Her

features were sharp, matching her tone, which conveyed the disdain of a meticulous bureaucrat for someone foolish enough to lose a passport.

Mrs Muir undid the buttons of her black suit jacket. The suit had clearly done her good service. It was smart, but well worn. She looked tired, a little haggard. She opened the file and peered at the contents.

'Where are you staying, Ms Berlin?' she asked. 'You haven't given us an address.'

'With a friend,' said Berlin. 'She's very private.'

Mrs Muir glanced up at her, then resumed her perusal of the file.

'It seems you are the subject of an investigation,' she said. 'We understand the Russian authorities will detain you here until the conclusion of those enquiries.'

Berlin stared at her. 'I haven't been charged with anything,' she said.

'It doesn't make any difference,' said Mrs Muir. 'We can't issue an Emergency Travel Document in these circumstances. They wouldn't let you leave, anyway.'

She took a thin sheaf of roughly stapled, photocopied documents from the file and pushed them across the table to Berlin.

'What's this?' said Berlin.

'A Prisoner Pack. An explanation of the Russian legal system and what services Her Majesty's government can offer if you are arrested.'

Berlin stared at her and Mrs Muir added, 'Just in case.'

Berlin gripped the edge of the table.

The guard stepped forward.

Mrs Muir raised a hand. 'There is absolutely nothing we can do in the current climate,' she said.

'What does that mean?' said Berlin. '*The current climate.*'

'It's a question of balance,' said Mrs Muir. 'Whitehall is currently engaged in negotiations with the Kremlin. These matters are very sensitive.'

'Are you telling me I'm a pawn in some diplomatic stand-off?' said Berlin.

'Each situation is assessed on its own merits,' said Mrs Muir.

'So that's a yes,' said Berlin. 'The police officer involved certainly didn't appear to be preoccupied with diplomacy.'

'But that's exactly what they *are* preoccupied with,' said Mrs Muir. She glanced back at the file. 'We're talking about an intelligence agency. Not the police. They seem to think you're a spy.'

The security guard steered Berlin through basement corridors to the employees' entrance. She was being put out with the rubbish.

Mrs Muir had made it clear that there was nothing they could – or would – do for her until the SVR, the *Sluzhba Vneshney Razvedki*, the Russian foreign intelligence agency, had completed its 'assessment'.

If Berlin's behaviour gave the Russians a reason to lock her up, they could. The implication was that they didn't need much of a reason and that she should count herself lucky to have avoided that fate up to this point.

Mrs Muir couldn't say how, or when, Berlin might find out why the SVR was interested in her. She suggested that they often approached matters in what she described as a 'tangential fashion', but someone might, probably, eventually, approach Berlin.

None of which sounded promising.

Berlin could see the river as she made her way down the narrow lane at the rear of the embassy. She turned right, away from where she knew Charlie was waiting. She needed some time to think through what was going on.

The embassy was cordoned off with concrete barriers designed to deter suicide bombers, and Charlie had parked at the other end of the block. She wouldn't be able to see Berlin leave.

The icy footpath was treacherous. The leaden clouds were low, threatening more snow. Berlin slithered up an incline towards a bridge, past a giant billboard advertising Heinz tomato sauce. The Cyrillic characters rendered the banal surreal.

Darting across the wide road, she was assailed by a cacophony of horns and abuse. The traffic roared and whined in her ears as it shot past. She raised a weak fist in defiance and sought a familiar landmark.

But she was lost; reality had gone soft at the edges. She was marooned in a shifting landscape of threat.

Bewildered, she made it onto the bridge and walked to the middle, where she stood gazing over the parapet at the shifting, groaning ice fifty feet below. She gulped for air.

A gentle hand tugged at her sleeve.

Berlin looked up into the concerned eyes of a woman shrouded in a fur hood. She glanced at the river, then back at Berlin, speaking very quietly in Russian.

'I'm sorry,' stuttered Berlin.

The woman patted her arm. Her cheeks, flushed pink in the chill air, wrinkled into a broad smile.

'Our visitor,' she said brightly. It was a warm word of welcome.

'Yes,' said Berlin. 'A visitor.'

She took the woman's proffered arm and together they crossed to the other side.

40

Fagan switched off his mobile, removed the SIM card and disabled the car's GPS. He had avoided cameras too, staying on the B-roads. He didn't want anyone tracking him.

The house he was looking for was somewhere down a lane, beyond a farm-style gate. He drove another half mile before he realised he'd gone too far; the lane was overshadowed on both sides by a thick briar hedge. He reversed back at speed. There would be tyre tracks all over the bloody place.

This time the gate was easy to spot because it was open. Fagan swore.

Magnus had spent what was left of the night in the sitting room hunched over Carmichael's laptop. He had tried to log in to his email, but the bastards had changed his password. Finally he created a new address using Carmichael's account.

Magnus had only a hazy idea of the Byzantine world of Russian domestic politics. But he had an encyclopaedic knowledge of the machinations of Whitehall, which helped.

His research took him to arcane blogs documenting

the connections between organised crime and the state in Eastern Europe. It opened up a vast web of relationships encompassing bankers, politicians, bureaucrats and senior figures from law enforcement agencies and the military.

Magnus threw his leads out there: a white Ford Transit van unloading something into a warehouse; a security company employee offering a bribe to someone to turn a blind eye; the fact that his source was now incommunicado in Moscow. Incommunicado was a bit over the top; she just hadn't returned his calls. But a bit of drama never hurt.

He had posted the information in forums and blogs frequented by sober academics, hacks and conspiracy theorists alike. The speed and volume of the responses he was soon receiving was astonishing, and most of it seemed to come from inside Russia itself.

Detailed profiles of the current personnel installed at the Russian embassy in London popped into his inbox and he was treated to more than one lengthy analysis of the *siloviki*, the former KGB officers who now ran the Kremlin. If his correspondents were to be believed, they also controlled nearly everything else in Russia.

There were a number of emails that described disturbing events in Istanbul, Dubai and Qatar.

Magnus now had a file of well-sourced commentary.

When a drawn, tousled Carmichael appeared at the door, Magnus was drinking the last dregs of the Scotch.

'Good morning, old darling,' he said. 'How are you?'

'I've been thinking, Magnus,' said Carmichael. 'We should be careful . . .'

A soft knock at the front door startled them both.

A visitor at this hour was unusual, not to say alarming. In fact, Magnus thought he might shit himself. Christ. Surely it couldn't be the bloody constabulary? Or Peter Green? He scuttled to the downstairs loo and left Carmichael to it.

He heard a few words exchanged through the front door, which he couldn't make out, then he heard it open. All he could think about was the short trip across the hall to that door. A strategic retreat was in order.

The sound of the front door closing was followed by footsteps passing the loo and heading down the hall. Magnus waited a moment, then crept out. He tiptoed to the front door and opened it with great care.

Peter Green was striding up the garden path.

Magnus backed up.

Green stepped inside and drew his gun.

Magnus thought he might pass out.

Green indicated the loo. Magnus had left the door open, for fear of making a noise. He did as he was told and went back into the toilet and Green gently shut the door after him. Magnus's heart was pounding, fit to burst.

A moment later he heard a couple of *pops*.

He held his breath.

The loo door opened. Green beckoned.

'Give me a minute, old darling,' Magnus croaked.

Marjorie Carmichael had made the mistake of marrying the other promising journalist on the quality newspaper where she hoped to make her name. It soon became clear that there was only room for one star cub reporter on *The Sentinel*, and in their household.

Marjorie had retired from the fray with good grace. She devoted herself to her twin boys, and to making her husband pay for her sacrifice every day of his life.

This morning she came downstairs with a spring in her step, hoping to find an exhausted, redundant spouse whom she could console, in a patronising way, and at least one son with a filthy hangover who would assist her.

She glanced into the kitchen, then made her way to the study. The warm glow of light beneath the door betrayed Carmichael's presence in his so-called sanctuary. Not today. Marjorie would pursue him with relentless, low-key concern and kill him with kindness.

She tapped at the study door and then opened it.

There was a man slumped across the desk. It wasn't Jolyon, but she couldn't say who it was, because he didn't have a face. She tried to shout for her husband, but it came out as a squeak.

She ran back to the kitchen and that's where she found him.

On the floor with a neat hole in his forehead.

4I

Berlin walked, staying close to the river, until her feet burnt and her cheekbones ached with the cold. Mansion blocks lined the embankment; solid, discreet and well maintained, they were set in gardens that reminded Berlin of London's elegant squares.

A woman in a fur was walking two borzoi hounds among the leafless trees. The silky, russet coats of the dogs perfectly complemented the woman's long, blonde tresses and the golden sheen of her own coat. The three stalked the swept path, heads held high.

Evidence of the sweeper – a twig brush, reminiscent of a witch's broom, and a long-handled spade – were propped up against a wall. Berlin saw her resting in a nearby doorway, swathed in municipal waterproofs, eyes closed, praying, no doubt, for the thaw.

Charlie's deception and the disappearance of the Gerasimovs paled into insignificance compared with the question of why she had attracted the scrutiny of Russian intelligence. With Major Utkin added to the mix the result was positively baffling.

If an agency was watching her, it was using someone with access and knowledge of two languages and cultures. Someone for whom duplicity was second nature.

In the present scenario, one candidate stood out.

Charlie flung open the door and greeted Berlin with a tirade worthy of an anxious mother waiting for an errant teenager.

'Where the hell have you been?' she demanded. 'I waited for hours at the embassy.'

The pot-bellied stove glowed with warmth, drawing Berlin towards it.

Charlie barred her way. 'What happened? Did you get a passport?' she said. 'I want some answers.'

Berlin pushed past her. 'You're not alone there,' she said. She huddled on one side of the stove. Charlie sat down on the other with Yorkie curled up on her feet. But it was not going to be a fireside chat.

Berlin needed to get a handle on Charlie if she was going to make any sense at all of the situation. She had to exploit the thin wedge of empathy that existed between them.

Charlie was a desperate, isolated woman. It shouldn't be too hard.

Berlin would take her back to the beginning. 'Tell me why you left England,' she said.

Charlie gave her a look that said she knew exactly what Berlin was up to and she was going to humour her.

'Have you ever heard of Operation Able Archer?' said Charlie.

Berlin shook her head.

'Nineteen eighty-three,' said Charlie. 'The last gasp of the Cold War. It was a NATO exercise simulating the escalation of conflict with the USSR, who took umbrage when the so-called exercise involved the deployment of Pershing II missiles on their doorstep. Moscow put their nuclear forces on alert.'

Berlin reflected that in 1983 she was probably too stoned to notice, or care.

'What difference did it make to you?' said Berlin.

'I'll tell you what bloody difference it made,' said Charlie. 'I had a double first in Slavic languages, but for years I'd languished in filing in the Foreign and Commonwealth Office. Tainted by my parents' politics.'

'The FCO thought you had divided loyalties?' said Berlin.

'My parents were left-wing,' said Charlie. 'And so was I. But so what? I was sick of greed. And Thatcher. So were a lot of other people.' She lit another cigarette. 'I never even knew my father,' she said bitterly. 'And my mother dumped me in a minor boarding school at the earliest opportunity and fled back to Russia.'

'The government didn't trust you,' said Berlin.

'What a joke,' said Charlie. 'In the civil service even a filing clerk is aware of people feathering their own nests, and bugger the public interest.'

'So you defected,' said Berlin.

'I'd already been effectively banished, anyway,' said Charlie. 'In fact, I don't think they even noticed I was gone at first. Probably thought I was on sick leave or something.'

'And how did Moscow react when you arrived?'

'Oh, they always made a big fuss of anyone who turned up from the West. Big propaganda coup. Made out I was some high-level Foreign Office wallah with lots of secret stuff. The daughter of valued comrades, etcetera, etcetera.'

'It must have been nice to have been wanted for a change,' said Berlin.

'They gave me an apartment, a car, a job translating signals, and a decent salary.'

'So what happened?' said Berlin.

'Nineteen ninety-one,' said Charlie. 'Suddenly communists were on the nose, particularly anyone who had fled the West saying it was decadent and corrupt.'

'So that was it?'

'More or less,' said Charlie. 'Drink?'

The evasion was obvious. Charlie's fall from grace owed its genesis to something more than the collapse of the Soviet Union.

'How have you lived since?' said Berlin.

'On my wits,' said Charlie.

From somewhere in the decaying apartment came the sound of a rhythmic thudding.

Berlin glanced down at Charlie's feet.

Yorkie snored on.

Charlie gripped Berlin's arm, trying to restrain her, as she kicked open the series of doors that lay between her and the source of the noise.

'For fuck's sake, get off me,' said Berlin. Charlie

wouldn't let go. She hung on for dear life, forcing Berlin to drag her down the long, dark corridor.

When they reached the source of the noise, the pounding on the other side of the door stopped.

The key was in the lock.

Berlin reached for it.

'Please,' said Charlie. 'Let me.'

Berlin stood back. Charlie unlocked the door and opened it.

A stocky young man in black trousers, a hand-knitted jumper and felt slippers was standing on the other side.

'This is Nikki,' said Charlie. 'Say hello.'

'Hello,' said Berlin.

Nikki walked straight past her and headed down the corridor.

'He's not very sociable when he's hungry, I'm afraid,' said Charlie.

Berlin felt further explanation might be in order.

42

Magnus couldn't stop blubbering like a baby. Green was driving. 'That will teach you to go sneaking out at night,' he said. 'Sir.'

'For Christ's sake, have some pity,' said Magnus. 'A man I've known for thirty years has just been gunned down in cold blood.'

'You'll be next if you don't start behaving,' said Green.

Magnus couldn't shake the sight that had greeted him when he'd finally got himself together to creep out of Carmichael's loo. He'd made for the front door, but couldn't resist looking back. Carmichael's study door was ajar.

A man was slumped across the desk. Blood was pooling and dripping onto the carpet. It wasn't Carmichael. But there had been something familiar about the chap; his few strands of hair hung pathetically straight down from his bald, pink scalp. Magnus couldn't think straight. It was all too much.

'Oh God, oh Jesus, oh Christ,' moaned Magnus. He blew his nose. 'How did this happen?'

'You used Carmichael's Internet account and his email, right?'

Magnus nodded.

'The traffic is monitored,' said Green. 'How do you

think *I* found you? We weren't the only people looking. You asked a lot of questions about certain people and events and you woke up a lot of bears. With sore heads.'

'The Russians killed Carmichael,' said Magnus.

'Who did you think it was?' said Green.

Magnus looked at him. 'Of course,' he whispered. 'It was the Russians. And it was all my fault.'

Marjorie Carmichael huddled in the back seat of the police car, flanked by her twin boys. They watched as ghostly figures, shrouded in white, drifted in and out of the house. Mist hung in the garden in ethereal patches, reflecting the rhythmic flicker of a rotating blue light.

Marjorie wondered why they didn't turn it off. The car door opened and an officer handed over three mugs of tea, mugs from her second-best set. She tutted and drew her cardigan tighter around herself. A sergeant approached.

Marjorie heard him ask the constable if everything was all right. He didn't wait for a reply. 'Back to the station,' he said. 'They're sending the heavy mob up from London to deal with this one.'

'Homicide?' said the constable.

'SO15,' said the sergeant. 'This is a burglary gone wrong, got it?'

The constable nodded. 'Got it, Sarge.'

'What's SO15?' asked Marjorie. One of the twins would know.

'Counter-terrorism,' replied the one studying political science.

She was so proud of her boys.

43

Charlie smoothed a cowlick of brown hair back from Nikki's forehead. 'My good boy,' she murmured.

The good boy appeared to be in his late twenties. It was difficult to tell. His moon face was pale and unlined. He had a sharp nose, which appeared to have been broken at some stage, and his eyes were of the same watery blue as his mother's. His dark eyebrows formed neat arcs, which gave him a wide-eyed expression.

Berlin and Charlie sat at the table watching him eat dumplings. He ate very quietly and with deliberate movements.

'Why do you keep him locked up?' said Berlin. She felt a bit uncomfortable, talking about him as if he wasn't there. But her attempts to engage Nikki in conversation had signally failed.

'I don't,' said Charlie. 'I was locking you out. He doesn't like to leave the apartment on his own, anyway.'

She had produced a packet of something that looked like ravioli, little pasta pillows stuffed with grey meat, and heated them up on the gas ring. '*Pelmeni*,' she said.

Berlin watched, amazed by the transformation that had come over Charlie. Her stout torso had metamorphosed into a nurturing bosom. The gravel voice had softened. She had even stopped smoking, leaning close to murmur endearments in Russian and English, urging Nikki to eat.

'He understands everything,' said Charlie, 'but he rarely speaks.'

Berlin wished more people would show such restraint.

Nikki's alabaster complexion was marred by a livid bruise along one jaw.

'What happened there?' said Berlin.

'Sometimes he becomes a bit rumbustious,' said Charlie. 'And hurts himself.'

Berlin found herself waiting patiently for further explanation, as if she too had been infected by this tender atmosphere.

But it never came.

Nikki stood up.

'Finished, Nikki?' said Charlie.

He nodded and trotted off, back to his wing, which Berlin had discovered contained the facilities she had believed were missing from the apartment. Now, at least, she might get a hot bath.

When he'd gone, Charlie turned to Berlin. There was no sign of her gentle demeanour. 'You must never tell anyone about this,' she said. 'There's absolutely no need for you to involve yourself in my and Nikki's affairs. Understand?'

'Calm down,' said Berlin. 'I have no intention of betraying you.'

Charlie lit up and took a deep drag on her cigarette. 'But?' she said.

'But we need to get real here, don't we?' said Berlin.

It was clear that Nikki was Charlie's Achilles heel. Whatever she feared, it had to do with him.

Charlie capitulated quietly.

'He was born that way,' she said. 'He was a perfectly normal baby, but then he started to miss certain stages. He didn't speak. He became fixated on things, had tantrums.'

'What's wrong with him?' said Berlin.

Charlie shook her head. 'Who knows,' she said. 'I had him very late. He was quite a surprise. Perhaps that had something to do with it. The delivery was very difficult. There might have been some neurological damage.'

The phrase 'on the spectrum' came to Berlin unbidden.

'It became more of a problem as he got older,' she said, sighing. 'So I educated him at home.'

'Couldn't he have gone to a special school?' asked Berlin.

'Don't you think I explored everything?' said Charlie, exasperated. 'People with congenital problems weren't very popular in the socialist utopia. Veterans with physical injuries were heroes, but even up to the eighties there was still some official reluctance to acknowledge that people with disabilities even existed in the USSR.'

'That's ridiculous,' said Berlin.

'People believe what they want to believe. Deformity was a capitalist deviation, or a product of evil or some nonsense,' said Charlie. 'It hasn't changed that much. Children born like Nikki are regarded as uneducable and dumped in institutions. I wouldn't put Yorkie in those places.'

'What did Nikki's father think?' said Berlin.

Charlie snorted. 'We met soon after I arrived in Moscow. Whirlwind romance and all that,' she said. 'We were married and had Nikki quickly. It became more difficult as he grew older, but we soldiered on until . . .'

Charlie seemed to drift away.

'Until what?' pressed Berlin.

'His father wanted to put him in an institution,' she said. 'I didn't agree, so I left.'

She got up and made a great show of cleaning up after Nikki's meal, banging pots, putting a kettle on to boil, eating the leftover dumplings. It was apparent that this was the end of the matter as far as Charlie was concerned.

Berlin had recognised the subtext in Charlie's story: she had abandoned family life and her privileges to protect her son. It would be useful, even essential, for someone in that position to have a 'roof': protection. From her husband. From the state.

'What would happen to Nikki if the authorities knew he was here?' said Berlin.

'Well, they don't,' barked Charlie. 'And they're not going to find out.'

'If your husband was so intent on institutionalising him, why hasn't he told them?'

'You'd have to ask him that,' said Charlie. 'Perhaps deep down he knows I'm right.'

'But if something happens to you, what will happen to Nikki?' said Berlin.

The words were out of her mouth before she realised she'd given expression to Charlie's greatest fear.

Charlie practically disintegrated before her eyes.

'I would do anything,' whispered Charlie. 'Anything. To take him home.'

Home.

44

Berlin quietly closed the front door behind her. Unable to assuage her aching limbs with vodka, she would try to quieten the insistent, gnawing beast that dwelt within her in time-honoured fashion: pacing up and down.

Apart from the lack of drugs, her most pressing problem was getting out of the country, but she also had to find a way of letting Del know what was going on without dragging Burghley into it.

Del had done her a big favour. It was difficult enough for someone with his background to break into an elite dominated by old-school ties, without mistakes tarnishing his reputation.

Burghley had instructed her in good faith.

Del would never knowingly put her in harm's way. She didn't need him for that; she was quite adept at finding her own way into trouble.

But the identity of the mysterious client was starting to worry her; it wasn't unusual for commercial interests to use a firm like Burghley to conduct these sorts of enquiries. Most firms just didn't have the expertise in-house. A third party was also supposed to be impartial, to report without fear or favour.

But there was another angle: it provided deniability. If the actions of the third party proved to be an embarrassment, or worse, the firm would simply claim they had never authorised such activities.

Del had told her the client was a firm she had worked with before. He should have added 'recently'.

Hirst. It had to be.

When she refused the bribe, then the offer of further shifts, they had put this scenario into play. How many of the seemingly unconnected events since then had been down to them? Fucking Hirst. She had seen something that could embarrass them: a breach in security, dodgy employees running a scam; something they didn't want her to see, anyway.

They could clean up while she was otherwise occupied.

She felt foolish. Humiliated. The client didn't want her expertise, they wanted her out of the way. Del had said something about them specifically wanting her on this job. She had been flattered by instructions coming from Burghley: a step back into clean, lucrative work involving a better class of lowlife.

Who was she kidding?

Berlin walked beside the dark, silent reaches of the canal until the cold became unbearable. At that moment she felt that the oblivion of hypothermia might at least release her from the relentless need that was making her skin crawl.

Sensing warm air she looked for its source.

It was seeping from a grille beneath her feet.

*

The press of bodies in the underpass was comforting; one wall was lined with tiny, brightly lit kiosks crammed with everything from tights and bras to religious icons and snacks.

The vendors were a disparate lot: stout, middle-aged women in woollen hats; thin young women in high vinyl boots and faux fur jackets; toothless babushkas exposing only their eyes and rosy cheeks to the elements.

On the other side of the underpass, men in ill-fitting suits and fur caps were pressed against the tiles selling items from battered suitcases: sets of cutlery, apparently fashioned from steel offcuts; felt-lined slippers; pen-and-ink drawings of domed churches.

The atmosphere beneath the ground was benign.

Berlin noticed a woman selling bags of lustrous persimmons. A delicate rose perfume drifted from one that had been cut in half. Berlin smiled and the woman offered her a bag of them, speaking in Russian, keen to make a sale.

Berlin was about to pantomime her apology for being unable to communicate, when the woman recognised the source of her diffidence. She plucked a fruit from one of the bags and pressed it into Berlin's hand.

The crowd surged, forcing Berlin on. She glanced back, over her shoulder. The woman waved. Berlin waved back, a taut sensation in her chest, a sharp reminder of what generous, benevolent contact with another human being meant. She thought of Bella, who understood the effort it took to behave normally in circumstances of deprivation.

When she emerged at the top of the steps that led from the underpass, Berlin melted into the reassuring crowds of cheerful Muscovites shopping and dining. Sharp, spicy smells drifted from cafés as their doors swung to and fro.

The Golden Arches presented themselves. Warmth, Wi-Fi, and a menu you could point at – this was probably as good as it was going to get.

The almost-tasteful McDonald's, a contemporary cube done up in olive green with a timber fascia, loomed clean and bright, defiant among mounds of grubby snow. This was not the McDonald's in Pushkin Square, Utkin's pride and joy, but it was bustling nevertheless.

When she reached the counter, Berlin made a dumb show of pointing at a picture of a burger. The girl raised an eyebrow and briskly pressed a key on the console.

'Do you want fries with that?' she asked.

Berlin nodded, sheepish. 'And tea,' she said. She wasn't prepared to brave McDonald's coffee, Russian or otherwise.

Berlin had eaten most of her fries before she found an empty seat beside a window. Outside, strings of coloured lights hung from the eaves of shops and bars, casting blue-and-red shadows across the faces of the crowd.

A sudden sweat caught her by surprise. She blew her nose on a napkin and wiped her brow with her scarf. Her flu-like symptoms had nothing to do with a virus.

Beyond the plate glass a girl in a knitted Peruvian hat with ear flaps, a dirty grey puffa jacket and scuffed Nikes was begging.

Berlin watched her thrust her paper cup at diners as they left the restaurant. Her pinched face and fingers were blue with cold. The stringy hair, expressionless eyes and quick movements as she avoided sharp elbows completed the picture.

After a couple of people tossed their change into the cup, the girl tipped the contents into her hand, assessed the haul, then dropped the cup into the slush.

She took off with the single-minded intent of a hunter in pursuit of quarry.

Berlin left her burger on the tray and followed.

The girl crossed a busy road, darting between the cars, and made for a shopping mall that bore the logos of Marks & Spencer, Zara and Top Shop, but she didn't go inside. Too many security guards.

Berlin hurried to keep her in sight as she skirted the mall and sped towards a car park. Beyond it was a large red M, signifying the Metro, and beyond that a stately building with twin domes, porticos inset with neoclassical figures and a high clock tower. It was a railway station.

The girl weaved her way through the cars and travellers, then turned sharply to the right and disappeared behind the station.

Berlin turned the corner. A door slammed. She was looking at a dismal expanse of broken concrete and a clutch of what looked to be abandoned workmen's huts.

The noise of the traffic was muted. In the silence, she could hear something scratching at a pile of ripped plastic sacks that lay beneath a blanket of ice.

Berlin walked very slowly, picking her way through the detritus of the construction site, hidden in the snow. A glow emanated from one of the huts. As she approached it, she could smell an acrid odour seeping from one of the hut's cracked windows.

She opened the door.

The needle was already embedded in the girl's groin. She gazed at Berlin with utter detachment.

In a small pool of light from a hurricane lamp, her two male companions were cooking a grey substance on a flattened Coke can, over a candle. One of them spoke to Berlin, but she didn't understand a word.

She closed the door behind her and squatted down. She was unafraid. Desperation trumped vulnerability. They recognised her for what she was; no-one with any sense would venture into this place unless compelled by a need they understood.

The girl's head lolled back. Spittle dribbled down her chin in a long string and hung there, suspended, until one of the boys wiped it away with the back of his hand.

Berlin put her hand in her pocket.

One of the boys started, alarmed, but when she withdrew it she was clutching roubles, not a weapon. He rocked back on his heels as Berlin gestured with the money.

The boy levered open the lid of a paint tin.

Berlin could see a bunch of old syringes nestled among rags and a bundle of small balloons. He reached inside.

Suddenly there was a loud crack and Berlin was knocked flat by the force of the door crashing into her back. She sprawled on the greasy concrete.

There was a torrent of Russian, then someone grabbed her coat collar and dragged her upright.

Utkin thrust his face into hers.

'What do you think you are doing, Miss Berlinskaya?' he hissed.

The girl was oblivious, but the two boys had scuttled into the furthest corner of the hut.

Utkin dragged her over to one of the boys, who shrank back against the wall, shrouded in an old army greatcoat.

'What do you think?' Utkin demanded of her. 'You think this is heroin?' He kicked out at the guttering candle and the hot tin.

Berlin tried to break Utkin's grip, but he cuffed her hard with his gloved fist. Her ears rang. She stopped struggling.

'*Krokodil*,' he announced, pointing at the sticky grey mess spilling across the floor with the toe of his boot. 'It eats you.' He reached down and yanked open the boy's greatcoat. 'From the inside.'

The swollen black stump at the end of the boy's leg had once been a foot. Corroded flesh hung in wizened hanks, the muscle beneath it glistening with the ooze of putrefaction.

The smell was of something long dead.

45

Major Utkin handed Berlin the flask. She gulped at the burning liquid as if it would scour her soul. The car rattled along, bouncing her against the window. Her reflection stared back at her.

She had insisted she hadn't been there to buy; she was just going to give some money to the girl. The major had dismissed this. She protested, but wasn't sure she believed it herself.

'*Krokodil*,' Utkin spat out the word. 'Cheaper than heroin. Mixing codeine, lighter fluid, iodine, industrial solvents. Result: scaly skin. Death soon. With luck.'

The buildings on either side of the road were old and low-rise, haphazardly fashioned from cast-concrete blocks. The doors and ground-floor windows were sealed with sheets of rusty iron.

Utkin had dogged her since their first encounter at the hotel. He wasn't psychic, and she hadn't seen any evidence of a team watching her. She recognised him for what he was, a lone wolf. Or in his case, a lonely bear.

There was only one explanation. She wound down the window, took her phone from her pocket and tossed it out.

Utkin tut-tutted.

It was a petulant act, but fuck it. It would put paid to Utkin's tracking. In any event, her phone was always backed up. And she still had the tablet in her coat pocket.

This thought gave her pause.

Tracking a phone was easy, even without the cooperation of the carrier. But a tablet would only be visible when connected to the Internet, unless you installed a bit of kit, an actual device secreted inside.

It would require expertise and more than just your telephone number or the phone's electronic identification number. The sort of expertise that was commonly found in intelligence agencies.

'Do you work for the SVR?' she asked.

Utkin snorted. 'I am policeman,' he said. 'Not SVR or FSB or GRU. Not *siloviki*. Policeman. Not more, not less.'

Not more, not less. A policeman with an unusual level of commitment to the job. Not very likely. Utkin was protecting his investment. Or someone else's.

He could be working for Hirst.

Utkin took a packet of cigarettes from the dashboard and lit one.

Ahead, a single lamp arched over a ramp that led underground. Utkin drove onto the ramp and pulled up beside a keypad on a crooked steel stanchion. He punched in a number.

A metal grille shuddered and rose slowly to reveal a basement bathed in yellow sodium light.

Berlin took another long pull on the flask to cover the fact that she really wanted to cry.

Utkin drove into the basement and turned off the car. He got out, took a bottle of vodka from a carton in the Ford's boot and stuffed it in his coat pocket.

Berlin got out too and stood nearby, listening to the motor tick as it contracted in the cold.

Utkin shut the boot, but it bounced open. He tried again, slamming it without success, so gave up.

Taking Berlin's arm, he led her to a heavy steel door set in a rough brick wall. It squealed as Utkin opened it. They stepped inside and the door swung shut behind them.

Dim bulkhead lights encased in wire cages flickered as they tramped down a corridor, then up a set of stairs. Berlin couldn't read the sign on the door at the top, but when Utkin knocked and it opened, she recognised the smell.

Utkin handed the vodka to a bow-legged woman in a headscarf. She was a clone of the babushka selling mandarins outside the railway station, but not as imploring. She muttered and glared at Berlin as Utkin strode past her. When Berlin hesitated to follow, the woman grabbed her with astonishing strength and dragged her inside.

Row after row of bodies lay on mortuary slabs. The pathology lab itself was antiseptically clean, but reminiscent of a museum display: 'Autopsy, 1965'.

Berlin anticipated an object lesson in the grave dangers of *krokodil*. As if she needed further persuasion.

Utkin motioned her forward to where he stood beside

a corpse beneath a grey sheet. He lifted one corner. The man beneath it had not suffered the depredations of the drug. He was solidly built and well preserved.

'Do you recognise him?' asked Utkin.

Berlin concentrated on the face and tried to ignore the fish-belly pale, vein-marbled flesh.

She shook her head.

'Allow me to introduce you,' said Utkin. 'Katarina Berlinskaya, please greet Vladimir Matvienko. Your interpreter. He was found in rubbish bin at airport with cardboard bearing your name.'

Berlin was aware that Utkin had paused in order to scrutinise her reaction. When she remained expressionless, he took her elbow, steered her across the lab and stood beside another body. Once again he lifted the sheet.

Berlin flinched.

'What about him?' said Utkin.

Berlin stared at Utkin, not at the deceased.

'For God's sake,' she said.

'Please, look close,' said Utkin.

He drew the sheet back to expose the torso. The man was short and bald, with the narrow waist and broad shoulders of a bodybuilder. But the angle at which his head lolled, and the bruising, indicated his neck had suffered trauma.

'He reminds me of . . .' She faltered.

'Yes?' said Utkin.

Berlin's mouth was suddenly parched. She swallowed hard and struggled to continue, but with no discernible effect.

'It looks like him, but it can't be Gerasimov,' said Berlin, clearing her throat.

'Yes,' said Utkin. 'It's him. Mikhail Gerasimov. Away on business, his wife tells me.'

He took a sweet from his pocket, unwrapped it and popped it in his mouth, then fished out another and offered it to Berlin. On autopilot, she extended her hand.

The cellophane shroud of the sherbet lemon twinkled in her palm. She stared at it, bemused, then slipped it in her pocket.

Utkin pointed at Matvienko, then at the other body, sucking on his sweet, contemplative. 'Both died by same hand,' he said.

'Forensics?' said Berlin.

'Detective work,' said Utkin.

'When was he . . . when was the body found?' she asked.

'Four days before you arrived,' said Utkin.

'So the man I interviewed . . .' said Berlin. The thought drifted away. Something was closing in on her, something indistinct, a grey, menacing shape flitting through a dark forest.

Utkin clapped his hands. 'Now the introductions are over,' he said. 'A toast.'

The babushka appeared, bearing a battered instrument tray on which were balanced three glasses and the bottle of vodka. Utkin poured. He handed a glass to Berlin and the attendant took her own.

To Berlin's astonishment he began to recite in Russian.

The cadence betrayed the source: a poem or incantation. Even in an unintelligible tongue the bitter lamentation resonated. When he finished the deep creases of the attendant's face were wet with tears.

Utkin looked straight at Berlin and raised his glass.

'I drink to you,' he said. 'And the dead.'

The glass slid from Berlin's numb fingers to the floor and shattered. Her knees buckled and she followed.

She was choking. She gasped for air and lashed out. Something hot dribbled down her chin. Berlin opened her eyes and met those of the attendant, who was peering down at her, clutching a small glass.

Utkin said something in Russian as Berlin struggled to sit up. The room was small and stuffy. She was lying on a shelf built into the wall, on a thin mattress. The attendant retreated and Utkin appeared in Berlin's line of sight. He drew up a chair and sat down.

'You have eaten very little. The climate is harsh. You are weak,' he said. 'Withdrawing.'

Berlin attempted to move off the shelf, but Utkin pushed her back. 'Let's talk,' he said.

Berlin considered asserting her right to silence, but she wasn't even sure she had that right in Russia. Besides, Utkin had nailed it: she was sick, friendless, and under scrutiny in a country she couldn't leave for reasons she couldn't fathom. She had nothing to lose.

The man who was supposed to meet her at the airport and the man she was to interview were both dead before she arrived.

The Potemkin village made sense now. Whatever game they were playing, the stakes were high; worth two murders.

Charlie had seemed equally surprised when they got to the apartment and discovered the couple had done a runner. She was just a minion.

Utkin seemed to read her mind. 'Someone did meet you at airport,' he said.

'Yes,' said Berlin.

'Who?' said Utkin.

'Charlotte Inkpin,' said Berlin.

'Tell me about her,' said Utkin.

Berlin was aware that the attendant was lurking in the corner, bent over a gas ring.

'Valentina,' said Utkin. The attendant shuffled over with a saucepan and a wooden spoon. The aroma was tantalising.

'Inkpin is British, about seventy. She defected during the eighties,' said Berlin.

'So. Traitor. Who does she work for?' said Utkin.

'I don't know,' said Berlin, 'but they're definitely local.'

She was struck by his use of the term 'traitor'. From the Russian point of view surely Charlie was the opposite. A patriot.

'Does she live alone?' asked Utkin.

'Yes,' said Berlin, without hesitation.

She gave him her best level stare.

'What do you want from me, Major?' she said.

'What have you got to offer, Miss Berlinskaya?' he said.

The attendant shuffled closer, scooped up a spoonful

of soup from the saucepan and brought it to Berlin's lips. The rich stock was ambrosia. Borscht.

Berlin's senses reeled. The last time she had tasted borscht, it had been Zayde holding the spoon to her mouth. Tears spilled from her eyes.

She could see Utkin was disconcerted by this sudden display of emotion, but his confusion was nothing compared to her own.

'Enough,' she cried. She knocked the spoon away.

The crimson liquid spattered the wall.

'What the hell is going on here?' she said.

Utkin and the attendant stared at her.

'That is very good question,' said Utkin. 'Perhaps you should ask your friend Inkpin.'

46

The twenty-four-hour café was heaving with Internet gamers. In the gloom scenes of carnage flickered across the intense, pale faces. It was the middle of the night, but time meant nothing in here.

Utkin had offered to drive her home, but she had walked – or rather staggered – out and eventually found a taxi. She just needed to get away. The presence of the Hard Rock Café, Dunkin' Donuts and faux antique street lighting implied that the driver had dropped her in a tourist zone. A sprinkling of shifty-looking touts in cheap suits, enticing obvious out-of-towners into clubs, completed the picture.

Her first challenge was to sort out the implications of Utkin's revelations on her own circumstances. If the subject of her due diligence job was dead before she arrived, Burghley's client clearly didn't know.

Or they had another reason for sending her. It wasn't just to get her out of the way. They could have sent her anywhere. It meant this was their turf, or they were confident they had more control of the situation here.

What 'the situation' might be was another question.

The youth in charge of the place, barely older than the adolescents he ruled, spoke English with an American accent.

The gamers ignored Berlin as she wandered among them, looking for a spare booth. She didn't need a huge screen, but she did need headphones. When she found a spot at the back she cleared a space among the crushed cans of energy drink, sat down and fired up her tablet.

Her email was inundated with spam.

She flicked to voicemail. Her phone had been crushed into a thousand pieces, but the number was still active and all her messages were available online. Disembodied data found another host.

A demon denied one body would possess another.

There were two messages from Peggy. That didn't surprise her. But the contents did. Peggy spoke with care, enunciating every word: she was passing on important information from a Mr Magnus Nkonde. It was important Berlin got in touch with him. A matter of life and death. Peggy paused.

Berlin could hear the fear in Peggy's voice as she continued: Mr Nkonde wanted her to know that the Russian embassy owned the van. Peggy swallowed hard and repeated it: the Russian embassy.

Berlin felt her own mouth go dry. That's why it was Moscow. It confirmed that Hirst, if she was right about their involvement, didn't simply want her out of London. They wanted her here, because they were working for the Russians.

Once she would have dismissed 'life and death' as Magnus's usual hyperbole, which had clearly terrified poor Peggy. But given the murders of Matvienko and Gerasimov, his warning deserved to be taken very seriously.

She had expected a chilly rebuke from Peggy about her failure to call over Christmas, not this. And if this wasn't bad enough, her second message was even more disturbing.

Peggy informed her that a man and a woman had come to the house and asked her about Magnus's telephone call.

How on earth had they found out about it?

There was a pause and Peggy sighed. She hoped that Berlin wouldn't be too angry. She had been very worried after Mr Nkonde called, so she had rung the police.

Berlin felt her blood begin to boil, but in the next moment it turned to ice.

Peggy added that she couldn't remember the woman's name, she was a detective, a DCI. But the man who came with her was Delroy Jacobs; she had remembered his name after they'd gone because it had finally rung a bell. They'd shown her a picture of someone called Carmichael. Peggy had seen him on the news. He had been murdered.

With a tremor in her voice Peggy asked Berlin to please get in touch as soon as she could. There was a pause, as if Peggy wanted to add something else, but thought better of it. Berlin listened to the silence for a moment and her mother's unspoken fear. Under the circumstances, Peggy had shown admirable restraint.

Berlin opened the BBC News site: Jolyon Carmichael had been shot in his own kitchen. A second deceased male in the house had yet to be identified.

An awful thought occurred to her: it could be Magnus. He must have been desperate to warn her if he had sought out her mother, which meant that for some reason he couldn't contact her directly. He had her mobile number. He'd left a message to call him before she flew to Moscow.

Alarm bells were going off all over the place.

She read on. The police had identified the weapon in the Carmichael murder as an Eastern European military sidearm, probably used with a silencer.

Christ. It's all about the Russians. Her head was spinning. What the hell had she been sent into and what was in that bloody van?

There was a link on the web page to a sidebar about Carmichael's newspaper. Berlin clicked it. *The Sentinel* had been bought by someone called Kalandarishvili. Great. She took off the headphones and dropped them on the table.

This was turning into a nightmare of epic bloody proportions. She had stumbled into some serious business involving Russians, who had had her shipped off to the mother country, where they dealt with their problems by incarcerating them. Or worse.

Berlin bought a can of Red Bull from the young headbanger in charge. He made sad gestures to convey he couldn't give her change from the five-hundred-rouble note, so she shrugged. Keep it. It would also cover her Internet use. His grin told her that she had fallen for the oldest trick in the book.

Back in the booth she picked up a flyer advertising the tour dates of an American pop diva. She turned it over and began to jot notes on the back, trying to weave the disparate bits of intel into a coherent scenario.

The van that Hirst's supervisor had lied about belonged to the Russian embassy; Gerasimov and the interpreter were dead; Charlie, pressured by her *krysha*, was a substitute; Carmichael, Magnus's former editor, had been murdered with an Eastern European weapon; Magnus himself, who had identified the van, was trying to get in touch with her; *The Sentinel* had been bought by a Russian.

Last, but not least, she was being investigated by a Russian intelligence agency.

Lies, deceit, duplicity. To hide what?

The night that she and Del had left Burghley's Christmas party the City had been full of Eastern European cigar-smoking revellers. Because the Russian president and his trade delegation were in London. How could she have forgotten that?

She peered at her notes, drawing solid arrows between items where she knew the connection and dotted lines where she didn't. Two things were immediately apparent.

First, the events were in the wrong order. The correct sequence was that she saw the van, she encountered the supervisor, she told Magnus about the van and he made enquiries. The term 'enquiries' sounded benign, but covered a multitude of sins.

Hang on. Did she speak to Magnus before or after the party? Christ, it was so recent, why was it so difficult to recall? Then she remembered the taxi that had miraculously pulled up right beside her and Del that night.

The driver had failed to turn on the meter. Was he waiting for them? Watching her, or Del, or both of them? What had they talked about in the cab? She wasn't paranoid. That had definitely happened *after* she'd seen Magnus in the Approach and no doubt he'd already begun to follow up her tip. Somehow, his intervention had acted as a trigger.

The second thing was more problematic and had nothing to do with her hazy memory. A piece of information was missing from her patchwork of arrows: what was being unloaded from the van?

There was no way she could work that one out, but the warehouse itself might add a piece to the puzzle.

She opened Google Maps and cruised around the images of the Park Royal estate. Warehouse 5B came into view. She zoomed in and found a name painted along one side.

A quick search revealed the company was registered. Her online account with Companies House, a hangover from the halcyon days of lucrative fraud investigations, was still active. She simply ordered the Current Appointments Report.

A link immediately arrived in her inbox. She clicked it and the document unfurled. Among the filing dates, company registration information and status details, one name stood out. The short list of directors included one M. Gerasimov.

Raised voices on the other side of the room broke Berlin's reverie. She had no idea how long she had been sitting there, trying to take in the fact that Gerasimov, the man she'd been sent to interview, and who lay in the mortuary, owned warehouse 5B.

The voices grew louder. She peered over the partition.

A man and a woman, their backs turned to her, were arguing with the youth at the front desk.

The boy gamers were paying attention to the altercation; they understood what was being said, and the looks on their faces indicated it wasn't good.

The woman began to wander among the booths, peering at the occupants. Berlin heard a crack and glanced up to see the youth at the front desk clutching his face.

Her colleague was enjoying himself.

One of the boys muttered something to Berlin in Russian. She shook her head and frowned, indicating she didn't understand. Another boy leant over and whispered in her ear.

'Go,' he hissed. 'They look for foreigner.' He pointed at an exit in the back wall.

This she understood.

She slid the tablet in her pocket and dropped to her knees. She wasn't the only one on the floor. A couple of blokes were weaving between the booths towards the exit.

Berlin followed.

The door was already swinging shut behind other fugitives. A shout indicated that someone had noticed.

Berlin had no idea if they were looking for her or pursuing illegal immigrants, but in the circumstances it seemed sensible not to hang around to find out.

47

Magnus had moped around the house all day. The evening he had spent drinking, and dozing, on and off, on his sofa. There wasn't much else he could do; Green wouldn't let him out of his sight, wouldn't let him go upstairs to bed, had even followed him into the toilet.

He opened one eye and looked at his babysitter, sitting upright in the armchair opposite. The man was a fiend. Magnus could see the sweat standing out on his brow, the slight but persistent twitch of his knee.

'Nasty cold, is it?' said Magnus.

Green scowled.

Magnus thought he should know better than to provoke a man with a gun, but he couldn't help himself. 'How much longer is this going to go on?' he said.

'Not long,' said Green.

'You mean until the talks are over, the trade deals are done, the prime minister and the president shake hands and the delegation flies out,' said Magnus.

'You should never have stuck your nose in,' said Green.

'That's my bloody job,' exclaimed Magnus. He stood up, fatigue fleeing as indignant rage swept through him. 'For Christ's sake,' he shouted, 'this is England!'

'Sit down,' said Green.

'What if I won't?' bellowed Magnus. 'Are you going to shoot me?'

'Sit down,' said Green. He stood up, walked over and shoved Magnus in the chest. Magnus fell back onto the sofa with a soft *whump*. It was the sound of his token resistance evaporating.

A mobile phone ringing caught them both by surprise. It was coming from Green's pocket, but it was the phone he had taken from Magnus.

Green took it out, glanced at the display, accepted the call and switched the phone to speaker. He handed it to Magnus and raised a finger in warning.

'Hello?' said Magnus.

'Magnus! Christ! I was almost convinced you were dead. Thank God. I got your message. What the hell's going on?'

The voice was distorted, but unmistakable.

'Oh, hello, old darling,' said Magnus. 'Have a good Christmas?'

Berlin crouched beneath the booths, between the legs of two lanky youths, trying to ignore the smell of their trainers. In turn, they were ignoring her.

She had let the back door close with a bang, while she stayed inside. The woman had dashed for it. She shouted something and her colleague had run out the front.

Meanwhile, Berlin had crawled back between the booths.

The denizens of the café resumed their activities in stolid silence. She began to appreciate that a habit of passive resistance, grounded in a deep mistrust of authority, was not readily turned around. A regime may change, but the instincts of its subjects do not.

'There's a terrible echo,' said Berlin. She was calling on Skype, crouched over the tablet, which was balanced on her knees, but the echo wasn't at her end.

'I'm in the bathroom,' said Magnus. 'Where are you?'

'I'm in Moscow,' said Berlin. 'What's happening, Magnus?'

'Not a lot,' he said.

'But you told my mother it was life and bloody death,' hissed Berlin.

'Oh, you know, I do carry on a bit,' said Magnus. He chuckled. He was almost certainly drunk.

'So the van belongs to the Russian embassy,' she said.

'Yes,' said Magnus.

'Well, here's the thing, Magnus,' she said. 'The warehouse belongs to Gerasimov.'

'Who?' said Magnus.

'Mikhail Gerasimov. The man I was sent here to interview,' said Berlin.

'Oh,' said Magnus.

Berlin was taken aback by this response.

'How much have you drunk, Magnus?' she said.

'A bit,' came the reply. 'When are you coming home?'

'I can't leave the bloody country,' said Berlin.

'Why on earth not?' said Magnus.

'They took my sodding passport,' said Berlin.

'I don't understand,' said Magnus. 'Who did?'

'A policeman. A Major Utkin,' said Berlin. 'They use

military ranks here. But he's not my only problem. The British Embassy tells me I'm also under investigation by Russian intelligence.'

There was silence at the other end.

'Magnus?' she said.

'I'm still here,' he said.

His reactions were getting weirder by the minute. She threw something into the mix.

'I see *The Sentinel* has been sold,' said Berlin. 'And Carmichael's been murdered.'

'Yes, there is that,' said Magnus.

He had to be really sozzled to react like that. He didn't sound drunk, but then with an old soak like Magnus you couldn't always tell.

'He's not the only one,' she said. 'Gerasimov is dead too.'

A tone cut in.

'Hello?' she said.

But she was speaking to dead air.

The connection had been broken.

48

Fagan sat in the Audi, watching the house and waiting for his mobile to be routed through a secure connection. 'Come on, come on,' he muttered.

Finally his call was answered.

'Gerasimov's dead,' he said.

His boss emitted a sound like wind punched out of a pillow. 'You're sure?'

'Well, I haven't seen the body,' said Fagan.

'When?'

'I don't know,' said Fagan.

'Our competitors will be working to move into this space. Do you think they were behind it?'

'It's possible,' said Fagan.

'Are our friends aware of this development?' said his boss.

'I don't know,' said Fagan.

'You don't know much, Fagan,' said his boss.

'Just that Berlin told Nkonde he's dead.'

He could hear his boss tapping a pen on a hard surface: probably a sleek marble desktop.

'Is that threat contained?'

Fagan glanced at the house. He could see Magnus peering at him from behind the chintz curtain.

'Yeah,' he said. 'Recent events have scared him shitless.'

'Good,' said his boss. 'What about her? She's a risk of a different order. Do you know where she is?'

'Moscow,' said Fagan.

'I meant a precise location.'

Fagan hesitated. If he said yes, he knew what would follow. If he said no, there would be hell to pay.

'I can get it,' he said.

'You know what to do.'

Fagan hung up and flicked the button on the glovebox. Open, shut. Open, shut. Open.

This is what happened when he tried to do things in a civilised fashion. Unlike others.

Magnus was astonished when he saw the Audi pull away. Green had even left Magnus's mobile behind. He wanted to cheer. Free at last, free at last. But instead he was seized by a sense of abandonment. He shivered, drew the curtains and turned on all the lights. He daren't leave the house.

He poured himself another stiff one and switched on the BBC News channel. Bombs were exploding in all the usual places, oppressive governments were turning water cannons on the usual protesters, and electricity prices were set to rise again.

Magnus turned off a couple of lamps.

He drained his glass and poured another. There was no doubt he was in danger; he shuddered, thinking of Carmichael.

He had an absolute cracker of an exposé, but he was

the one exposed: no lawyer, no editor, no gun. Not that he would have a clue what to do with a bloody gun.

His mobile rang and he jumped. He picked it up as if it might explode. He'd read about bombs in phones.

'Yes?' he said.

'Magnus Nkonde?'

The accent was thick, but the pronunciation perfect.

'Yes,' said Magnus.

'Joseph Kalandarishvili here,' said his caller. 'Forgive the intrusion at such a late hour.'

'Not at all, not at all,' spluttered Magnus. He was painfully aware of the obsequious note in his voice. At any other time a call from the new proprietor of *The Sentinel* would have been more than welcome. But in the current circumstances he didn't know what it might signify.

'Your recent enquiries have come to my attention,' said Kalandarishvili. 'It's an interesting story. But there are one or two things I'd like to clarify.'

Magnus hesitated. He gulped his Scotch.

'I appreciate that you are in a difficult position,' said Kalandarishvili.

'You don't know the half of it,' said Magnus.

'I'm sure,' said Kalandarishvili. 'But we are willing to offer you every protection and will give you whatever undertakings you require in writing.'

'Carmichael—' began Magnus.

'I'm not Carmichael,' said Kalandarishvili sharply.

That was an understatement. The chap was a billionaire; his security arrangements practically amounted to a private army.

'Of course,' said Kalandarishvili, 'there will be a permanent position on staff. I'm sure you'll agree that sort of standing in the press confers its own protection. In Great Britain.'

Magnus closed his eyes. He had a vision of himself as a thrusting young reporter, fearless, dashing, a force for good.

'Naturally, my editor will ask for full disclosure. In return we can offer you every assurance,' said Kalandarishvili.

Magnus hesitated, suddenly timid. He could see his father, shaking his head in disappointment. Behind him, the choir belted out 'Jerusalem'.

'Every protection?' said Magnus.

'And your own column.'

Magnus opened his eyes.

49

Berlin lay on the floor near Charlie's wood stove, racked by stomach cramps, sweating and retching. She had taken her last buprenorphine on Christmas morning. The old year was dying, and she felt as if she might go with it. She'd had no opportunity to taper her withdrawal.

The half-life of bupe was longer than other opiate agonists, which meant it took longer to reduce its concentration in her bloodstream – which meant withdrawal took longer.

There had been no dawn. She had found her way back to Charlie's through a freezing mist that had obscured the brief, miserable passage of night to day. Then she'd collapsed.

Each time a wave of symptoms swept over her, she thought they were at their most severe. But the next spate of nausea, anxiety and pain was inevitably worse.

She had been here once before, withdrawing in circumstances not of her choosing. On that occasion the final decision, to continue withdrawal or not, had been taken out of her hands. She had been given opiates without asking for them and she had been in no state to refuse.

A burning log crackled and spat, sending sparks up

the makeshift chimney. Smoke leaked from fissures in the cast iron, coalescing into spectral shapes that loomed over her.

Her imagination was fevered, she had no doubt, but there was no denying she was haunted. Lenny and Zayde danced before her, calling a tune out of her Russian blood.

'What's that music?' she groaned.

Her mother's face came close to her. 'Klezmer,' she said, 'don't dance to his tune. He weeps but he wouldn't fight for his country.'

Berlin felt her sweat-soaked thermals chilling. Her teeth chattered.

'What time is it?' said Berlin.

'Time for you to go back to sleep,' said Charlie. 'Where did you go? Where on earth were you all night?'

The ability to distinguish between friend and foe, predator and prey, had deserted Berlin. Charlie was her lifeline.

'Please,' she whispered. 'Get me something.'

'Can you wait until I take Nikki out for his walk?'

Berlin began to laugh. The illusion of autonomy, to which she had clung for so long despite all evidence to the contrary, was crumbling.

She was marooned on a strange planet, dependent on a bizarre shape-shifter and her mute automaton son.

Lenny and Zayde executed a frenetic jig. The delirious rhythm consumed her.

50

Magnus was woken by the noise of the newspaper dropping onto the doormat. The paper always arrived just after six. He was grateful for this comforting reminder that life went on, despite one's own struggles.

His heart was in his mouth. Anyone would think he was a cub reporter desperate to see his first byline.

Kalandarishvili had wanted to ensure the story was solid; it had to be, if he was going to ignore a DA-Notice. Magnus had explained everything. The new proprietor was left in no doubt as to the veracity of the information.

He picked up *The Sentinel* and unrolled it. His heart beat a little faster. The headline leapt out at him: *Cover-up*. The byline was his. He scanned the columns, delighted. Just a few tweaks by a sub. All good.

Then he realised they had added a final paragraph.

He couldn't believe his eyes. Dear God, what had he done?

Fagan was woken by his mobile. He was curled up on the back seat of the Audi and was so stiff he could barely move. He grabbed his phone from the floor.

'What?' he said.

'Get over to Park Royal and make sure the goods are still secure,' snapped his boss.

Fagan managed to sit up. He massaged his neck. 'What the fuck?'

'Where are you, Fagan?' said his boss. 'Have you seen the news? Worst-case scenario.'

'You're fucking kidding,' said Fagan.

'Get over there.' His boss hung up.

Fagan pulled himself together and scrambled into the front seat. The car started the first time and he accelerated out of the car park, spraying gravel. He glanced in the rear-view mirror. A dark shape was streaming across the gunmetal-grey clouds, a fast-moving phalanx.

Fagan blinked.

He'd frightened the ducks.

Fagan had to exercise every ounce of restraint he possessed not to speed down the North Circular Road. The last thing he wanted was to attract the attention of the constabulary.

He turned off towards Park Royal. The traffic was lighter here and he quickly arrived at the periphery of the site. A lot of places would close between Christmas and New Year.

A cluster of warehouses loomed; he did a circuit, to make sure there were no vehicles parked behind the control room that shouldn't be there. All clear. He killed the headlights, rolled into the car park and eased to a halt in the shadow of the building.

Reaching under his seat, he found what he wanted

buried deep in the springs: a spare ammunition clip. He got out of the car and shut the door carefully, then padded across the concrete apron and up the ramp to the door. He tried the handle. It was unlocked. He stepped inside.

The grey walls of the corridor seemed to contract to an infinite pinpoint. He controlled his breathing as he walked.

The chain of fluorescent lights above him hummed in the silence as he reached the door to the control room, which stood slightly ajar. Somewhere a generator whined. A rat trapped in the ducts above him squealed and scrabbled away from a sudden blast of heat.

Fagan felt the warm air caress the back of his neck. He poked the door open with his toe. A familiar dank, ferrous odour assailed him.

Raj's shirt glistened, scarlet in the glowing lights. His throat had been slashed by someone standing behind him. No sign of a struggle. Fagan glanced up at the monitor. There was a gap at the bottom of warehouse 5B's roller door.

He kicked over a chair.

51

Berlin dragged herself up on one elbow and gazed around the room. She groaned. 'Christ. What time is it?'

'How are you feeling?' said Charlie. She was sitting at the table with a pair of scissors and a pile of old newspapers. She appeared to be making strings of paper dollies for Nikki, who sat at her elbow.

'Never better,' said Berlin.

'It will pass,' said Charlie.

Berlin got up but felt weak, so immediately went and sat down opposite Charlie and Nikki at the massive dining table.

Charlie was trying to make the dollies dance. Berlin reached across the table and took one end of the chain as Charlie held the other. Together they made the dollies bob up and down.

Charlie gave her a shy smile of gratitude.

Nikki was entranced.

After a while Charlie rose and went to the stove. She returned with a large bowl of soup and plonked it in front of Berlin. 'Dig in,' she said. 'You've got to keep your strength up.'

Berlin did as she was told. The soup disappeared quickly. It helped. Reasonably clear-headed, but restless, she began to patrol the apartment. A sensation of exposure seized her, as if she'd been prodded and poked, invaded, used and abused. A specimen abducted by aliens.

She tried to focus, forcing herself to sit down, turn the tablet on and deal with her email.

Buried among the spam was a message from Del. It said baldly, 'Leave now. Go to the airport and get the first flight out. It doesn't matter where you go – we'll arrange another flight on to London.'

That was it. Not a word of explanation or even a friendly salutation.

The next email grabbed her attention immediately – it was from the British embassy. A crisp note from Mrs Muir informed Berlin that her request for an Emergency Travel Document had been expedited and the requisite papers were waiting for her at Domodedovo Airport.

Presumably she was no longer of interest to Russian intelligence. She could leave.

So that was it. Here today, gone tomorrow.

It put her teeth on edge. She had been lied to, shot at, manipulated, pursued. Now she was supposed to go home and forget any of it had ever happened.

'What are you going to do?' asked Charlie.

Berlin looked up.

'You should go home,' said Charlie.

Del, Mrs Muir. Now Charlie.

It was as if the sun had suddenly appeared from behind a rain cloud. She was dazzled. Bloody, but unbowed.

52

Berlin paid the taxi driver, grabbed her bag and made her way across the concourse to the Departures Hall. It was busy, but there was no queue at the British Airways information desk. The man and woman behind the counter were sitting some feet apart, staring at their computer screens.

'Excuse me,' she said.

The man, who wore a badge naming him as *Barry, Customer Service*, barely managed to drag his eyes away from the screen.

'Yes?' said Barry.

'Is this where you collect Emergency Travel Documents?' said Berlin.

'Are you flying with us?' said Barry.

'Yes,' said Berlin. 'I was supposed to leave on the 27th.'

Barry raised an eyebrow. 'Yesterday.'

Berlin tried to smile.

'Name?' said Barry.

'Berlin,' said Berlin. 'Catherine.'

Barry's fingers flashed across a keyboard. He peered at the screen, frowned, then went and consulted with his colleague. She pointed at a drawer. Barry opened it and brought out a file.

Berlin was surprised to see it contained a number of clear plastic pouches. Names were written on the pouches in large black letters.

Barry flipped through the pouches, then returned to his computer. 'You're not here,' he said.

'I must be,' said Berlin. 'I was told by an embassy representative I could collect my documents at the airport.'

Barry adopted a stance that Berlin recognised as one he had been taught when dealing with a difficult customer. He cocked his head, as if he were listening to her, and smiled. It was more of a rictus.

'I'm sorry, madam,' said Barry. 'Your name isn't in the computer and there are no documents waiting for you in the file. Perhaps you would care to wait while I double-check.'

Barry sauntered off through a door in the wall behind the counter.

Fifteen minutes later he hadn't reappeared. No doubt Barry was taking the opportunity to make himself a coffee and take a break. The woman glanced at Berlin a couple of times, with a look that said, 'Are you still here?', but she said nothing.

Charlie wandered about the apartment, feeling a little lost. To her chagrin, she had to admit that she would miss Berlin. It had been nice to have some company from the old country for a while, even if she had been a right royal pain in the bum. Her mobile rang. 'Yes,' she said warily. She listened in growing disbelief. 'But she's gone,' she said. 'To the airport.'

The cursing at the other end of the line was so loud that Charlie was forced to hold the phone away from her ear. Finally it stopped.

'Yes,' she said. 'Of course I will. But I can't see why she would come back . . .'

Her caller hung up.

Berlin was about to shout at someone, anyone, when Barry returned. He'd been gone twenty minutes.

'I'm sorry for the delay, madam,' he said. 'I can't contact the duty officer at the embassy at the moment. Perhaps you'd like to take a seat?'

Berlin was in the process of deciding whether Barry had also made himself a sandwich, when he glanced over her shoulder.

Berlin turned to see what he was looking at.

A man and a woman were striding across the terminal, weaving through the passengers and making straight for her. The last time she'd seen them was at the Internet café.

Berlin ran.

She had a good fifty-yard start, but it wouldn't have done her any good had she not remembered Charlie's sneaky route to the service bay.

The emergency exit was propped open, just as it had been that first morning. She ran towards it, a surge of adrenalin giving her a kick she hadn't felt in a long time.

The woman was gaining ground.

Berlin ran through the exit, slammed the door and yanked the bolt across.

The Russian words on the back had been conveniently translated into English: *This Door Must Not Be Locked.*

Spurred on by the rattling and hammering on the other side, Berlin took the stairs two at a time and ran into the cargo bay. A lone forklift truck was executing a three-point turn. Its yellow warning beacon was spinning and it was emitting a high-pitched signal.

The pulsating light and the noise gave her the cover she needed to cross the service apron and run around the corner of the building to the car park.

A few rows away someone was hauling a suitcase out of his boot. He handed it to a smartly dressed businessman hovering impatiently nearby. The businessman strode away.

Berlin slowed down and approached the driver, who was getting back into his car.

'*Chastniki?*' she said, holding up a fistful of roubles.

The man frowned, then smiled. 'You want lift?' he said.

Berlin slid into the passenger seat and didn't look back.

The helpful driver dropped her near the canal. She walked beside it, looking for water. The moon's reflection failed at the line of demarcation between ice and liquid. When she reached a darker patch, she bent over the parapet and let something slip from her hands.

The tablet barely made a splash.

Her feeling that she hadn't just been caught up in a random immigration sweep at the Internet café had proved correct. She had been using her tablet. The bright, shiny new device that had arrived after hers had been nicked.

It came via Burghley, but a device could have been planted by the client, the front-runner being Hirst.

They'd failed at the café, so they had set up the airport scam. The Russians weren't the only people she had to worry about. The British were after her too.

She had reached the point where there was no-one she could call on for help without putting herself, or them, at risk: anyone could be watching or listening.

The ice crept across the water, sealing the breach. The canal was once again a seamless grey mass; all traces of its recent rupture had been obliterated.

Berlin's spectral status was now absolute. For all intents and purposes, she was dead.

She walked back to Charlie's, a ghost of her former self.

The fighter

53

Delroy waited impatiently in the Cheshire Cheese, a bog-standard pub in Crutched Friars, underneath the railway arches. Hirst's representative didn't want to meet at the office, or during business hours. He was looking to distance the company from Burghley and its subcontractor. As if somehow this was all Berlin's fault.

Del hadn't actually met him before; everything had been done at the last minute, over the phone. But when a tall bloke in an expensive suit walked in, he looked straight at Del and nodded, then went to the bar. He brought back two doubles, put one in front of Del and offered his hand.

'Peter Green,' he said.

Del took his hand and shook it without any warmth. 'Delroy Jacobs.'

The Sentinel was spread out on the table.

Del couldn't restrain himself. He went straight for it. 'You knew that Berlin and I went back a long way,' he said. 'You knew she wouldn't question the gig if it came from me. You were watching her.'

Green sat down. 'We were protecting her.'

'I should have paid more attention,' said Del. 'One of the partners told me the job was coming and to run with it. That was it. I thought it must have been because of Christmas.'

He took a long drink. He could see Peter Green wasn't going to say anything. He was all corporate restraint.

'I *wanted* to believe it. But I've been around long enough to know that when a job from a big client gets flicked to the new boy, it's because he will be easy to sacrifice if it goes pear-shaped.'

Del jabbed a finger at *The Sentinel*. 'And it has gone pear-shaped, hasn't it, Green?'

'Don't blame yourself,' said Green. 'Your boss says jump, you say "How high?" We're all the same.'

'Berlin trusted me,' said Del. He gulped his Scotch.

'You should know, Jacobs, your firm has the confidence of the Ministry. They all went to school together.'

Del realised that Green was trying to tell him something. 'There's no paperwork, no contract? It's all been done on a nod and wink through the old boys' network?' he asked.

Green nodded, confirming it.

'What about the fee? Berlin's advance, her expenses?' said Del.

'I imagine someone gave you a Post-it note with the bank account details?'

Del stared at the bottom of his empty glass.

Green went to the bar. When he returned with two more doubles, Del drank his down. He wasn't drinking to savour the flavour.

'So when did you last hear from her?' asked Green.

'There was a message not long after she arrived.'

'The one that said the job was going okay?' said Green.

'She emailed the interview transcripts, too. I forwarded them to your office.'

'Anything else?'

'She'd left the hotel.'

'A heads-up at that point would have saved us all a lot of trouble,' said Green.

'Why would we bother the client with that sort of detail? She changed hotels, no big deal.'

'But it was a big deal,' said Green.

'It was only when she mentioned the interpreter that a flag went up,' said Del. 'I just didn't put it all together.'

'She didn't use the bloke you'd booked?'

'No,' said Del. 'It was someone called Charlie Inkpin. I thought he must be one of Gerasimov's people.'

'Right,' said Green. He finished his drink and glanced at his watch. 'I'm sorry, Jacobs, I have another . . .'

'Not so fast, Green,' snapped Del. 'I sent Berlin to do a straightforward job that was a sham.'

'It wasn't,' said Green. 'We had to do due diligence on a prospective business partner.'

'But you must have known that if this got out, Berlin would be in the worst possible place.' Del picked up *The Sentinel* and thrust it at him.

'Steady,' said Green. 'It only got out because she couldn't keep her mouth shut. We were just asked to keep an eye on the warehouse.'

'Who by?' hissed Delroy. 'The so-called Ministry?'

Del could see the smooth company-man façade was crumbling. Green's knuckles were white. He was sweating.

'We've done everything we can,' said Green. 'The

British embassy is moving heaven and earth to find her. We're giving them every assistance.'

'Hirst knew about that unscheduled delivery,' accused Del. 'Christ! According to newspapers the fucking British government knew! Where did the tip-off come from?'

'The intel was offered to us to sweeten a business deal. We just passed it on.'

'Jesus,' said Del. 'It's all about money.'

'Fear was a factor, too,' said Green. 'A quick exit from Russia was necessary. The source knew Whitehall would expedite the process for someone who brought a little something with them.'

'So where is your source now?'

Green looked down at his drink.

Del took a deep breath. 'Oh no,' he said. 'Of course. Gerasimov.'

'It's all about national security.'

'Bullshit,' snapped Delroy. 'It's all about the so-called national interest. Which means the City. It's not the same thing.' Delroy thumped the table.

A few patrons looked around.

Green stood up and strode away.

Delroy leapt up and ran after him. He grabbed Green as he was opening the door and they spilled out onto the pavement. Passers-by gave the two men a wide berth as they tussled.

'What about Berlin's interest in staying alive?' shouted Del.

'I'm sorry, mate,' said Green. He tried to extricate himself.

'You're not my mate,' said Del, fierce. 'What happened here? What are we going to tell her mother? Oh, sorry, we sent Berlin to Moscow on a job and it doesn't look like she's coming back. What are you going to do about it?'

'What the fuck can I do about it?' said Green. He punched Del in the sternum. Del staggered, winded.

Green held on to him and got right into his face. 'Do you want to be next, Jacobs?' he whispered. 'Or Linda and the baby? You need to start coming to terms with the fact that it's over.'

He pushed Del up against the wall and let him go.

Del's knees buckled and he slid to the ground.

Green straightened himself up and walked away.

'What?' gasped Del. 'What do you mean, "it's over"?'

Fagan glanced back at Delroy Jacobs, slumped against the wall of the pub. The bloke had been exploited, and he knew it. A strange sensation gripped Fagan. After a moment he identified it as empathy. It wasn't helpful.

Berlin's last known position was a canal in the middle of Moscow. It wasn't conclusive – she was a smart operator.

It wasn't quite over, but thanks to Jacobs it soon would be.

54

Mrs Muir regarded the man and woman who stood in front of her with ill-disguised contempt.

'This is the best you can do?' she said. 'A civilian who doesn't know the city or the language manages to give you the slip. Twice.'

The woman shuffled, shamefaced.

'We could ask the locals for help,' ventured the man.

'Brilliant,' said Mrs Muir. She arched an eyebrow. 'We know how that will end.'

'Why haven't we got backup? This is highly irregular. I don't understand what we are supposed to do if—'

'Behave like professionals,' said Mrs Muir.

Their faces hardened. Their eyes conveyed exactly what they thought of her, sitting in a nice, warm office, giving them orders. Mrs Muir was unconcerned. She was used to it. The problem nowadays was that life imitated art, and mediocre art at that, far too often.

The men failed to shave, apart from their thick skulls, then bought designer suits and thought the job was half done. The women, bitter at being patronised by their inept older male colleagues, just wanted to shoot someone. They were loose cannons, in every sense of the word.

'Our involvement is off the record, so we can't employ

the usual methods. That would require a paper trail. Do you understand? Just find her.'

The two operatives stared at their feet.

'Why are you still here?' said Mrs Muir.

They stomped out.

The old-fashioned phone on her desk rang. She kept it as a reminder of simpler times. She picked up and listened. When she replaced the receiver she turned to her computer and set up a query. While the servers in some remote, heavily fortified location were doing their work, she considered her options.

Delegation was perhaps not the wisest choice, given the unreliability of her subordinates. Sometimes, if you wanted a job done, it was easier to do it yourself.

Her team would report a fruitless search. They had tried, and failed. They wouldn't be covered in glory, but they were used to that. Failure was the best option, officially. The computer pinged: a result.

Unofficially, she now had other plans.

55

Berlin limped out into the bright Moscow day. She felt stronger; she had slept more soundly. Anyone tracking her electronically now had a problem.

Charlie hadn't seemed that surprised to see her back again; in fact, she was almost enthusiastic about Berlin's reappearance. Had she known about the airport set-up?

The tension in Berlin's damaged tendon eased as she lengthened her stride, following the curve of the canal, which would guide her back to where she had begun.

When she reached the main road, cops on motorbikes were holding back vehicles and pedestrians to allow a motorcade of black limousines to pass unimpeded. Russian flags fluttered on the bonnets. The traffic was gridlocked in all directions. She shuffled from foot to foot, trying to keep warm among the crowd of scowling, grumbling Muscovites.

It was clear that their chagrin was directed at the occupants of the vehicles, but it made her nervous.

The chemicals were leaching out of her system and fear was colonising the empty places. It was the kind of terror that chased out normal, everyday anxiety about such things as not speaking the language, getting lost in a strange city or being a person of interest to shadowy authorities.

These things were trivial by comparison.

This was the kind of angst that could only be kept at bay with action. She had to do something. The sweats and weakness would claim her again at some point, but she would just have to ride it out.

In the meantime she would find out what the hell was going on: her self-respect rested entirely on her professionalism. If she lost that, she might as well retreat into a pleasant narcotic haze until the day she died.

The arse-covering exercise was over – theirs and her own.

The image of her grandfather came to mind: posing in his long johns, bald head cocked and fists raised. She would follow Zayde's example.

Come out fighting.

Artem, the hotel manager, was very surprised to see her. He took a step back behind the reception desk as if she were infectious.

'How may I help you?' he said.

The lobby was bustling with European businessmen checking out. An American tour group was checking in.

'I can happily make a scene here, or perhaps we could go somewhere more private?' said Berlin.

From the hasty fashion in which he lifted the barrier, allowing her to pass beyond the desk, his choice was clear.

Artem didn't sit, nor did he invite Berlin to do so. No-one was going to bring blinis.

She had returned to the place where it had all started, only a few hours after she had arrived in Moscow.

Without Utkin's intervention she would never have known that Charlie wasn't the interpreter assigned by Burghley. The major had taken her passport and her drugs, but he hadn't asked her for anything except information.

All his actions since their first encounter had kept her out of trouble. It had dawned on her that if Utkin wasn't actually her friend, he was certainly the least of her enemies.

'What do you want?' said Artem.

'I want you to make some calls and find the policeman that was here. Major Utkin. Then let me speak to him.'

'Why don't you just call him yourself?' asked Artem.

It was a reasonable question. If she hadn't lost the piece of paper with his number on it, and thrown away her mobile, she wouldn't have to take this circuitous route. The stress had obviously got to her and she had made some stupid mistakes.

'I lost my mobile,' said Berlin. 'I don't have his number and my Russian consists solely of *da, nyet* and *vodka*.'

Artem sighed, sat down and picked up the phone.

56

The gilded dome was Berlin's beacon. More copper than gold beneath the slate sky, it was the only one she could see with four blue domes standing sentinel around it. Utkin's description of the place they were to meet was apt.

Artem had clearly known where to look for the major, and after a couple of brief conversations he was put through and handed the phone to Berlin.

Utkin had been solicitous; he'd asked if she had come to the hotel alone and how she was feeling. His directions had been clear – he'd told her to keep to the road – and she had left the hotel with a small sense of achievement.

Every investigation was about making the small connections and letting them build into the big picture.

The policeman was the first piece of the puzzle.

Berlin made for the dome as quickly as possible, but the footpath was treacherous. Short, tentative steps seemed to work best on the ice. Her Peacekeeper boots were standing up to the snow well, but it had never occurred to her that she'd be doing so much walking. Del had told her that the interpreter would have a car that would be at her disposal. So much for that.

In fact, he hadn't told her anything she really needed to know. That's what it looked like. There was a very good chance that the client had blindsided Burghley too, relying on its impeccable reputation to deflect any suspicions she might have harboured.

Utkin had said it should only take her twenty minutes to reach the church, which he had described perfectly. She followed the road around a bend and up a hill, looking down on a large frozen pond and a track around it that led up to the sheer, whitewashed wall of the fortification. That was the short cut she would have been tempted to take.

Something trotted along the track that ran beneath the wall. It could have been a Shetland pony, but it was a brindle mastiff. Even at this distance, Berlin could see the drool hanging from its jowls. At the end of a very long rope was an old man. It looked as if the dog were leading him.

She was grateful that Utkin had emphasised the necessity of sticking to the road.

Finally she reached a pair of massive timber gates. Beyond them were whitewashed buildings reminiscent of a medieval village, with the exception of the church, which loomed over them.

Berlin was an atheist, but she was moved by the dignity of the grand building in its somewhat tatty state. She admired persistence. The enduring legacy of faith always amazed her, and the testimony of its mute, corporeal manifestations was never less than impressive.

A faded wooden sign beside the gates was in Cyrillic,

but beneath it a plastic box held damp, yellowing tourist maps of Moscow sights. '100R' was scrawled on the box. Two quid. There was no-one about.

Berlin hesitated, then took off a glove, fumbled in her pocket and found the required fee. She was her mother's daughter.

A small symbol on the map informed her that the church, a *katholikon*, was the first in Moscow, built in the fourteenth century. The fortification was constructed in 1640. It was the Novospassky Monastery, the Monastery of the New Saviour.

She hoped it would live up to its name.

The gloomy interior of the labyrinthine place of worship was the perfect setting for a brooding policeman. He patrolled the walls, peering at the icons. Berlin walked with him.

'History of this place is history of Russia,' said Utkin. 'But no tourists come.'

'Why not?' said Berlin.

'Kremlin, Kremlin, Kremlin,' said Utkin. He spoke with disdain.

'You know the monastery well?' said Berlin. The urgency of her situation seemed to have dissipated in the atmosphere of candle smoke, incense and dusty parchment.

'I worked here long time ago,' said Utkin.

'You were a monk?' said Berlin with surprise.

Utkin chuckled. 'After revolution, Bolshevik prison. Later, drunk tank. That was my time,' he said. 'I was cadet. Then soon it was museum. Church got it back in

1991.' He made the circular motion with his hands. *History: the wheel turns.*

Berlin found the flat iconic images oddly compelling. She gazed into the almond eyes of the Slavic Christ and thought of the pink baby Jesus.

'Can you tell me any more about my grandfather?' she said.

'Very likely he did hard labour,' he said. 'His *nakolki*, his tattoos . . .' He stopped walking and turned to her.

'Yes?'

'That isn't why you contacted me.'

They were standing in darkness in an alcove decorated with a faded fresco. A shadow moved swiftly in the periphery of Berlin's vision.

Berlin took a step closer to Utkin and leant in, as if about to kiss him. 'No. But before we go any further,' she whispered, 'do you carry a gun?'

It was Utkin's turn to be surprised. 'Yes,' he muttered. 'Of course.'

'Then I strongly advise you to draw it,' said Berlin. 'Because someone just came in through that side door. With a weapon in his hand.'

They both shrank back further into the alcove. Footsteps approached softly from behind the altar and another figure emerged into the flickering candlelight, meeting up with his colleague.

Their shapes huddled together, indistinguishable in the shadows. A hiss of whispers rose into the dome above them. The pair then separated and began a systematic search. It was only a matter of time before they reached the alcove.

A heavy iron grille hung about four feet from the wall, protecting the fresco. It created a cell between the two massive columns that formed the recess.

Utkin nudged the grille with his hip and, to Berlin's amazement, it silently swung open. His stint at the drunk tank had paid off.

It was tight, but he and Berlin were able to squeeze beyond it. Utkin pushed the grille back into place and they crouched together behind the pillar.

Berlin smothered a giggle. Utkin frowned at her. It wasn't funny. Her reactions were all over the place.

Footsteps approached, paused, then moved on.

Berlin craned her head. She couldn't see the men, but it seemed they were no longer concerned with keeping a low profile. Their voices carried in the empty stone space.

'What are they saying?' whispered Berlin.

'He made mistake. No-one here,' Utkin whispered.

A door creaked and a shaft of light fell across the flagstones, then disappeared as the door closed behind them.

Berlin and Utkin crouched in the dark alcove under the saint's baleful gaze, waiting.

57

Charlie thought she was hearing things. A knock on the
door. But the second time there was no mistake. One of
the most dreadful sounds. There was no point in ignoring
it. She swore, strode to the door and flung it open.

A middle-aged woman gave her a wintry smile.
'Charlotte Inkpin?' she said.

Charlie stared at her.

'Allow me to introduce myself,' said the woman. She
was holding a black briefcase. She offered Charlie her
other hand. 'Mrs Muir.'

Berlin sat in silence beside Utkin. The wide road ran
parallel with the Moskva. They were driving in the direction of a massive statue of a man on the prow of a galleon.
It loomed out of the water, the rigging towering above
them. Peter the Great. A useful landmark, Charlie had
said. She was right.

They drove over a bridge. Utkin pulled up in front of
an archway under a broad flight of stone steps. A bloke
leaning against the wall nodded at Utkin and he drove
slowly through the narrow gap. They followed a route
down, marked by concrete pillars. At each level the air
became danker and the temperature rose.

When Utkin finally stopped and turned off the motor, Berlin could hear the drips of condensation hitting the car's roof.

'They were looking for you,' said Utkin.

Berlin nodded. 'I think so,' she said.

'Do you know why?'

She hesitated. She could see furtive figures darting about, caught in the blue bars of fluorescent light, getting in and out of cars, ignoring each other.

It was a dead zone. No signals could penetrate at this depth, in either direction. There was no quick escape route. You came down here with someone you trusted, or not at all.

'The official at the British embassy told me I was being investigated by the SVR,' admitted Berlin.

'That's why you asked me,' he said. 'I should have realised.'

Even in the dim light Berlin could see his pupils dilate. He rubbed the back of his neck, where no doubt his bristles were standing on end.

'I thought it was over,' said Berlin.

'It's never over,' said Utkin. 'Maryna Gerasimova. Colonel, SVR.'

'Jesus,' said Berlin. 'Do you think she murdered her husband?'

Utkin gazed out of the window. 'Not with her own hand,' he said. 'So now, Miss Berlinskaya, tell me everything.'

There was no point in being coy. 'I think it all started when I was working in the CCTV control room on an industrial estate in London,' she said. 'I saw two men make a delivery to a warehouse. It didn't appear on any schedule.'

'You were suspicious?' said Utkin.

'It was odd, that was all. But alarm bells began to ring when the supervisor offered me a bribe to keep quiet.'

'That's unusual in London?' said Utkin.

Berlin shook her head. 'It was what he said that surprised me; he said they were stealing from the warehouse. But I knew they had actually unloaded something.'

A poxy night shift at a miserable north London industrial estate had led to all this.

'The bloke who was supposed to work the shift in the CCTV control room, someone called Raj, had called in sick at the last minute. I imagine they were confident that he would turn a blind eye.'

'Most people would, yes,' murmured Utkin. 'I'm guessing you didn't keep quiet.'

'I passed the information on to a friend, a journalist. He found out the van belonged to the Russian embassy.'

'What was in it?' said Utkin.

'That's a very good question,' said Berlin. 'Whatever it was, it's unleashed a shitstorm.'

Utkin raised a questioning eyebrow.

'It's an expression,' said Berlin. 'A lot of trouble.'

Mrs Muir sat at Charlie's table. The file that she had produced from her briefcase was open in front of her.

Charlie sat opposite her, rigid, as Mrs Muir perused the file.

'. . . and we see here that you have a son,' she said. 'And where is he?'

She looked up at Charlie.

Charlie felt a sweat break out on her top lip, despite the frigid temperature. She licked at it.

'I'll just go and get him, if you like,' she said.

'There's no need,' said Mrs Muir.

'No, really. You should meet him,' said Charlie.

She stood up and, with much less equanimity than she felt, crossed the room. She had to do something, and fast. She closed the double doors behind her and slipped her phone out of her pocket.

Utkin had produced a bottle of vodka from his endless supply in the boot of the Ford. Berlin longed for a good single malt. She took a swig and handed it back. Utkin drank deeply, then wiped the back of his mouth on his sleeve.

'The reporter's former editor, Carmichael, has been murdered,' said Berlin. 'And the newspaper has been bought by a man named Joseph Kalandarishvili.'

'Ah,' said Utkin. 'I know of him.'

'You know I was sent to interview Gerasimov.'

'Who was already dead,' said Utkin.

'I don't think they knew that,' said Berlin. 'There was another angle.'

'They wanted you out of the way,' said Utkin.

'It was more than that. I'm here for a reason.'

As she said it out loud, piecing it together for Utkin while huddled in this subterranean realm, the conclusion was inescapable. If she became a threat, they wanted her where they could shut her down, permanently, and control the subsequent investigation.

From the way Utkin was looking at her, he was reaching the same conclusion. Very likely, she thought. After all, he was a detective.

'I think I might be the only one who can identify the men in the van,' said Berlin. 'Apart from the supervisor, of course.' Her memory of the two stocky, unshaven men with identical pudding-basin haircuts was vivid.

Utkin nodded. 'You said intelligence firm sent you here.'

'But they were acting under instructions.'

'From who?' said Utkin.

Berlin could see the fifty quid lying on the console and smell the threat that had accompanied it.

'Hirst Corporation. The world's leading international security solutions group.'

She was a risk, and she had been managed. Hirst was protecting Gerasimov's warehouse, which the Russian embassy was using for an illegal operation.

Hirst had the perfect cover: a legitimate job in pursuit of a business venture, undertaken by a respected, impartial third party – Burghley.

But if something went wrong, the only witness to the warehouse delivery could be eliminated by their Russian partner.

No doubt there was no paper trail of Hirst's request that Burghley use Berlin. That decision would rest on Del's shoulders.

She looked Utkin in the eye and laid it out.

'Find the men from the church and arrest them,' she said.

It was a challenge and a plea.

'What?' protested Utkin. 'We didn't even see them.'

'There must be cameras in the area,' said Berlin. 'They didn't walk there. Find the car and you'll find them. Men carrying guns aren't beginners; they'll have history, previous convictions. You could track them down.'

Utkin shook his head, his expression grave.

'You misunderstand. If they are SVR, even if I could find them, they would laugh at me. Arrest them for what? *You* are criminal here.'

'For God's sake, do you want to catch this killer?' said Berlin. 'You're after whoever murdered Matvienko and Gerasimov. The men looking for me could have useful information. At the very least.'

Utkin frowned. 'But there's only one connection,' he said. 'You.'

The way he said it gave Berlin the chills.

'You're wrong,' she said. 'Gerasimov owned the warehouse in London.'

Utkin started the car. 'Where can I drop you?' he said.

58

Charlie sat at the table with her forehead resting on her arms, her eyes shut tight against the awfulness of it all, struggling to breathe. Her chest ached with the effort. She couldn't take much more.

Nikki sat next to her and gently stroked her hair. She was always amazed and grateful when he showed such sensitivity. She sat up and he wrapped his arms around her. A shoulder to cry on. She hadn't had one of those for a very long time. Leaning into him, she began to weep.

'My dear boy,' she said. 'It will soon be over.'

Berlin thought it was less than gentlemanly of Utkin to dump her in the middle of a metropolis when she was being pursued by armed thugs.

Her assumption that she was in central Moscow could, of course, be entirely wrong. The city was vast and gave no quarter to strangers. In that respect it reminded her of London.

She focused on Peter the Great in the distance. He would guide her back to the canal, and thence to Charlie's. As if that were a refuge; the woman could be one of her enemies. They seemed to be multiplying.

Only two people knew what she'd seen at the warehouse:

Magnus and the supervisor. It was very unlikely that Magnus would have mentioned her name to anyone.

Gerasimov was dead before she arrived. The revelation of the deception, the Potemkin village, confirmed it. Perhaps, like Berlin, he had also known the identities of the men who made the delivery to the warehouse.

Gerasimova and the lookalike little commodore had been forced to put on a show when they found out she was coming to interview him. If Gerasimov hadn't appeared, it would have sent up a flag.

But to whom? Hirst? Maybe. Their joint venture would have died with Gerasimov. It was a necessary condition, but not sufficient.

Gerasimov's death would have come out sooner or later; Hirst could find another partner. Something of much greater significance than a company merger had to be on the line.

Berlin was surprised to find the chain on the gate hanging free. Exhausted, she limped up the garden path and into the lobby. In the murk it was able to hide its dilapidation and project a semblance of its former grandeur.

Each rise of the broad staircase challenged her sore Achilles tendon. When she finally reached Charlie's imposing entrance, the door stood ajar. Stepping inside, she crossed the vestibule and entered the reception room.

The reek that assailed her was familiar. The room was dark, except for the glow from the wood stove.

Berlin felt for the switch and flicked on the electric chandeliers.

Charlie was sitting at the table. Nikki was beside her.

A dark line joined them, as if they'd been struck by lightning which had scorched a continuous pattern across their chests.

Berlin moved closer. The streak was damp. Blood.

Charlie looked to her left.

Berlin followed her gaze.

Mrs Muir lay on the floor, her throat slashed. Blood had pooled around her.

The bloody line that joined Charlie and Nikki was spatter thrown from a knife at the end of its arc.

Then Berlin noticed something lying on the table.

It was Mrs Muir's tongue.

'They thought she was you,' said Charlie.

59

Berlin sat on the stone steps beneath the faded pink portico, trying not to think about Mrs Muir. The poor woman's death had given Berlin a chance at life: if Berlin's would-be assassins thought she was dead, she was safe for the moment.

It was an uncharitable thought. But not quite as uncharitable as to wonder how they could have confused her with the desiccated civil servant.

It was a thought she decided not to pursue.

Mrs Muir's hideous death couldn't be reported to the police, or the embassy, without exposing Berlin. Struggling with nausea Berlin had rolled up the threadbare rug on which Mrs Muir lay and dragged her to the furthest wing of Charlie's apartment. The temperature was in their favour.

The tongue she had delicately scraped off the table with an old *Pravda* and dumped in the garden, after which she had quietly been sick. No doubt scavengers would consume both. There was no shortage of them.

Charlie thought it was unlikely anyone would know of Mrs Muir's visit. Mrs Muir was intelligence. Accordingly, she would have played her cards close to her chest. She had come alone for a reason.

She would be missed, but no-one would necessarily know where she had gone. Her colleagues would eventually assume the enemy had got to her, one way or another.

Berlin remembered an article about a Russian defector, Oleg Gordievsky, who claimed there were as many Russian spies in London now as during the Cold War.

Gordievsky had been the KGB's station chief in London and operated as a double agent for more than ten years. When his superiors became suspicious they recalled him. The Brits smuggled him out in the boot of a diplomatic vehicle.

In 2007 Gordievsky had been awarded the Order of St Michael and St George by the Queen. In Russia he had been awarded a death sentence.

A wheeze and shuffle heralded Charlie.

'Mind if I join you?' she said.

She sat down and lit a cigarette.

Her hands shook and she was deathly pale. Hardly surprising: a woman had been murdered in her living room.

'How on earth did she find out I was here?' murmured Berlin.

There was a long silence. Not companionable. They were both still stunned.

'She had my file with her,' said Charlie, finally. 'She knew everything. I suppose it makes sense they would keep track of someone like me.'

Berlin let this sink in. 'Are defectors always spies?' she said.

'Not invariably,' said Charlie. 'But it does tend to go with the territory. One has to offer one's host something.'

A sacrifice.

'The tongue. What was that all about?' said Berlin.

'It was a warning,' said Charlie. 'Not to wag mine.'

Charlie lit another cigarette from her stub.

Berlin nearly asked for one.

Charlie had insisted that it was a coincidence that the killers had turned up while Mrs Muir was there. Berlin didn't believe that for a moment. Charlie had tipped them off.

'What's the *siloviki*?' asked Berlin.

'Where did you hear that?' said Charlie. She glanced left and right, as if someone might be lurking in the bushes, listening. It was clear that just the word made her nervous. '*Men of power.*'

'Men of power?' echoed Berlin. 'Like the old boys' network?'

Charlie's chuckle was grim.

'In the old system it was the party apparatchiks who ruled. In Yeltsin's time he empowered the oligarchs. But when Putin's turn came, he appointed his old KGB comrades to run the police, the military, the bureaucracy and, of course, the so-called new intelligence services. They're all still there. Collective noun: *siloviki.*'

Berlin could see why the analogy with the old-school tie didn't really work. The prospect of two damaged women, both past their sell-by date, challenging these men of power seemed unlikely.

'Look, Charlie,' said Berlin. 'There's something I should say.'

'What?' said Charlie.

'Thank you,' said Berlin.

'Don't mention it,' said Charlie.

But it looked like something else was on her mind.

'I wonder if I might ask you a favour in return,' she said.

Payback had come up fast.

'Take Nikki back to England with you.'

Berlin was gobsmacked. 'You can't be serious.'

'I'm not well,' said Charlie. 'He needs proper care.'

'I can't even get myself back to England, let alone him,' said Berlin. 'And have you seen the state of the National Health Service lately? He might be better off here.'

'Hardly!' said Charlie. 'He'll just end up in some ghastly asylum or prison.'

'This is ridiculous, Charlie,' said Berlin.

'You owe me this much, Berlin. I saved your fucking life!' she shouted.

Berlin stared at her. The woman had gone mad. She was also aware that Charlie could still give her up to the people who had murdered Mrs Muir.

'How would I get him out?' said Berlin.

'All you have to do is make it to a border with an EU country and find a way across,' said Charlie. 'Illegals do it all the time. The borders are porous. It's not like they would shoot you, even if you were spotted.'

'For God's sake,' said Berlin. But Charlie had it all worked out. She ranted on.

'There would be a lot of bureaucratic shenanigans, but finally the British would have to give you a new passport. In the meantime, you claim asylum for Nikki.'

When she fell silent, Berlin couldn't look at her. She fixed her gaze on the frozen canal. Conversation over.

Charlie finally got the message. She huffed and puffed as she got to her feet.

'One good turn deserves another.'

She shuffled away, back into the lobby.

Berlin tried to ignore Charlie's chagrin and think through the larger issues; for a start, how she got into this shitty mess and who sent the people who came to kill her?

Charlie had admitted she was working for her *krysha* when she acted as Berlin's interpreter and when she gave her shelter. Berlin believed her when she said she didn't know Gerasimova or the commodore, but there was clearly a connection between them and the *krysha*.

Perhaps the killers had also done Charlie a favour. What if Mrs Muir had something on her and Charlie saw a chance to rid herself of a threat?

Who said a problem is just an opportunity in disguise?

Yuri made his way down the corridor, clutching two coffees from Starbucks. He wondered how his men could have missed Utkin and Berlin at the monastery, given the tip-off from Artem. They were worse than useless.

But at least they'd finally caught up with her. He hoped that would please Maryna and her talk of 'loose ends'.

At the moment she was in his ear about the risk posed

by Misha's stand-in. The little bastard was making a nuisance of himself, looking for more money, then spending it on vodka and boasting about working for 'the authorities'.

That's what you got when you used a criminal database to pick a lookalike.

Yuri pushed open the door to Utkin's office with his foot and plonked one of the coffees on the desk.

Utkin looked up from a very old file he was perusing.

He regarded the coffee with distaste.

Yuri knew that Utkin thought it very *New Russian* to spend good money on such beverages. Perhaps it had been a mistake.

'You should be scaling back your workload, old friend,' he said.

'No-one will shoot at me here,' said Utkin. 'At least, it's not very likely.'

Yuri laughed.

'You seem cheerful,' said Utkin.

Yuri sipped his coffee and smacked his lips with satisfaction. 'A bad peace is better than a good quarrel,' he said. He didn't want to give the impression he still needed Utkin's approval.

Utkin said nothing, deadpan.

It made Yuri nervous. 'I've got some good news for you, old friend,' he blustered. 'Your case is solved.'

'Which case is that?' said Utkin.

'Mikhail Gerasimov,' said Yuri.

Utkin stood up. 'It's not possible. The body hasn't even been formally identified yet,' he said.

Yuri took a step back. He held his coffee in front of him, as if it were a talisman to ward off evil. He was aware of Utkin's clenched fists.

'I'm telling you, it is. And don't forget who is the senior officer here,' he said. 'You should be thanking me.'

'And who was responsible for his death?' demanded Utkin.

'An Englishwoman who arrived recently. Someone sent by British intelligence,' said Yuri.

Utkin froze. 'You have a witness?'

Yuri was backing up. He was halfway out of the door now.

'Certainly,' he said. 'Maryna Gerasimova, his wife. Who is . . .'

'I know who she is,' snapped Utkin. 'And this Englishwoman is in custody, I assume.'

'No,' said Yuri. He was in the corridor now. 'She's gone.'

Utkin strode towards him. Yuri began to walk away quickly.

'Gone where?' shouted Utkin.

Others in the corridor stopped to watch. A few people stuck their heads out of their office doors.

'Fled. Back to England, I imagine,' called Yuri, and disappeared around a corner.

Utkin strode back into his office and slammed the door. It bounced open. He kicked it shut again.

Utkin sat down at his desk and thought about Yuri, who had come to him as the junior partner in their working relationship. They had grown close, almost like father and son, but from the beginning it had been clear that Yuri was meant for higher things. He wasn't a better policeman than Utkin, but he had better contacts.

What was his connection to Colonel Gerasimova?

Yuri had become an aloof, nervous man, so insecure that he still wore a uniform, a rare sight among people of his rank in the criminal division. He was almost certainly moonlighting too: he kept disappearing out of the station at odd times, and he avoided Utkin as if he had the plague.

Utkin reflected that a secret did not always create a bond between those who kept it. Often it drove them apart.

When Utkin's marriage imploded, he and Yuri had shared too much. Yuri had said nothing, but he became distant. He had never used what he knew.

But there was always a first time.

60

Berlin mounted the stairs slowly. She was drained and her feet were frozen. The cold had finally driven her back inside, although she thought she could still detect a whiff of blood in the air. She entered the vestibule and sat down on a small bench to drag off her boots.

In the apartment, she heard Charlie's mobile ring. She heard Charlie mumble a curse. The mobile stopped ringing.

'*Da*,' Berlin heard her say. Then emphatically, '*Nyet.*'

There was a pause.

'*Nyet*,' said Charlie again. She sounded strained.

Berlin waited, boot in hand, to see where the conversation was going. A long silence ensued. Finally, Charlie called out, 'No point hanging around out there, Berlin. You can come in now.'

Berlin dropped her other boot and left the vestibule. Charlie was sitting on a chaise, wrapped in her tatty furs.

'Who was that?' said Berlin.

'Who do you think?' said Charlie.

'Your *krysha*,' said Berlin.

Charlie nodded. 'Checking up. Making sure your body hasn't been left lying around.'

Berlin padded over to the wood stove in her socks, sat down and rested her feet on it.

'Don't do that,' said Charlie. 'You'll get chilblains. You look like shit, if you don't mind my saying so.'

'Those blokes were sent by him, weren't they?' said Berlin.

Charlie nodded.

'Did they kill Gerasimov and the interpreter at the airport?' said Berlin.

'No doubt,' said Charlie. She lit a cigarette.

'So why won't you tell me who it is?' said Berlin.

'What difference would it make?' said Charlie. 'There's nothing you can do.'

Berlin changed the position of her feet on the stove. But there must be. She had to know. It was her only chance of working out why corpses were piling up around her, which might go a long way towards helping her to avoid joining them.

She and Charlie had reached a stalemate. Somehow Berlin had to find a way to flush out the 'roof'.

Berlin sat to one side of the stove, watching Charlie smoke while reading an ancient guide to the great gardens of England. Nikki had been sent to his room for a nap with the promise of a long walk that night.

'You never take him out during the day,' said Berlin.

'He becomes over-stimulated,' said Charlie. 'It's uncomfortable.'

Berlin wondered if the discomfort was hers or Nikki's.

The stove was struggling against the many draughts and the high ceiling. Berlin flexed her numb toes and moved her feet closer to the heat.

A greater puzzle was Utkin's reaction when she had told him that Gerasimov owned the warehouse at Park Royal. Gerasimov was safely tucked up in the morgue. He wasn't a threat. Utkin had made another connection, and one that apparently disturbed him.

He was pursuing a killer, but that had always been the case. That was how he had found Berlin: her name had been emblazoned on the sign that was in the skip with Matvienko's body. Burghley had arranged the interpreter and would have informed Gerasimov. But Gerasimov was already dead.

So they didn't call him. Or if they did, they left a message. Or sent an email. Which someone with access found.

Someone close or someone clever?

'Mind if I use your computer?' she asked Charlie.

Charlie sighed. Berlin had never seen the device in question, but she knew it must exist.

'Be my guest,' said Charlie. She raised herself up a couple of inches and reached beneath the cushion on her chair. The notebook computer she produced was a ruggedised, military-grade model: thin, tough and very high-end.

Berlin made no comment. She was past being surprised by Charlie.

Berlin couldn't access her email without betraying her location and, more fundamentally, the fact that she was still alive. She was in no doubt that someone, somewhere, had been monitoring her account. But it was unlikely that anyone would think to flag activity on her Companies House login.

The link was still there on her account page. She'd

already paid for the report so she wouldn't have to risk using her credit card. She scanned the list of office bearers of the company that owned the warehouse. There it was. Gerasimov, M.

Berlin was aware that Charlie was pretending to read, but was watching her out of the corner of her eye.

'Charlie,' said Berlin.

'Mmmm?' said Charlie, feigning deep interest in her tome.

'What was Mrs Gerasimova's name?' said Berlin.

'What do you mean?' said Charlie. 'That is her bloody name.'

'Her first name,' said Berlin.

Charlie put her book down. 'Why do you ask?'

Charlie hovered around Berlin as she dragged on her boots.

'Where are you going?' said Charlie, clearly alarmed.

'I thought you were anxious to see the back of me,' said Berlin.

'Yes, no. Not like this. I mean, what about Nikki?' said Charlie.

'I'm not leaving Moscow,' said Berlin. 'Too much unfinished business.'

Charlie was wheezing so hard Berlin thought she might pass out. 'What do you mean?' said Charlie. 'You shouldn't go out during the day. They might see you.'

Berlin stood still and looked her in the eye. 'Who are "they", Charlie?' said Berlin. 'Who are these animals, who can slit a woman's throat and cut out her tongue?'

Charlie couldn't meet her gaze.

Berlin pushed past her and out the front door.

'You're not well,' called Charlie, as Berlin strode down the stairs. 'You're rambling.'

Berlin kept going, resolute. She was displaying more confidence than she felt. There was a good chance Charlie was right.

Charlie heard the front door slam. She fumbled in her pocket for her cigarettes, lit one and stood there smoking furiously. It was all getting out of control.

Berlin was unpredictable. God only knew what she was getting up to out there. Everything was at risk. Nikki's future. She had to do something, and quickly.

She went back to the table, where she'd left Nikki's dollies and her phone. The phone wasn't there.

She hunted among the detritus that littered the surface of the immense table, but without luck. She checked her pockets, the chaise, the floor.

Berlin had taken it.

'Oh bugger, oh Christ, oh bloody hell,' she mumbled.

Berlin wanted to know who was trying to kill her. If she used the phone to try and find out, they were all dead.

A pre-emptive strike was needed.

She hurried down the wide hallway and peered into Nikki's room. He was fast asleep. Yorkie was curled into the crook of his arm. They were inseparable.

Gently, she turned the key in the lock.

*

Berlin had never seen Charlie move so fast. She didn't even bother to hang the chain back across the gates.

Berlin watched through the railings as Charlie hurried to her car, opened the creaky driver's door, got in and tried to start it. She tried again. Berlin put her hand in her pocket, touching Charlie's mobile, as she heard the useless click of the starter motor turning over.

Berlin had no idea what the cables were that she had yanked out of their sockets and tossed into the bushes, but they were obviously important.

Charlie got out of the car, slammed the door and strode off down the road. The stout figure with the distinctive waddle was an easy target. Berlin moved out from behind the undergrowth of the wasteland next door, and followed.

61

Magnus took the tablets the nurse offered and swallowed them with a sip of water from the straw she put in front of his mouth. He fell back on the pillow.

'I'm terribly sorry,' he said. 'I seem to be having a bit of trouble . . .'

'You're in the Royal London Hospital,' said the nurse. She drew back the curtains around his bed.

'What happened?' croaked Magnus.

'The police found you in the gutter in Bethnal Green Road. You said you were on your way to Berlin. They called the ambulance.'

'A blackout.'

The nurse looked at him with professional compassion.

'It's happened before,' she said.

Magnus nodded. He covered his face with his hand.

He heard the nurse walk away. The tears leaked through his fingers.

Something on his bedside table vibrated. He realised it was his mobile. For a moment, he couldn't remember Peter Green returning it. Had he had a hand in this?

Magnus blew his nose and looked at the phone. It was another call from Berlin's mother. He had no doubt the poor woman would be out of her mind with worry. He stuffed the phone under the pillow.

Green had warned him about 'mixing it' with the other parties involved. It was all his fault, but what could he do about it now? What had been going on while he was drinking himself into a self-pitying stupor?

A television, suspended from the ceiling, hung over the end of the bed. He fumbled around until he found the controls at the end of a long cable, switched it on and flicked through the channels until he found the news.

There were a number of items of little interest: flood, famine and war. Then the newsreader introduced a 'developing story' about the Russian delegation. They cut to some anonymous civil servant being interviewed outside Whitehall. Magnus increased the volume; the little parasite was mouthing platitudes about the 'unsubstantiated rumours that were damaging the country's interests'.

Magnus fumed. The one person who could substantiate them was in mortal danger, if they hadn't got to her already. He groaned.

The nurse popped her head around the door. 'Everything all right, Mr Nkonde?' she enquired. 'Is the medication working? Can I give you something else to help you doze?'

Magnus glanced at the TV. The civil servant was still banging on and saying nothing; in the background Magnus spotted a pusillanimous MP sneaking into the building, head down. Magnus recognised him at once.

'Mr Nkonde?' said the nurse.

Magnus grabbed his mobile from beneath the pillow, threw back the bedclothes and stumbled out of bed.

'Stick your bloody pills,' he shouted. 'Call me a cab!'

62

Berlin watched as Charlie entered an upmarket Euro café and approached the counter. A moment later a young waitress handed her a phone.

The café was one corner of a T-junction. Across the busy road, hoardings and scaffolding, which seemed to be ubiquitous in Moscow, hid a new development.

Meanwhile, on the opposite corner, directly facing the café, a sprawling, decrepit public building of some kind was undergoing renovation. Berlin secreted herself between the massive pairs of columns that supported the wedding-cake tiered tower above its barred entrance.

She was hidden, but had a direct line of sight into the café through its large plate-glass window. Its other customers – smart, intense young men, women absorbed in their smartphones, well-dressed ladies who lunched – wished to be seen.

The urbane habitués came for the casual dining, the rustic ambience and the affluent multicultural patrons: foreigners. This metropolitan class was global; their counterparts in London behaved in an identical fashion.

Charlie finished her call, handed back the phone and retreated to a corner of the café where she could keep her back to the wall while watching the door.

Berlin dropped back just behind the point where Charlie's gaze was fixed. She was waiting for someone.

Berlin stamped her feet and remembered why she hated surveillance, and why she was no good at it. There was a good chance that she would suffer frostbite if she had to stand here too long.

Twenty minutes later, by which time she had lost all sensation in her feet, Berlin saw Charlie half-rise from her seat.

A short, thin, middle-aged man was approaching the café. He walked quickly, with diminutive, almost mincing steps. His face was grey and his eyes downcast. His hands were thrust into the pockets of his long leather coat.

He walked into the café and saw Charlie waving. At that moment he paused and took a long look around the café and through the window to the street outside.

Berlin shrank back. She felt as if the man's eyes were on her, but knew that she was safely hidden.

She was surprised. She had been expecting some muscle, a caricature of a Russian villain – not this insignificant little shit. This was the man who had arranged the deaths of Gerasimov and Matvienko, then sent two thugs to kill her?

He was a picture of nondescript evil.

Charlie's *krysha*.

Charlie was long past being cowed by Yuri's anger.

'Why did you insist we meet?' he said. 'This is unacceptable.'

'I've lost my phone,' said Charlie. 'And I'm sick of being fobbed off. You made promises. It's time to keep them.'

'Or what?' sneered Yuri. 'You'll go to the police?'

'We have an expression in English,' said Charlie. 'There's more than one way to skin a cat.'

'I thought you were a good Russian citizen,' said Yuri. 'We have an expression too: beware of a silent dog and still water.'

Yuri may have been only one man but he had power, and power behind him.

Charlie bent forward, gripping the edge of the table with both hands.

'You think you can send your brutes to slaughter a woman in my own home and expect me to just go on living there as if nothing's happened?'

Yuri frowned.

Charlie figured it could go one of two ways: his next victims would be her and Nikki, although there were real risks for Yuri if he took that route; or he would try to placate her.

She couldn't afford to seem too desperate, in case he became suspicious. She adopted a more conciliatory approach.

'Please, Yuri,' she said. 'We've known each other a long time. You understand my circumstances.'

'Only too well,' said Yuri. He sighed. 'These are difficult times for all of us, Charlie.'

Charlie relaxed a little. Things were going in the right direction.

Yuri lowered his voice. 'But you have to do one more task for me.'

Charlie opened her mouth to remonstrate.

Yuri raised a finger in warning. 'Do this, then I swear on my mother's grave there will be passports. For both of you.' Yuri crossed himself in the Orthodox fashion.

Berlin watched the man stand and walk away. Charlie remained at the table with her head in her hands. Whatever had transpired, it hadn't been good news for Charlie.

The man left the café and hurried across the road.

Berlin followed.

63

There was no sign on the building that betrayed its purpose. Even if there had been, it would have meant nothing to Berlin.

But the CCTV cameras, the blank windows, the iron bars and the silent individuals protesting outside with placards, cowed by officers with batons, indicated that this was a government building, and perhaps an important one.

The man in the leather coat had slipped in through a side entrance. There was no point in trying to follow him – the door had a keypad entry.

Instead, Berlin circled the block, looking for a public entrance. It didn't look as if there was one. There was a pair of spiked gates that opened onto a concrete yard, which a woman in overalls was hosing down.

More officers appeared from another door. A police station. Must be. The Scotland Yard of Moscow. It didn't look like the sort of place where you could walk in and report a burglary.

But she had to get inside; she could identify the *krysha*, who was obviously a cop, but she didn't have a name and she wasn't going to drag Charlie down here. If she could raise Utkin – and no better place to start than police headquarters – she could describe the man behind the murders. Utkin would find him somewhere in this building, sooner or later.

On her fourth time around, she turned the corner as the last of the demonstrators were being thrown into a police van. They were no longer silent, but screaming in agony as cops beat their arms and legs with long batons.

Berlin could hear bones breaking from fifty yards away.

The officers were all dressed in black camo gear. There were as many of them as there were demonstrators. They were having a high old time, laughing as they tossed the protesters into the vehicle.

Berlin ran over, snatched up one of the fallen placards and raised it high above her head. She had no idea what it said. The officers looked bemused. One shouted at her.

'Free Nelson Mandela!' cried Berlin.

There was a brief silence.

The officers looked at each other, then two advanced and grabbed her arms. Berlin didn't say a word as they berated her and demanded responses in Russian. Her silence was enough provocation.

They invited her to step inside the van.

It was a short trip in utter darkness, punctuated only by moans. Berlin heard the grinding sound of heavy metal gates. The van lurched to a halt, the doors were flung open and the demonstrators were dragged out one by one.

Berlin was separated from the others. The officers shouted at her. Her failure to speak or gesture appeared to be read as insolence. She was shoved and slapped for her trouble. The woman in overalls thought it amusing to play the hose over her, splashing her colleagues. They jumped back, cursing.

It occurred to Berlin that her standards of personal hygiene and dress had slipped to such an extent that they might think she was a mad bag lady, or the Russian equivalent. Although she didn't have any bags.

Her hair was matted and unwashed. Beneath her long black coat, which was smeared with mud, she was wearing a dishevelled business suit, both her shirts and both sets of thermal underwear. All of which had been slept in. Her black eyes had faded to jaundiced rings.

She was frogmarched to a desk, behind which stood a severe, matronly woman in a neatly pressed uniform. The matron spoke to her, in Russian. Berlin remained mute, dripping.

One of the officers slapped the back of her head, hard. At this point she decided to deploy her meagre Russian.

'Utkin,' she said. Then slowly and very loudly she said, 'Utkin.'

She prayed that she had pronounced it correctly.

The matron looked at the officer who had slapped her. He shrugged and muttered something.

The matron shouted at him and the two officers grabbed Berlin's arms again and dragged her away.

Berlin thought a rough translation might be 'Get her out of my sight.'

64

Fagan sat in his car beside Fairlop Waters, staring at the forest of masts swaying and gently clanking against each other in the breeze. The pipe was still warm in his hand. His phone lay on the seat beside him.

People were dropping off the radar. Everyone was acting as if he didn't exist. He didn't: there was no paper trail, no email, and all phone calls had been routed through servers that would scrub the records. There was nothing to connect him and them. Which usually suited him. But something felt wrong. He gazed up at the stars.

His boss was maintaining radio silence. He picked up the phone and rang again.

This time someone picked up, but didn't say anything.

'Hello,' said Fagan.

There was a crackle. Old equipment.

'This is no longer a direct line to the party you are calling. That party is on extended leave. Please don't call again.' Then they hung up.

Fagan wound down the car window and threw the phone into the lake. He flipped open the glovebox and prepared another pipe. He needed to draw a line under the job; he was personally exposed. He just wouldn't be comfortable until he knew they had a result. Certainty.

But who could he turn to for information?

In the dream-haze that soon enveloped him, something took shape behind his eyes. A name that drifted through soft clouds and whispered to him. And when he woke up, he was amazed to find he hadn't forgotten it.

Fagan drove to the airport and parked in a blind spot, just beyond the reach of the CCTV. Popping open the boot, he lifted the floor and retrieved the bag he always kept there, just in case. He slipped the Makarov out of his shoulder holster and put it in the now empty space, dropped the floor back into position and shut the boot.

He had seriously underestimated Berlin, but at least he knew where to start. It had come to him in a dream.

Fagan almost chuckled.

He turned up his collar against the chill evening. It took Odysseus ten years to make it home after the Trojan War. At least he had had a home to go to.

It was goodbye to his difficult wife and his surly boys in Chigwell. He would miss his family.

But he had another one.

Fagan strode towards the terminal and disappeared.

65

Utkin peered into the gloomy basement cell through the spyhole. A prone figure huddled beneath a thin blanket. It would be below freezing in there.

'What do you want me to do with her?' asked the desk officer in a clipped tone that conveyed her disapproval.

She was old school. Utkin knew that messy situations involving foreigners were anathema to her.

'What did she say?' he asked.

'Nothing. Just your name,' she said. 'Over and over. Very loudly.'

Utkin considered his options.

'I'm busy,' he said.

'So what should I do?' said the desk officer.

'Just leave her there,' said Utkin.

He snapped the spyhole shut.

'Until when?' said the desk officer.

'Until I say so,' said Utkin.

Berlin was aware that someone had been watching her. The four-inch-thick steel-plated door admitted no sound, but there had been a very subtle shift in the shadow on the rough wall.

They had taken her cash and Charlie's mobile. Her neck

was bruised and her shoulder painful from the manhandling. But her gamble had paid off: the *krysha* had revealed himself.

Charlie's anxiety whenever the police were mentioned was entirely rational; she was in thrall to a senior police officer who presumably could easily have her detained and Nikki put away.

The only question was how long she herself would be locked up before Utkin appeared and she could trade her information for her passport and buprenorphine.

After all, holding a placard didn't make her an enemy of the state or justify her detention. She was just a confused, perhaps disturbed, tourist. Make that a definitely disturbed tourist.

She reached out from beneath the blanket and pressed her fingertips against the coarse stone. Perhaps Zayde had once done the same.

The walls that contained her also provided a strange kind of respite; there were no drugs to be found here. It wasn't even an option.

She felt as if every cell in her body was interrogating her at every moment, demanding that she answer the question: why are you doing this? It had been difficult to remember why, but in this frigid, claustrophobic bunker it was purely rhetorical.

Now she had no choice.

Utkin went home. He just wanted to cook himself a meal and have a few drinks. He had been forced into moves he would never have taken but for her rash actions. English women were crazy.

He took the wooden box down from the shelf. He poured himself another shot, drank it and brought the box close to his cheek. He could still discern a faint scent, the fragrance of sandalwood, after all these years.

He opened the box. Three cellophane sweet wrappers twinkled up at him. He had no doubt that another would soon join them. He embraced the guilt like an old friend. There was no-one else to comfort him.

66

The building was very quiet. It was New Year's Eve. Utkin had returned to the station in the early hours of the morning, after the shift change. Desk staff were prohibited from overtime, due to budget cuts.

The long holiday would begin tomorrow – a week of celebrations and family get-togethers that would continue until Orthodox Christmas Day on 7 January. The country was being run by priests and thugs now. Of course, the country had also been run by priests and thugs in the old days, except the priests were called cadres and the thugs worked for the Committee of State Security.

Now they worked for the deepest pocket.

The holidays were shorter in those days, but there was more certainty: the source of inequity was privilege, acquired through position in the Party. Now corruption was at street level – everything revolved around money, and the influence it could buy.

Utkin knew which he preferred.

He shot the bolt on the cell door and opened it.

Berlin slowly manoeuvred herself into an upright position.

'I have been detained without charge,' she said.

'Very likely,' said Utkin. 'But this is country where

innocent men can be beaten to death and then tried and convicted before judge. You are lucky.'

The liquid slipped down Berlin's throat. She couldn't taste it and she didn't try. She wouldn't have cared if it were actually an industrial solvent. She gulped it down and held out her tin mug for more.

'He was thin, hunched and grey-faced, with a big nose,' she said. 'He met with Charlotte Inkpin, then came straight back here.'

Utkin poured her another drink from the battered flask and slipped it back in his pocket.

'Where am I?' she said.

'Petrovka 38,' replied Utkin. 'The Main Department of Internal Affairs of Moscow.'

'Police HQ,' said Berlin.

'That,' said Utkin, 'and more.'

Berlin got his drift.

Sensation began to return to her limbs. Utkin had led her from the cell through a labyrinth of corridors to a room that appeared to be set up for interrogation. She doubted that the dark stains on the floor were spilt tea.

'You believe this police officer arranged the murders of Gerasimov and Matvienko,' said Utkin. 'Very serious charge.'

'He's Inkpin's *krysha*,' she insisted.

'*Krysha?* What do you know of such things?' said Utkin.

'Charlie explained it to me. She just did what she was told: she picked me up at the airport, drove me around, interpreted at the interviews. He forced her to let me stay with her after you intervened at the hotel.'

'Why would this woman conspire with a murderer?' said Utkin.

Berlin hesitated. There was nothing to gain from exposing Charlie's secret.

'He has something over her,' she said. 'I don't know what it is.'

Utkin clasped his hands together, apparently deep in thought.

Berlin began to shake. She couldn't remember when she had last eaten.

'What is this officer's motive?' said Utkin.

'His roof has something over him, I imagine,' she said. 'That's how it works here, isn't it? Leverage, obligation, fear.'

'All these roofs,' said Utkin. 'Now we have village. So who do you think stands over this officer?'

'I think it might be Gerasimova,' said Berlin.

Utkin folded his arms and raised an eyebrow.

'I jumped to conclusions when I checked the Companies House records,' said Berlin. 'The owner of the warehouse is identified as M. Gerasimov. I assumed it was Mikhail. But I think it's Maryna.'

Petrovka 38 was creaking back to life. The skeleton night crew had gone home. The next shift of officers, required to work over the holidays, were yawning resentfully and making their way slowly to their desks.

Utkin carried the two cups of Starbucks coffee very

carefully. He had queued for thirty minutes and paid a small fortune for them. He nudged open the door with his foot and walked into Yuri's office. 'Breakfast,' he announced.

Yuri stared at him. 'Don't you ever go home?' he said.

'What for?' said Utkin. 'I am not a lucky man. By the way, how are Daria and the girls?'

'Fine,' said Yuri. 'What is the meaning of this?'

He pointed at the coffee, which Utkin had placed on his desk.

'The gesture of an old friend,' said Utkin. 'We have grown apart, Yuri Leonidovich.'

Yuri's confusion was evident.

'Forgive the intrusion,' said Utkin. He retreated to the door.

Yuri stood up. 'Wait,' he commanded.

Utkin froze.

'I'm sorry,' said Yuri. 'I meant, thank you.'

Utkin nodded and continued his retreat. He paused in the doorway. 'Oh,' he said. 'I nearly forgot. The suspect in the Gerasimov case. She hasn't gone back to England.'

'What?' said Yuri. 'How do you know?'

'She was arrested yesterday,' said Utkin.

Utkin watched Yuri's grey pallor drain to white. He gripped the edge of his desk.

'It's not possible,' he said.

'Yes it is,' said Utkin. 'I saw her. Drunk and disorderly.'

'Where is she?' said Yuri.

Utkin glanced at his watch. 'Is that the time?' he said,

and strode off down the corridor. He could hear Yuri crashing into his desk as he followed. He imagined the coffee spilling. What a waste.

'Major Utkin!' shouted Yuri. This time it was a command.

Utkin turned. 'Yes, sir?' he said.

'Where is she?' said Yuri. He was breathing heavily, as if he had run a mile.

'There was nothing in the system,' said Utkin. 'I believe they let her go.'

67

Berlin limped into the apartment.

Charlie dropped her spoon into her soup and stood up. 'I thought you'd gone,' she exclaimed.

Berlin sat down before she fell.

'What on earth are you still doing here?' said Charlie. 'You should be moving on.'

'But I haven't even seen the Kremlin yet,' said Berlin.

'You're a fool, Berlin,' said Charlie. 'I don't know what you're up to, but you should get out while you can. And take my boy with you.' Her wheezing was worse than usual. She came and took Berlin's hand, softening her tone.

'My dear,' she said. 'You don't value your life enough. This is your last chance. Don't you understand that?'

Berlin tried to move away, but Charlie hung on. 'Mrs Muir told me an SVR Colonel was running the operation you disrupted,' Charlie said.

'Gerasimova,' said Berlin.

'Acting with the highest authority.'

'The *siloviki*,' said Berlin.

Charlie nodded. 'They don't fear the law. They *are* the law. You saw the result lying on that table.'

Berlin shrugged her off. 'What have I got to lose?' she said. 'I'm already dead.'

Yuri went home to kiss his daughters. Daria would be at work, but there was no school. It was crisp and clear. The last day of the year. The blue sky could fool you into believing it was the beginning of something, not the end.

The market near his home was still open. He went in and bought a huge bag of groceries: cheese like string, for his youngest, who loved it; chocolate for the teenager, who would complain it made her fat; and persimmons for his wife.

The apartment was warm. The girls were watching TV, talking on their phones, playing on their computers. Multitasking. Most incredibly, in separate rooms. He had grown up in a two-roomed apartment with his parents, his grandmother and his two brothers. No-one complained. Privacy was bourgeois.

His father had fought in the Great Patriotic War, defending the motherland. Millions had died, a fact conveniently forgotten by Russia's erstwhile allies. If Russia had fallen, the West would have followed. It was an object lesson in the shifting nature of alliances.

For his father, the war was never really over. The enemy just spoke a different language.

'Tell your mother I may be delayed at work,' he said. He put on his cap and saluted his children.

They stared at him as if he were mad.

'Be good, work hard. Happy New Year.'

*

Gerasimova stared at the computer screen, watching prime minister's question time on the BBC News site. An Opposition MP had alleged that Britain's intelligence services were engaged in a cover-up of recent activity by the Russian delegation.

A British citizen, who could identify the participants, was in Moscow, unable to leave. She was being pursued by the authorities there and at risk.

The MP sat down.

The prime minister rose. 'These are scurrilous rumours,' he began. There were loud boos. 'This is the high price we pay for a free press. If the Honourable Member has any evidence to support these wild allegations, let him produce it. All he and his cronies have done is manage to insult the Russian president and cost this country millions in lost trade opportunities . . .'

The tumult in the House grew. The Speaker called for order. Gerasimova shook her head in disbelief.

'. . . all because of a personal vendetta by the proprietor of a newspaper, who is himself in exile from Russia because he is being pursued by the authorities for tax evasion. If they have a witness, let them produce her.'

The prime minister sat down.

Gerasimova wondered again at the inability of the British government to control their press. The liberal democracies had failed; they offered sanctuary to foreign freeloaders who wished them ill, and were paralysed by their fear of feckless public opinion. Nationalism was a dirty word to these effete states.

The Russian government was not afraid of international

disapproval. They were used to it. The embassy in London had issued a statement saying that the allegations were politically motivated. No British citizen was being sought by Moscow authorities.

Gerasimova reflected that this was because the British citizen was dead.

Her mobile rang and she picked up. It was Yuri.

'Maryna,' he whispered. 'How will you ever forgive me?'

68

Berlin ate her share of the tinned *kasha*, a kind of porridge, that Charlie had dished up for the three of them. It was a meal conducted by the light of a hurricane lamp. Charlie was of the opinion that the snow had brought down the power line, which was no doubt illegal and would not be repaired until the thaw.

It was still daylight, but with the windows blacked out the gloom inside was pervasive. No-one spoke. Nikki never uttered a word anyway, so his silence was unremarkable. But Charlie's forced cheerfulness had evaporated. She couldn't keep it up now. She seemed preoccupied.

It added to Berlin's sense of foreboding.

'You don't have to worry about your *krysha* any more,' she blurted out.

Charlie looked at her, impassive, her eyes blank.

'He's in the hands of the authorities now,' said Berlin.

Charlie's lips twitched. She put her hand to her mouth. She shook.

Berlin realised that she was laughing. 'Oh, for God's sake,' Berlin said, and shoved her bowl across the table and stood up. 'I'm going out. This is a madhouse.'

*

Berlin limped down the sweeping staircase and immediately wished she'd never left the warmth of the stove. She was disturbed by Charlie's sceptical reaction.

Berlin had flushed out the rat-faced officer, so surely Utkin would act. He was driven by his pursuit of a killer; she was just driven.

As she stood for a moment beneath the portico the cold air cleared her head.

Soaring cranes on building sites across the canal reached out to each other across the slate sky, keeping a mournful balance, swaying slightly in the wind, closer to God than the ancient domes that swelled beneath them.

She was a junkie. Her perception was shot, her guesses were wild. She couldn't rely on her own judgement.

She'd missed something.

Charlie glanced at Berlin's bowl on the other side of the table. It was still half full.

'Waste not, want not,' she said. She reached over and pushed the bowl towards Nikki.

'Eat up, darling boy,' she said. 'You'll need your strength. A walk tonight. A journey tomorrow.'

Something lying beside Berlin's bowl caught her eye. It was her own mobile. Berlin must have left it there. She scrolled through the log. Berlin hadn't taken it to make calls.

Good Christ. The realisation struck Charlie with full force. Berlin had set her up. That's what she'd meant when she had said that her *krysha* was in the hands of the authorities.

Charlie ran from the apartment and took the stairs as fast as her legs would allow. But by the time she emerged onto the portico there was no sign of Berlin.

God only knew what the woman had done now, but whatever it was it could only make matters worse. She hurried down the path, squeezed through the gate and peered up and down the road, but Berlin had gone.

There was no way to warn her.

69

The traffic was more chaotic than ever. Berlin noticed that the shoppers streaming in all directions were clutching huge bags of food; queues were spilling out of the shops and on to the streets. Everyone was preparing for midnight. The excitement was palpable.

Brilliantly lit skyscrapers jostled the heavens: pinnacles of luminosity, bright blue against the black sky. Stalin would have been proud.

Massive, silent screens carried images of luxury vehicles hurtling across the desert. Strings of pearls glistened in store windows, draped across tiny, exquisite shoes and handbags.

Berlin felt a pang of nostalgia for Soviet utilitarianism, which was ridiculous, because this was her first visit. The European Mall beckoned, offering the bounty to be acquired by individual enterprise, not collective endeavour.

Across the busy boulevard the McDonald's was packed.

The girl was outside the door, begging with her paper cup, just as Berlin knew she would be. They were all creatures of habit. Berlin waited for the lights to change and crossed over.

The girl recognised her immediately. She stood still,

glancing over Berlin's shoulder, probably to see if the fat policeman was lurking behind her.

'Do you speak English?' asked Berlin.

The girl didn't respond, but she didn't run away and the look in her eyes was alert, intelligent.

'I'd like to give you a thousand roubles,' said Berlin, quickly.

A slow smile spread across the girl's face. She had understood every word and knew it was a test. She got the joke.

'For what?' she said.

The girl said her name was Anna. She led Berlin back across the road and into the railway station behind the Mall. Berlin was astonished by the beauty of the iron and glass dome and the huge, elaborate murals. Her failure to have paid this extraordinary city even the slightest bit of attention suddenly depressed her. Clarity had its downside.

Anna weaved through the throngs of passengers to a line of small kiosks, where she ordered hot pastries filled with cheese. Berlin paid for them.

They sat nearby on upturned crates and ate in silence.

Anna showed no signs of the agitation that Berlin would usually have associated with a street junkie who was chasing. It was also clear, when Berlin had the opportunity to look at her in a decent light, that she wasn't a girl. She was a young woman in her mid-twenties, her wasted flesh evidence of years of neglect.

'Where did you learn English?' said Berlin.

'At school, then at university,' said Anna. 'I was student of biochemistry.'

She gave Berlin a wan smile, aware of the irony.

'No more *krokodil*?' said Berlin.

Anna shook her head, sombre. 'Pasha died,' she said. As if that explained everything.

Anna was getting clean. She was begging for money for food, not dope. Hence their visit to the kiosk.

The frail young woman brushed the crumbs from her grubby jacket. 'What do you want me to do?' she said.

70

Yuri could hardly meet Maryna's stony gaze. His men, stinking of alcohol, stood as far away from her as possible. Their celebrations were premature. She beckoned them forward, but her eyes were on Yuri. They shuffled closer. She pointed at a photocopy of Berlin's passport photo on her desk.

'Is that her?'

The men peered at the picture.

'It could be . . .' muttered one.

'Is that her?' reiterated Maryna.

'No,' said the other one. He looked at Yuri, his eyes pleading for support. 'We had an address and a description. She was English and the right age.'

'Lieutenant Colonel Lukov's contact, the old fat one, was present. She confirmed the target,' added his colleague.

'What did you do with the body?' said Maryna.

The two men stared intently at the floor.

'Get out,' she said.

After his men had gone, Yuri expected Maryna to give full vent to her anger. But she barely raised her voice.

'The other matter?' she asked.

'Everything is ready for tonight,' said Yuri, eagerly. Perhaps she realised it wasn't really his fault.

'Good,' said Maryna. 'Now go and end this.'

Yuri didn't move. 'How will I find her?' he said.

Maryna swivelled her computer screen to face him.

It displayed a map of Moscow. She pointed to a dot pulsating in one corner of the screen.

'There was activity less than thirty minutes ago on one of the accounts. So start there.'

She began to shuffle papers on her desk.

He was dismissed. His heart was bursting.

'Maryna,' he said.

She looked up. 'I don't think I heard you correctly,' she said.

'My apologies, Colonel,' said Yuri. He put on his cap and snapped out a salute.

71

Utkin sat in his car and watched the front of the Internet café. The heater wasn't the best. The Ford was from the car pool and had been treated poorly, like most police vehicles. Nobody wanted it, so they didn't mind Utkin using it as his personal transportation.

Business wasn't brisk, but he had seen a few slouching youths coming and going. Terrible. They should have been celebrating with family, preparing dinner after the fireworks.

Revellers were erupting from clubs and restaurants nearby, singing the national anthem. That is, those able to remain upright. They were all heading for Red Square, to watch the fireworks. He glanced at his watch. Berlin and the drug addict had gone into the café nearly an hour ago. He took another sip from his flask.

A black van pulled up. The side door slid open. Two men in camouflage and balaclavas, clutching automatic weapons, jumped out. One ran down the street and turned into an alley.

Yuri got out of the front, glanced left and right, and strode inside. The other man took up a position at the entrance. No-one could get in or out.

*

Yuri shoved the cold metal barrel into the nape of the girl's scrawny neck. The wasted junkie raised her arms very slowly. He grabbed her by the hair and threw her to the floor.

The computer she had been using presented him with an image of a monkey running uphill while trying to avoid the rocks that were raining down on him.

He jiggled the mouse. Behind the game Berlin's email was sending another 'Happy New Year' message.

Yuri glared at the girl at his feet. 'Are you sending these emails?' he asked.

'It was like that when I got here,' she said, dismissively. 'The last person must have forgotten to log off.'

Yuri sneered. 'And who was this person?'

The girl shrugged.

Yuri raised his boot above her face.

'I don't know!' exclaimed the girl. 'A foreigner.'

'And who are you?' he demanded.

'No-one. I was begging, that's all.'

'Where?'

'Outside the McDonald's at the Mall of Europe. She gave me some money.'

She was telling the truth.

He let his boot fall anyway.

From her position in the shop doorway across the street, Berlin had watched Charlie's *krysha* enter the café. The sharp smell of gunpowder hung in the air. The continual pealing of bells, the crack and whine of fireworks and the surging, cheering revellers gave her great cover. She needed it. If she was seen, it was over.

But she had had to find out if she could trust Utkin. Now it was clear she couldn't.

The rat-faced policeman knew she was still alive and kicking in Moscow or he wouldn't be looking for her in the café. It had been less than an hour since she had logged on to her email and sent a message. Fast work. They clearly had access to sophisticated signals intelligence.

He wouldn't be in there long.

Sure enough, he reappeared and scanned the street.

She shrank back into the shadows. Even at this distance she could see his body was taut with rage.

Berlin suddenly realised that Charlie might bear the brunt of it. Something had to be done about this bastard. But she was on her own. Utkin had given her up.

The bloke who had run down the alley to the rear of the café came back. The *krysha* conferred with the two men for a moment, then they got into the back of the van and he got in the front. It took off at high speed.

Berlin left the doorway. A vehicle was cruising past, the driver intent on the road ahead.

Utkin.

Berlin stepped back smartly.

The vehicle accelerated, following the van.

Utkin had used her for bait. Berlin didn't know what his game was, but she was a pawn in it. At least she had found out before she made another move.

She was concerned about Anna, but couldn't risk going into the café. The young woman was tough. It was cold comfort. It meant Berlin was no better than Utkin.

She cut through an alley and at the other end walked

into the midst of a raucous, happy throng. She let them carry her along. At least now she had the true measure of her enemies. But that was all she had.

While logged on to her email she had collected one from Magnus with the subject 'Can you ever forgive me?' The body of the email contained nothing but a link to *The Sentinel*. She clicked it and read:

The Russian president has cut short the trade and security talks and returned to Moscow overnight following this newspaper's exclusive revelations about suspect shipments to a north London warehouse.

We approached the president's office for a response before publishing, but our request for an interview was declined.

Whitehall has allowed the Russians to leave the country, despite knowing that members of the delegation were responsible for the alleged illegal activity.

A D-Notice, seeking the cooperation of the press in not disseminating this information, has been invoked by the government.

However, we do not believe issues of national security are at stake. Millions of pounds in deals were on the table during the talks. This government has demonstrated that its priority is trade, not justice.

She hadn't known about the D-Notice. It was rare for a newspaper to defy one.

A reliable source saw a Ford Transit van, registered to the Russian embassy, making the delivery in question to a Park

Royal warehouse owned by Russian interests.

Hirst Corporation, the company providing security at the site, declined to comment except to say that no irregularities had been reported at Park Royal.

The supervisor had been there to guarantee that there was no email, no phone call, nothing to evidence the 'irregularity'. Hirst had all their bases covered, as she had expected.

The last piece of the puzzle fell into place in the final paragraph.

The source, Catherine Berlin, a respected financial investigator, witnessed the events at the warehouse. She is currently in Moscow, where she is being sought by the authorities. The British embassy did not respond to our requests for information, citing privacy issues.

Ms Berlin is the only independent eyewitness able to identify the participants in the warehouse delivery.

She'd been thrown under a bus.

The killer

72

Berlin hoped that Charlie was still awake, or would be woken by her knocking. The woman slept like a log. She was relieved when she saw that the front door of the apartment was actually ajar. She pushed it open.

Two suitcases, one large, one small, were waiting behind it. The coat hooks were empty. From inside the apartment came the sounds of shuffling. Activity in the middle of the night. It looked like a moonlight flit.

Could it be that Charlie had betrayed her, not Utkin? She had saved Berlin's bacon in a desperate attempt to get her to take Nikki back to England. But when Berlin had demurred, perhaps she'd decided to come clean and try her luck with the *krysha*. She'd said she would do anything.

Did the suitcases mean the *krysha* could grant Charlie's wish?

She stepped back from the front door, leaving it ajar.

Berlin crouched in a corner of the vast, gloomy lobby and listened to Charlie and Nikki come down the stairs. She heard Charlie's phone ring. After a brief conversation in Russian, she hung up.

Berlin flattened herself against the wall.

Charlie hummed as she buttoned Nikki's coat tight and pulled his woollen hat down over his ears. Then she grasped his hand and they marched out of the building.

They weren't carrying the suitcases.

Berlin followed. This wasn't just Nikki's constitutional. It was well past midnight and below freezing. The Zaporozhets was still out of action. Charlie wouldn't venture out without a reason.

Wherever they were going, it was a preamble to a longer journey.

Berlin had no problem keeping the odd couple in sight, striding through the deserted streets, arm in arm, during the early hours of New Year's Day. Charlie kept glancing at her watch.

The pair made their way over the footbridge across the canal and turned to the right. There was no moon, and they were avoiding the well-lit main roads.

After about a mile they turned into a housing estate. Blocks of flats surrounded a basketball court and a children's playground. There were more lights here.

Berlin avoided the open spaces and stuck close to the buildings.

The blunt shapes of the carnival-themed playground rides, buried beneath three feet of snow, created a landscape peopled by grotesque monsters. She imagined that at any moment they would lumber into life, eager to feed their evil appetites.

She realised that she was more than a little light-headed,

disoriented by cold, exhaustion and other things: this was not a tapered withdrawal.

Charlie and Nikki proceeded around the perimeter of the estate and came to a halt in the deep shadow of an entranceway to a block of flats.

Berlin advanced as close as she dared. They were standing beneath an overhang, to one side of a path. It was so quiet that Berlin could hear Charlie wheezing.

At the sound of a vehicle approaching, Charlie touched Nikki's sleeve and they stepped back further into the lee of the building. Berlin took their cue, and stepped back too.

Headlights swept across the carnival monsters, caught dancing in the beams. A black Range Rover pulled up beside the path leading to the entranceway.

The car door opened and a man stumbled out of the passenger seat. In the pool of yellow light from the car's interior, Berlin saw that it was the little commodore.

Mikhail Gerasimov's stand-in.

He called out to the driver in a jocular fashion, slammed the car door and began to make his way unsteadily up the path. He was obviously very drunk.

The Range Rover took off. As it swept past Berlin she caught a glimpse of the driver. Everything seemed to be happening in slow motion. The swirling snow was a strobing light, each movement a staccato animation.

Charlie had stepped out of the shadows and approached the little commodore, who was leaning forward, peering at her. They spoke in Russian, and at first Berlin thought she was there to assist him. But then she gave him a shove. He staggered back, frowning.

Charlie advanced a few steps. He raised his arm to ward her off, but she persisted. The little commodore grunted, said something in Russian and struck her.

In the next instant Nikki came hurtling out of the shadows. Berlin barely had time to register what was happening. His silent fury was vented in a series of vicious blows. The little man wasn't even able to cry out. He fell to his knees.

Berlin saw him reach inside his jacket, but the gun was only in his hand a moment before Nikki kicked out and it flew through the air, coming to rest in a drift of snow.

Nikki grasped the little commodore's neck with both hands. The crack of splintering bone echoed around the playground. The little commodore swayed for a moment, then fell forward.

No lights went on. There were no sirens. It had all happened in a matter of moments. Berlin realised she was holding her breath.

The only sound was Charlie's wheezing as she waddled over to take Nikki's hand. He opened his palm. Charlie put something in it and they strolled away, arm in arm.

They didn't look back.

Berlin waited until they disappeared into the darkness, then exhaled and tried to breathe normally. After a few minutes she reluctantly approached the body.

His face was a pulpy mess. The area around him was stained with blood and urine. The smell of faeces hung in the air. There was no point taking a pulse, even if she could overcome her horror. The angle at which his head was resting left no doubt he was dead. She backed away.

Something on the ground nearby caught her eye. She picked it up, then went and retrieved the gun from where it lay, half buried in a drift. It was a baby Glock: slim, lightweight. She slipped it into her inside pocket.

It began to snow.

73

Berlin approached Charlie's dark, silent lair warily. In her mind's eye she played back what she'd seen: Charlie had provoked the little commodore until he had lashed out. Then Nikki attacked him. It was a practised manoeuvre. They'd done it before.

Nikki was Charlie's strength and her weakness.

Had her *krysha* blackmailed her into deploying Nikki, her secret weapon, as and when he saw fit? On pain of her son being taken away and incarcerated? Now that didn't seem like such a bad idea.

The gate creaked as Berlin pushed it open. She looked up at the crumbling façade and blind windows. It was the perfect setting for what dwelt within.

Berlin took the stairs slowly and hesitated when she reached the door of the apartment. Her heart was thudding, even though there was probably no reason for her to be afraid. Charlie had had plenty of opportunities to use Nikki against her.

Nevertheless, there was something unnerving about the prospect of being in the same room as someone you had just watched choke a man to death.

She took a deep breath and opened the door.

Nikki was sitting at the table, eating a plate of dumplings. Charlie was stretched out on a chaise, smoking. They were both still wearing their outdoor clothes and boots. Ready to move on.

Berlin stepped inside and closed the door behind her.

Charlie looked up and exhaled a cloud of smoke.

'So now you know,' she said.

Berlin went straight to the dresser and poured herself a shot of vodka, then took the bottle and her glass to the table and sat down.

Charlie might be mad, but she wasn't stupid. She had been a spy, probably still was, and counter-surveillance went with the territory.

'Your son's a serial killer,' said Berlin.

It was a stupid thing to say, and Charlie just laughed. With great wheezing and panting she levered herself off the chaise, shuffled over to the table and poured herself a large drink.

'Down the hatch,' she announced, and knocked it back.

Berlin waited for some kind of explanation, but she was not prepared for what came next.

'After the revolution this building was converted into apartments for important cadres and Party members.'

Berlin stared at her. A history lesson seemed less than appropriate, given the circumstances.

'They added internal walls,' said Charlie. 'To create connecting passages, a labyrinth that could accommodate a man, who was then able to travel between apartments and floors at will. Watching through peepholes. Ensuring everyone was toeing the Party line.'

Nikki kept eating, seemingly untroubled.

Charlie walked over to one of the walls and tapped it. 'The walls had ears,' she said.

'Why are you telling me this?' said Berlin.

Charlie launched herself at Berlin, grabbed her arm and yanked her out of her chair. 'Nothing could be more important,' she cried.

Berlin allowed herself to be dragged to the far corner of the room.

Charlie reached out and placed her palm flat against a panel formed by two elaborate, faded gilt borders, but before she could demonstrate further, they both heard the sound of footsteps on the stairs.

Charlie flew the length of the room and bolted the inner door, then hurried straight back to Nikki.

'Come, darling boy,' said Charlie, taking the spoon from his hand. Nikki stood up and Charlie led him quickly to where Berlin still stood beside the panel. She put Nikki's hand in Berlin's. 'We don't want him upset, do we, Berlin?' she said. 'They're coming.'

The footsteps had reached the vestibule.

Someone knocked at the inner door.

Charlie leant against the panel. It slid open.

'Just in case,' said Charlie.

'For God's sake,' protested Berlin. 'This is insane.'

The knocking became an angry banging, accompanied by loud commands in Russian.

Charlie shoved Nikki into the narrow space. He kept a tight grip on Berlin's hand and she had no choice but to follow.

'Be a good boy,' said Charlie. She leant forward and kissed his cheek, then stepped back and touched the wall.

The panel slid back into place.

The darkness was absolute. Berlin was suddenly grateful for Nikki's tight grip. He inched forward. He seemed to know where he was going and it occurred to Berlin that this might be a drill that he and Charlie had practised.

The noise from the other side of the wall was muffled, but clear.

Berlin heard the distinct sound of someone kicking in a door. Then she found herself standing directly in front of one of the peepholes. It seemed to be recessed into a frame or border, and it gave her a surprisingly complete view of the room. She blinked and put her eye closer.

Charlie was standing beside the door. She glanced back at the wall, then opened the door. The rat-faced man, her *krysha*, now in uniform, stood in the doorway, breathing heavily.

'That was unnecessary, Yuri,' said Charlie. 'I was asleep. We're both very tired, as I'm sure you appreciate.'

Yuri gathered himself and looked around the room. He barked something in Russian. Berlin caught the word 'Nikki'.

'Locked up in his bedroom,' said Charlie. 'So you have nothing to fear.'

Yuri responded in Russian.

'No,' said Charlie. 'I won't speak bloody Russian. I've had it up to here with this bloody country. Just give me the passports, Yuri, we're all square now.'

Berlin was aware that Nikki had sat down. His shape

emerged as her eyes became accustomed to the darkness; he had drawn his knees up so that he could rest his head on his arms. He appeared to be dozing. There was something to be said for whatever was wrong with him.

Berlin looked back through the peephole. The *krysha* – Yuri – grabbed the bottle of vodka from the table and took a long swig. She realised he was already drunk.

When he put the bottle down he unclipped his holster and drew his gun.

Charlie took a step back.

Berlin could barely hear over her pounding heart.

'You promised,' said Charlie. 'I . . . we . . . did everything you asked. You swore you'd get us passports so we could go home.'

'That was before you lied to me,' said Yuri. 'The *Anglichanka* is still alive.'

'Ridiculous,' said Charlie. 'Anyway, why would you care? You didn't kill anyone. You never get your hands dirty. Life can go on for you.'

'No more loose ends.' At each word he smashed his fist down on the table. 'You made me lose respect of woman I love.'

Charlie's chuckle was hollow. Berlin was terrified for her. 'You lot are all the same,' said Charlie. 'Everything has always got to be a bloody tragedy. I'm so tired of the Slavic soul.'

Berlin had the element of surprise. She considered using it, and the Glock. But only for a moment.

Yuri cocked his gun and shouted something in Russian. There was the sound of boots running through the apartment.

He hadn't come alone.

Charlie picked up the vodka and poured herself a drink.

Two men in black camo gear stomped into the room, dragging the furled rug. Berlin gave up the idea of a shoot-out. She peered at the men: thick mops of blunt-cut brown hair framed faces that bore a strong resemblance to each other. They could be brothers.

The last time she had seen them they were standing beside a van on the Park Royal estate, smoking.

The shock was like a blow. She shuddered.

The men dumped the rug at Charlie's feet.

It unravelled and Mrs Muir rolled out.

Charlie raised her glass in a silent toast.

'Who is this?' said Yuri.

'Don't they know?' said Charlie. She indicated the two men. 'Don't tell me they bumped her off by mistake? Good help is so hard to find these days, don't you agree?'

One of the men stepped forward and smacked Charlie in the mouth. She reeled back, but didn't fall. Her glass was still in her hand.

Berlin glanced at Nikki. If he woke up and realised Charlie was being assaulted, it was all over.

Yuri tried a different tack with Charlie. 'This is foolish, Charlotte,' he said. He pointed at Mrs Muir. 'Who is she?'

Charlie muttered something in Russian that he clearly didn't find complimentary.

Yuri flinched, as if she had struck him. 'We'll find out. You're familiar with our methods. Whoever she is, you will be prosecuted for her murder.'

He gestured to the two men. 'Take her,' he said.

The thugs stepped forward.

Charlie took a step back. 'Where to?' she cried. 'Petrovka? Lubyanka? It doesn't matter. I'll never get out alive.' She looked directly at the wall, as if she could see Berlin. 'One good turn deserves another,' she said.

Then she gulped the vodka, tossed the glass over her shoulder and with astonishing speed and grace ran to the window and flung herself through it.

A gust of freezing air swept through the room.

Berlin clapped a hand over her mouth, holding back the bile that surged into it.

Beside her, Nikki slept on.

74

Silence. Berlin found herself staring at the shattered window. Yuri and his two men stood frozen, shocked. A shard of black glass fell from the window frame and released them all from the moment.

Berlin shrank back from the peephole.

She heard Yuri mutter an order, followed by shuffling. She looked back.

Yuri was alone in the room with Mrs Muir's body. He hadn't moved an inch.

The night was very still. Noises drifted through the broken window: the gate squeaking, a motor starting. Yuri had sent his thugs away.

He put his gun and cap on the table, staggered to the sink and threw up. When he'd finished, he rinsed his face with cold water and wiped it on his sleeve, then hesitated, as if he'd just remembered something.

He picked up his gun and cap and walked out.

Berlin could hear him marching down the corridor that led to Nikki's wing. She wondered if they should make a run for it; it was pointless. They should sit tight. When Yuri found Nikki wasn't in his room, maybe he would leave.

Berlin's optimism was stillborn in a tumult of yapping. She had forgotten about Yorkie.

The little dog burst into the room and ran around in circles, tiny paws scrabbling on the parquetry as he tried to bite his tail. He must have been shut up in Nikki's room. Now that Yuri had inadvertently released him, he was going to make his presence felt.

Berlin cursed silently as the motley little dog dived under the furniture and between the chairs, bouncing up and down while emitting high-pitched barks. Looking for his master.

Yuri came back into the room.

Berlin held her breath.

Yorkie suddenly stood very still, quivering and sniffing the air.

He ran at the wall.

Nikki woke up.

75

Utkin gazed down at the body which lay near the entranceway, half buried in snow. The man had taken a beating. He ordered the floodlights to be angled so that he could take a closer look at the face.

The crushed cheekbone and smashed nose made it difficult to discern the features. Nevertheless there was something familiar about him. He knelt and gently lifted the jaw to examine the neck.

Utkin sighed, then with ponderous movements got to his feet and called for a torch. Backing away from the body, he began to sweep the beam across the snow, moving in concentric circles, careful not to miss an inch.

He was some yards from the scene, and beginning to think he'd been mistaken, when he heard an officer hail him.

'Major,' called the officer. 'There's a witness.'

'Where?' said Utkin.

'Up there,' said the officer, pointing at a third-floor window.

Utkin could just make out a wizened face pressed against the glass.

'He says he saw the victim get out of a very smart black car. It drove off and that's when the attack took place.'

'Did he see the assailants?' said Utkin. He held his breath.

'No,' said the officer.

Utkin exhaled. His breath hung in the air.

Utkin sat in his car and watched as they loaded the body into the mortuary van. The floodlights winked out. A thin veil of white was creeping across the bloody ground.

He needed another opinion. There was something missing. He'd taken a photo of the victim with his phone. Only one person could confirm his suspicions. He doubted he would receive a warm welcome, but he had to try.

If he was right, the victim would close the circle.

He was getting close. He had a feeling it would soon be over.

76

Berlin and Nikki sat side by side on the moth-eaten chaise. Yuri stood as far away as possible, his arm extended to its fullest length, levelling the gun at them.

In his other hand Yuri held his phone, pressed to his ear, conversing in a low voice in Russian. He knew she didn't understand a word, but he was clearly aware that Nikki did. He seemed to be familiar with Nikki and apparently credited him with an understanding of what was going on. He was right.

For his part, Nikki had shown no fear of the *krysha*. Or of anything else, for that matter.

Berlin could see the sweat standing out on Yuri's top lip, despite the snow swirling through the broken window and settling on the furniture. He was waiting for someone.

Nikki appeared untroubled by Charlie's absence and barely seemed to notice the mutilated corpse on the floor. Yorkie was lying in his lap, enjoying a tummy tickle.

Berlin kept her eyes averted from poor Mrs Muir and tried to think through her next move. She was all out of ideas, apart from following Charlie through the window. Anger, disgust and fear were fighting for the upper hand. A lifetime of hard-won detachment was dissolving.

The first day of the new year. But not for Charlie.

A warm hand clasped hers. Surprised, she looked down. Nikki insinuated his fingers between hers and squeezed gently. It was strangely reassuring. Berlin squeezed back.

There was a soft knock at the door. Keeping the gun on Nikki and Berlin, Yuri backed out into the vestibule and opened it.

Gerasimova, whom Berlin had seen so recently dropping the little commodore off to die, strode right past him and into the middle of the room. It occurred to Berlin that he wasn't the first person she'd had eliminated. Nor would he be the last.

Yorkie sat up on his haunches and growled.

Gerasimova didn't glance at Berlin or Nikki. She went straight to Mrs Muir's body and stood beside it. Her flared nostrils and rigid shoulders betrayed the effort it took for her to look down. But when she did, it wasn't for long. She took Yuri aside and muttered something in his ear.

He turned and pointed an accusing finger at Berlin.

'You are working for British intelligence,' he said.

Berlin's first reaction was: *That's ridiculous.*

'Yes,' she said. 'I am.'

Berlin wasn't entirely sure if British intelligence officers would actually acknowledge their status, except under torture, but her gambit had so far proved successful. It had postponed summary execution.

Yuri and Gerasimova had engaged in an intense conversation. He had made some phone calls, but was clearly frustrated by the lack of response. Of course, it was New

Year's Day. Most people would be drunk or asleep. He had kept his gun on her throughout.

Berlin had followed up her confession by quickly suggesting that they would naturally want to avoid exacerbating an already tense diplomatic situation. Or not, at any rate, without further consultation.

Now Gerasimova was on the phone, trying her luck.

Pieces began to fall into place: Yuri provided local, unofficial support to Gerasimova's activities; she owned the Park Royal warehouse, perhaps on behalf of the SVR, which had provided a location in London for them to hide . . . what?

Not Mikhail Gerasimov. He had been murdered in Moscow. Then, very inconveniently, Berlin had been sent to interview him. So they had procured a stand-in and dispatched Berlin's interpreter. Yuri had prevailed on Charlie to take on the role.

The ruse would have worked, except Utkin had connected the dead interpreter, Matvienko, to Berlin. When she'd told him she was to interview Mikhail Gerasimov, she had given him a link between the two. Utkin believed Gerasimov and Matvienko were victims of the same killer.

He was wrong. They were victims of the same killers, plural; Nikki, sitting next to her, petting his dog, and his mother.

Yuri had accused Charlie of making him look a fool in the eyes of the woman he loved. Gerasimova had to be that woman. But Berlin still didn't understand the connection between that and the delivery to the warehouse.

But one thing was apparent: the situation was spiralling out of Yuri and Gerasimova's control.

Gerasimova hung up and spoke to Yuri. He bit his lip and muttered something.

'Very well,' she said to Berlin. 'You will be detained as an enemy agent.'

They had all trooped downstairs and were now standing beside the Range Rover. It was still snowing. Berlin stood close to Nikki and shivered.

Yuri, gun in hand, was arguing with Gerasimova. It seemed to be about who should drive. Berlin's perception might be compromised, but she knew a domestic when she saw one. She had been right about that relationship.

In the end, Gerasimova got into the driver's seat; Berlin and Nikki got in the back, as directed, and the chagrined Yuri sat in the front, next to Gerasimova, turning to keep his gun on her.

Utkin drove up to see a Range Rover speeding away. It was the only vehicle on the road and in a hurry. What could be so urgent on New Year's morning? It would wait. The car was familiar and he knew exactly where to find it when he was ready.

But first he needed to establish the identity of the latest victim. If his intuition was correct, it would tie it all together.

The blizzard was closing in, but even from the car he could see something had been going on: the snow on the path had been churned into icy ridges.

He got out, bracing himself against the wind.

The gate was wide open.

Through the swirling white curtain he could see a trail had been trampled through the frozen vegetation. He followed it into the garden.

Snow was drifting against something solid, forming a mound. He took a step and heard glass crunch beneath his feet.

There were two people who could confirm his suspicions about the dead man on the estate.

He took a few more steps and blinked the snowflakes from his lashes. The mound resolved into a body.

Utkin fell to his knees and gently wiped the snow from her face.

Now there was only one.

77

Berlin and Nikki were locked in a bedroom in an apartment that seemed to belong to Gerasimova. It was telling that they hadn't been taken anywhere official. Yuri couldn't risk taking her to the police station: awkward questions would be asked.

Nikki had stretched out on the unmade bed with Yorkie and gone to sleep. It was his default setting: the sleep of the innocent. Berlin envied him. Perhaps a conscience free from guilt could cure her insomnia.

Although that might not be a problem for much longer.

Soon after they'd arrived there had been a lot of noise and activity in the rest of the flat: phones kept ringing and voices were raised. But for about the last fifteen minutes there had been an ominous silence.

Berlin looked out of the window. The street, eight storeys below, was very quiet. In the distance a fortress glowed, formidable and beautiful. See the Kremlin and die.

There was an old photo in a cheap frame on the dresser. Berlin picked it up. A young man, a boy really, was grinning at the camera. He was wearing a uniform that was too big for him. An older man had his arm around the boy's shoulders. He had a proud, faraway look in his eyes.

Berlin put it down and began listlessly opening and closing the dresser drawers, just looking. Peering into other people's lives. It's what she did. She could hear Peggy saying, 'And look where it's got you.'

Gerasimova knew catching a British agent could be a turning point in her career. If she *was* a spy.

Berlin could be exchanged for one of their agents, held by the British. Or she might have value as an asset; Gerasimova might even be able to turn her. Then her superiors might overlook other errors of judgement. Gerasimova glanced at Yuri.

While she had been busy with the necessary enquiries, he had been drinking. His usefulness was coming to an end. It was sad, but true. She had never misled him. He had understood her priorities from the beginning.

Unlike Misha. He had never grasped that her advancement and the interests of her country were aligned. When he had betrayed her, he had betrayed her in other ways, not simply as his wife. And yet at one time there had been real passion between them. The fury she had felt could only have grown out of that.

She was fond of Yuri, but he was becoming a liability. To her, and to Russia.

Utkin made his way slowly down the empty corridor towards his office, one hand resting on the wall. He felt their presences all around: the dead were an unbearable weight on his shoulders, grinding him down, so that he felt he might sink through the floor to join them.

He didn't turn on the light, just closed the door behind him and went and sat behind his desk. In the gloom it took him a moment to see the note that someone had left, pinned beneath a mug emblazoned with a faded red star.

He fumbled for his glasses and slipped them on.

Someone had taken a message. His caller had left a long telephone number he didn't recognise, but no name. He stuffed the note in his pocket, then felt beneath his desk drawer for a key he had taped there long ago.

It unlocked the steel cabinet in the corner.

He had kept the Avtomat Kalashnikova oiled and cleaned but hadn't used it since the Afghan War. A legendary version of the weapon, its existence was even doubted by some people. It was a modified AK47, shorter, with a folding stock.

Much easier to conceal.

He was going to pay an unofficial visit to the owner of the Range Rover. An unofficial weapon might prove very useful.

Berlin blinked in the shaft of light that fell across the bed. She had fallen asleep next to Nikki and Yorkie, but had no idea for how long. Her mouth was dry and her skin was burning. Familiar worms wriggled in her brain, demanding to be fed.

Propping herself up on one elbow, she saw that it was Maryna who stood in the doorway.

'Colonel Gerasimova,' said Berlin.

The colonel had recognised Mrs Muir because they moved in similar circles.

Gerasimova came further into the room and switched on a lamp. Nikki stirred. Yorkie rose, hackles up, growling at the colonel. Berlin made a move to get off the bed.

'No, no. Stay there,' said Gerasimova. 'Be comfortable.'

Berlin sank back down. They must have been ordered to treat her with some respect. It was a good sign.

Gerasimova walked around the bed to Berlin's side.

Through the open door, Berlin could see Yuri sitting at a table with a bottle of vodka, eyes downcast.

'Why did you kill your husband?' said Berlin. 'Is divorce illegal in Russia?'

Gerasimova looked stung.

'This wasn't about some petty marital dispute,' she said. 'He was a traitor.'

Berlin thought she heard Yuri groan.

'So your husband objected to the drug trade?'

'Drugs?' snapped Maryna. 'What are you talking about?'

'Your warehouse. Yuri's thugs. The president's plane. You're just common drug dealers,' said Berlin.

Gerasimova's eyes glinted. 'You addicts disgust me,' she said. 'One-track minds.'

Someone had helped Gerasimova with her homework.

'If it wasn't drugs, what was it? Enlighten my drug-addled brain,' said Berlin.

'Terrorists,' said Gerasimova.

Berlin struggled to take in this information. 'What do you mean?' she said.

'Chechens. They wanted martyrdom. Their wish was granted.'

The room seemed to tilt slightly.

There were bodies in the crates.

'Your government was foolish enough to give them asylum, despite the risk,' said Gerasimova. 'And my husband was foolish enough to betray our operation to eliminate that risk.'

Berlin stood up. Yorkie began to bark furiously.

Gerasimova shoved her hard in the chest and she fell back. 'I have something for you, junkie.'

It was a syringe.

'What's going on?' said Berlin. 'Do you know who I am?'

'Yes,' said Gerasimova. 'I know precisely who you are. No-one. Nothing. You are disavowed.'

She held up the syringe and depressed the plunger.

Berlin watched the liquid travel up the barrel and spurt from the needle. A hotshot. They were going to give her a lethal overdose, then dump her body somewhere with a needle hanging out of her arm.

Nobody would be surprised.

The syringe in Gerasimova's hand glinted in the light from the other room. Yuri called out something, his mournful tone apparent despite the slurred words.

Gerasimova turned her head a fraction, as if to answer him.

Berlin reached inside her coat for the Glock. She sprang off the bed. So did Yorkie. The little dog flew straight at Gerasimova and bit her face. She cried out and careened into Berlin as blood poured from her cheek.

Berlin staggered, trying to draw the gun with one hand and keep her balance with the other, but she was weak and ill-coordinated. She went down in a heap.

Through the door, she saw Yuri stumble to his feet.

Nikki had sat up and was watching Yorkie bounce up and down, snapping at Maryna. She shouted something in Russian, took a step back, then made a fatal mistake: she kicked out.

Her boot connected with Yorkie, who yelped as he flew across the room and hit the wall.

Yuri laughed, briefly. He stopped when Nikki sprang off the bed and threw himself at Gerasimova. She went down hard, next to Berlin.

Yuri rushed into the room, scrabbling to draw his gun. He had already been drinking when he got to Charlie's, hence his failure to search Berlin. Now he was utterly drunk.

Berlin got to her feet, drew the Glock and pointed it at Yuri's head.

'Drop it,' she shouted above Gerasimova's screams.

Yuri, befuddled, let his gun fall to the floor.

'Kick it over here,' she demanded.

He did as he was told.

Berlin didn't dare take her eyes off him, but the noise, a rasping gurgle, indicated that Nikki still had Maryna in his grasp.

Yuri was aghast.

'Stop him, stop him!' he shouted at Berlin.

She didn't know how.

Suddenly Maryna was silent.

Nikki stood up. He approached Berlin and for a moment she thought she was next. He stuck out his hand, expectant.

Berlin felt a surge of fear. Then something clicked. She reached into her coat pocket and there, tucked into a corner, she found the sweet Utkin had given her.

She dropped it into Nikki's bloody palm.

He unwrapped it, popped it into his mouth and let the cellophane wrapper fall to the floor.

The sickly sweet aroma melded with the scent of drying blood.

78

Yuri dropped to his knees and crawled across the room to where Maryna lay.

Berlin kept the gun on him, in case his grief suddenly turned to rage. He raised Maryna's head from the floor, cradled it in his hands, and kissed her.

Nikki had picked Yorkie up from the corner and carried him into the other room. The little dog was tougher than he looked. He was trembling, but set about licking the blood from Nikki's hands.

The only sound was Berlin's ragged breathing. She struggled to control it, to remain calm and think through her next move.

If she simply left the apartment, Yuri would soon follow and mobilise half of Moscow's police to catch her.

If she called the police herself, it would be Yuri's word against hers. He would have an answer for everything, if indeed she lived to tell her side of the story.

She couldn't rely on Utkin. He had only one motive: catch the killer. It would make little difference to him that the murderer seemed incapable of intent. To a policeman, a result was a result.

Yuri was kneeling beside Maryna, sobbing now, holding

her hand. Berlin took a few steps closer, bringing the gun close to his head.

She saw his shoulders tense as he waited for the shot.

The gun wavered in her hand. She drew it back and struck.

Yuri fell forward, out for the count.

Berlin snatched up his weapon, put both guns in her coat pockets, and went into the other room.

Two mobiles and a wallet lay on the table. She grabbed the phones, emptied the wallet and tore the landline connection from the wall. There was no telling how long it would take Yuri to come round. His colour wasn't good, but he was still breathing.

Where were the damn car keys? She checked the kitchen, but there was no sign of them. Finally she was forced to go back into the bedroom, roll Yuri away from Maryna and search her pockets. Bingo.

She stood up and backed away from the bodies.

The syringe was still in Maryna's hand.

Nikki had been too fast, too powerful and too brutal for her.

Nikki. What the fuck was she going to do with him? If she abandoned him, she was leaving him to the wolves. He'd go straight to an institution of the sort that Charlie had feared most. He couldn't fend for himself. He'd die, or go feral.

Charlie had insisted that he wasn't to blame for what he'd done. He'd had no choice. And she had sacrificed her life for him in a last doomed, desperate bid to give Berlin options: a chance to escape and take Nikki with her. If Yorkie hadn't given them away, it might just have worked.

Berlin found herself looking again at the syringe in Maryna's clenched hand. The barrel was full. It could be decanted. Reduced to smaller, safe doses.

Who was she trying to kid? She had no bloody choice, either. She raised her foot and stomped down hard. Through the sole of her boot she felt the syringe shatter. The sensation jarred every cell in her body.

Nikki looked up at her.

'Let's go home,' she said.

One good turn deserved another.

79

Berlin ran into the basement car park and pressed the key fob. At the far end of a line of upmarket vehicles, a Range Rover's headlights flashed. There was the reassuring soft clunk of locks releasing.

Getting out of the basement was easy. The same fob activated the security grille. The steering wheel, brakes, accelerator and gear lever were all familiar mechanisms. It was a car; she could drive. Here endeth the easy part.

Nikki sat beside her. Yorkie was on the back seat. They were both sitting up, quite perky, ready to enjoy the ride.

The glowing green digits on the dash read minus nine. Berlin cranked up the heater and reminded herself to stay on the wrong side of the road.

Her sense of direction was reasonable. From the apartment window she had seen the Kremlin. She drove towards it. The heavy vehicle required only a surprisingly light touch to steer. She welcomed the feeling that she had some control, even if it proved to be temporary.

The black sky was turning gunmetal grey. Dawn.

Utkin pulled over and parked opposite the entrance to the apartment building. There was no sign of the Range Rover in the street, but no doubt it was in the underground garage.

He slid the weapon inside his coat, got out and gazed up. He hoped the lift was working. This interview would not be conducted in the receptionist's cubicle.

The door to Colonel Gerasimova's apartment remained resolutely closed. Utkin knocked again. He bent close. He could hear something faint. It sounded like moaning.

He took a step back and kicked just below the lock. There was the sound of wood splintering. He took two steps back, drew his gun and charged at the door, shoulder first.

The place looked as if a whirlwind had passed through it. 'What the hell?' said Utkin.

Yuri lay on the floor, clutching his head and groaning.

Utkin strode through the apartment. When he got to the bedroom door he stopped dead. The scene in there was horrific; he felt as if he were passing through the circles of hell, each more forbidding than the last.

The cellophane wrapper peeked out from under the bed, mocking him. He walked in, snatched it up and strode out of the apartment, leaving the door wide open.

He could hear Yuri calling after him, weakly, 'Sasha . . . Sasha.'

He hadn't called him that for years.

The lift seemed to take for ever to reach the basement. Utkin took the weapon out from under his coat and held it ready. The doors opened.

Berlin had no vehicle and she would need one to beat a hasty retreat from the carnage she had left in the flat.

Utkin stepped out and made his way quietly along one wall. There were at least a dozen black Range Rovers, but none was the one he sought.

He ran back to the lift.

He would wring the truth out of that bastard Yuri.

But by the time he got back to the apartment, Yuri had gone.

The Range Rover flew along. Nikki had climbed into the back seat with Yorkie. Berlin dropped one of the phones into the hands-free dock. The phone chirruped. A smiley face appeared on the screen. It was a risk, but she absolutely had to have a phone if she and Nikki were to get out of this godforsaken country alive.

The windows were tinted and the muddy slush she had smeared over the number plates would have frozen to a crust by now. That would help.

But the luxury vehicle would have every technical and anti-theft advantage; they could easily be a pulsating dot on someone's screen. She couldn't afford to try disabling the electronic gizmos, for fear of triggering an anti-mobilisation device. Besides, she wouldn't know where to start.

The only thing in her favour was the fact it was New Year's Day. When Yuri regained consciousness, it could take him a while to get a search up and running, particularly if he was concussed. She should have given him another whack, to make sure.

80

Delroy lay awake, staring at the clock radio. He had been watching the numerals flip over for hours. He had run the job himself: the instructions had come through him, he had made all the arrangements, and in accordance with the client's requirements he had prepared the brief for Berlin.

Nothing had to be signed off by a partner. No questions had been asked. A file number had been allocated and a budget established. His delegation, the amount of money he could sign off on, had been increased to cover Berlin's expenses.

They had jokingly said that it was so he wouldn't have to bother his bosses during the holidays.

There were no-one's fingerprints on this assignment besides his own. It was his fuck-up. He was responsible for everything. He had let Berlin down in the worst possible way.

Everyone was convinced Berlin was dead. Delroy had a feeling that for some parties this had come as a relief. It left the field clear. No loose ends. Berlin was the very definition of a loose end.

Delroy turned over, holding back his tears. He didn't want to disturb Linda. They had stayed up for New Year, hoping they could sleep late. The baby would probably have different ideas. He was almost dozing off when his mobile rang.

Berlin only knew two phone numbers by heart. She flicked to speaker. Her call was answered on the second ring.

'Delroy Jacobs,' came a soft voice.

Tears welled up and clouded Berlin's vision, which wasn't helpful when she was steering half a ton of four-wheel drive through a strange city on icy roads.

'Del,' she said. 'It's me.'

'Jesus Christ, Berlin,' said Del. His voice came through the speaker loud and clear. He was so surprised to hear from her he had obviously forgotten to whisper in order not to wake up Linda and the baby.

Berlin laughed.

'Where are you?' said Del. 'Are you okay?'

'I could use a drink,' said Berlin. 'But apart from that, I'm fine.'

'Thank God,' said Del.

She could hear him choking up. She loved him to bits.

'Del, I've got to get out of Russia,' she said.

'What's all that noise?' asked Del. 'Are you in a car?'

'Yeah. I'm driving it,' said Berlin. 'There are some people on my tail. I have to get to the closest EU country.'

'No, no,' said Del. 'That's crazy. Go to the embassy.'

'That's the last place I'm going,' said Berlin. 'Just find me a route and text it to me. Start from the Kremlin. It's the only place I know that I can find.'

'I'll do my best, but . . .'

'Del?' she said. 'I have to turn the phone off soon. I'll turn it back on one last time after ten minutes. Did you capture this number?'

'Yes,' said Del. 'Look, hang on. What the hell's happening? Who's after you?'

'Everyone,' she said.

Berlin switched the phone off and took it out of the dock. The SIM was still active, but she couldn't afford to destroy it.

She kept driving towards the pool of light reflected off the clouds, to the heart of the city she had to escape.

81

Utkin opened the sandalwood pencil box and dropped the cellophane wrapper in with the others. He shut the lid, then picked it up and threw it at the wall.

The box lay on a threadbare rug, forlorn, discarded.

Utkin shuffled across the room and picked it up.

He shuffled back again. Back and forth, his felt slippers slid across the linoleum.

He was at a dead end.

When his phone rang, he didn't recognise the long number. Then he remembered the message at the office. He'd returned the call from his mobile, which he never blocked. There was no point. He wasn't hiding.

'Utkin,' he said.

'*Zdravstvujtye, Major,*' came the response.

Utkin was surprised.

Berlin kept the motor running so they didn't freeze to death. Nikki seemed oblivious to the cold. To most things. She glanced at him. He was gazing at the floodlit onion domes of St Basil's, the tips of which appeared to float above the lofty red wall that surrounded the Kremlin.

'So,' said Berlin. 'Here we are.'

She was talking to herself really, but she noticed a slight

shift in his expression. There was no reason to think he didn't understand every word. He just chose not to respond. Or, at least, not in any way that you could recognise unless you knew him very well.

Perhaps Charlie, over-protective, had encouraged him to remain in a state of suspended animation. His apparent lack of reaction to her absence might indicate relief. It was an awful thought, given what Charlie had done for him.

A cramp in Berlin's leg travelled through her and rattled her bowels. The sudden pain made her gasp. She might have made a poor choice when she crushed Maryna's syringe, although God knows what Maryna had cooked up.

It could have been *krokodil*.

Maybe she had simply acted out of fear. Self-preservation. She turned on the mobile to save herself from further introspection. A text message arrived with directions: highway numbers, a map, even a list of what appeared to be petrol stations.

Del had done a good job. The border with Belarus was the closest to Moscow, but it wasn't in the EU. It had to be Latvia. There was a border crossing at Terehova, just over seven hours from Moscow. The road appeared to run pretty much straight there. It was a numbered motorway, so she wouldn't need to understand any Cyrillic letters.

The tank was three quarters full, but no doubt the Range Rover was a gas guzzler. They would have to stop once, but at least she could turn the phone off now.

She remembered sitting in her father's, Lenny's, Morris Minor. It was before she and her mother moved out into the house in Leyton, leaving Lenny in the flat above the shop in Bethnal Green.

He always drove. Peggy would cling to her seat, which really annoyed him. Berlin and Zayde would be in the back.

Lenny, a fan of American gangster films, would look over his shoulder at her, grin and say, in a bad Bronx accent, 'Hold tight, kid. We're gonna break for the border.'

Her loving grandfather, who it now turned out was a gangster, would shout, '*Vpered! Forward!*'

Peggy would tut-tut.

'Hold tight, Nikki,' said Berlin. '*Vpered.*'

82

The doctor had given Yuri tablets for the pain. He had taken a handful, but his head still throbbed. He sat in the back seat, clutching it, as they cruised past the European Mall.

He was sick, but the nausea that gripped him did not stem from the pain in his head: he had lost everything. He tried not to think about Maryna. 'Pull over,' he barked.

The car veered abruptly and stopped. Yuri cried out at the jolt.

The two men in the front turned to look at him, concerned. 'What shall we do?' said one.

Yuri couldn't bear to look at them. 'Get out,' he said. 'Find that girl, the fucking junkie. It won't be hard. I broke her nose. Don't come back empty-handed.'

When they had gone, he allowed himself to weep.

When he was done, Yuri blew his nose and lit a cigarette. The bitch had taken the Range Rover. But unluckily for her it had a state-of-the-art anti-theft satellite tracking system.

He called the firm who had done the installation and managed the tracking. He had the password and full user privileges, so was able to quickly respond to all the security checks. He listened as they implemented the activation process and real-time data collection.

When they had finished, he hung up and flipped open the computer that was lying on the seat beside him. All the information would be routed directly to him. Hirst Corporation offered the most advanced facility of its kind.

If the Englishwoman was stupid or desperate enough to keep using the vehicle, Yuri wouldn't be far behind. And what other options did she have?

Eventually he would catch up with them. No-one else would have access to this information. Utkin wouldn't dare issue a general alert for the car. He had too much to lose.

Yuri would find her and the cretin and make an end to it. He would do it himself, to honour Maryna's memory.

He would finally be the man she had always wanted: one who would kill for her.

Utkin struggled to read the open map, which he couldn't really see without his glasses. Clear sight was wasted on the young. He didn't need a route, anyway. There was just the one road to follow.

The sandalwood pencil box lay on the passenger seat beside the map. His gun rested on his hip. Heavy, but comforting. Old faithful. Just like him.

Loyalty was a much-derided notion these days.

The M9 exit loomed ahead and he crossed lanes in readiness. They had at least an hour's start on him. The Range Rover was fast, but it was hungry. Even with a full tank, they would have to stop for gas or risk running out.

The car juddered as he accelerated. He spoke soothingly to it, muttering endearments. Together they had come far. Together they would go that little bit further. Six hundred and twenty kilometres.

The Ford was very economical. He had a plastic container of petrol in the boot for emergencies. He could piss in a bottle.

Nothing would stop him now. His quarry was within his grasp. He had everything he needed to end this whole ghastly murderous spree.

He would finish it, whatever it took.

83

Berlin had negotiated the Moscow ring road and found the highway, the M9. It was divided by a concrete median barrier, which was a blessing. There was enough traffic to keep the tarmac clear of ice and snow, but it wasn't hectic, probably because of the holidays.

It gave her some time to think. If she was right, this whole sordid business challenged even her ingrained cynicism. Treason for profit. The currency of national security – loyalty, accountability, shared values – had been replaced by cash.

There were any number of things that could go badly wrong now; even to call what she was embarking on 'a shot in the dark' was being generous. People were unpredictable. They didn't always make the choices you expected. They never made the choices you wanted.

The first thing that went wrong was the highway. It ran out. After about a hundred kilometres she found herself driving down a narrow dual carriageway. She switched on the phone briefly and checked Del's instructions; it was definitely the right road.

The hard shoulder on either side was obscured by walls of snow, broken only where lorries had skidded off the road and jackknifed. The drifts around the rigs indicated nobody was going to try to get them out until spring.

The tarmac itself was lunar, pocked with craters large enough to get lost in; ribbons of frozen brown sludge formed ridges that challenged even the all-terrain tyres of the Range Rover. The steering wheel slipped through her clammy hands as the car juddered and jolted.

Massive transports thundered towards them, blinding her with dazzling arrays of headlights. Those behind her overtook with a roar, careless of oncoming traffic.

She had no time to think about anything except keeping herself and Nikki alive.

Yuri had alerted all five traffic police units stationed along the M9. The first three had responded: there was no sign of the vehicle.

Yuri knew the lazy bastards wouldn't be venturing out to check. They would be sitting with their feet up on the heater, or drinking in a disreputable highway trucking establishment.

Beyond Moscow he had no authority. He was relying on goodwill or, more likely, the overweening ambition of some peasant who wanted a transfer into the big city.

He kept his eyes on the road. The conditions were shocking, even for a local. Speed was down to eighty kilometres an hour at the most. He didn't dare take his eyes off the road for long enough to check the computer screen, but the Range Rover had been on the move for nearly three and a half hours.

She would have to stop soon.

*

Berlin found herself driving through a gleaming white tunnel of swaying, snow-laden trees. The glare of the headlights bounced off the swirling blizzard. There was nothing to mark her lane. It was absolutely terrifying.

She wasn't even sure if she was still on the road. Her tongue was thick with fear and nausea. Nikki and Yorkie slept on. A dome of light appeared in the distance. She glanced at the fuel gauge. Pit stop.

She pulled in beside a pump, turned off the motor and rested her head on the steering wheel.

Nikki and Yorkie roused themselves.

When she climbed out of the car, so did they. The little dog went off to make its yellow mark in the snow. Nikki looked at Berlin.

'Go to the loo,' she said. She pointed at the glowing icon above a door in the main building and unhooked the pump.

The garage was similar to those found on English motorways, except there weren't any crisps. Berlin paid for the petrol and bought a handful of chocolate bars and a cup of tea. She wasn't about to risk the coffee.

While she was sipping the hot, sour liquid she saw Nikki walk past the enormous plate-glass window with Yorkie tucked under his arm. He seemed to be watching something. Berlin approached the window, following the direction of his gaze.

The lights on the two police vehicles were pulsing, the red and blue alternately tinting the snow.

One was blocking the exit, the other the entrance.

She went outside.

Nikki turned and looked at her with an expression that she could have sworn was dismay.

A policeman was standing beside his car with his weapon drawn.

'Get in the car,' she said gently.

Nikki did as he was told.

The policeman marched up to her and, without saying a word, knocked her tea out of her hand. Then he dragged her to the Range Rover, opened the door and thrust her into the passenger seat. He held out his hand.

Berlin gave him the key and fob.

He walked around the car, got in and drove them to the back of the garage. When he got out he took the key with him, but left the electrical system on.

There were no lights at the rear of the building. It was dark, with visibility even more limited by the snow. The dashboard bathed the interior in an eerie green glow. It matched the awful silence.

84

By the time Yuri arrived the locals were unhappy. He thought it unwise to deal with his problem in their presence. They might see an opportunity to put him in their debt. He expressed his sincere thanks for their splendid work and cooperation, and demonstrated his gratitude with a significant donation to the local police football team.

The traffic cop handed over the key and fob.

Yuri sent them on their way, then drove around the back, pulled up in front of the Range Rover and took his gun from its holster.

He pressed the fob.

Berlin heard the soft clunk of the doors unlocking. She brought her fist down hard on the central locking button.

Outside in the snow, Yuri pressed the fob.

The locks popped open.

Even over the howling wind she could hear him laughing.

'Get down and stay down,' she said.

Nikki obliged by sliding to the floor, taking Yorkie with him.

Berlin experienced a heightening of the senses. Possibly

the kind that preceded death. She found herself able to move with lightning speed, anticipating the movement made by Yuri as he pressed the fob. She turned on the headlights.

She could see his eyes. He was tiring of the game.

She kept one hand on the central locking button and with the other she took Yuri's gun, a heavy old thing, with a worn red star on the handgrip, out of her pocket.

She couldn't use it in the car for fear of a ricochet. It was pointless trying to shoot through the windscreen.

Yuri would open the door and when he did one of them would go down first. She had a fifty-fifty chance.

Berlin released the button. The locks popped.

Yuri didn't move from his position between the two cars. Instead, he turned to the boot of his vehicle and opened it. He gestured with his gun.

Berlin flicked the headlights to high beam.

Anna lay in the boot, gagged and bound.

Yuri put the gun to her head.

He had anticipated Berlin's armed resistance.

She opened the door and tossed out his gun. It was a gesture, that's all. Even if she had a machine gun, she wouldn't have used it. And Yuri knew it.

Connections create vulnerabilities: it was a rule Berlin had forgotten.

He motioned for her to get out.

Berlin climbed down, closing the door behind her.

She could see Anna's thin body quaking with fear or cold or both. But the light had gone out of her eyes, dulled by resignation.

'Walk,' commanded Yuri. He pointed towards the forest.

'Let the girl go,' said Berlin.

His weapon didn't have a silencer. He looked around and gritted his teeth. He was apparently anxious to avoid attracting attention. 'Move,' he said.

Berlin stood her ground.

Yuri hesitated. He left the boot open and stepped out from between the vehicles, but before he could advance any further towards her, a car appeared from one side of the building, catching the little scene in its headlights.

Yuri froze.

85

Utkin could see the boot of Yuri's car was open, but he couldn't see what was in it. He saw Berlin, but couldn't see the interior of the Range Rover, which was dark.

He got out of his car and raised a hand in a friendly gesture, addressing Yuri. 'What have you been up to?'

'Don't come any closer,' said Yuri.

Utkin stomped through the snow. He didn't look at Berlin. She couldn't understand what they were saying anyway.

'Why would you fear me, Yuri?' he said. 'I am an old man. Your junior in rank. You have relationships I can only imagine.'

'The only relationship that meant anything to me is over,' said Yuri.

His sweaty pallor was that of a man at the end of his rope – liable to be impulsive, to make mistakes.

Utkin softened his tone.

'What about your daughters?' he said. 'You love them, don't you?'

Yuri rubbed his sleeve across his eyes.

'Why did you do it, Yuri?' he said. 'Was it for the motherland?'

'It was for Maryna,' shouted Yuri, waving the gun about.

Utkin took a backward step.

'She was the one with pure motives,' said Yuri. He was ranting now. 'I was always weak, weak, weak. But still, it would have been all right. Then *she* interfered.' He pointed the gun at Berlin.

'Yuri,' said Utkin. 'I must ask you to bring her in for questioning.'

'She's an enemy agent,' said Yuri.

'All the more reason to keep her alive,' said Utkin. 'She may have valuable information.'

Yuri growled.

'A quick death is too good for her,' he said.

His eyes were glassy. He was listening only to an inner voice. Utkin moved forward a little. He had to keep Yuri talking.

'What happened to Mikhail Gerasimov?' he asked.

'He was a traitor,' said Yuri.

'And your mistress's husband,' said Utkin.

'He was exploiting his knowledge of Maryna's work,' insisted Yuri. 'He deserved to die.'

'Why didn't you kill him yourself?'

Utkin took another step forward.

'I'm warning you,' said Yuri. 'Stay out of this.'

He cocked the gun.

Utkin sighed, shrugged, kicked at the snow.

'Very well,' he said. 'Have it your way. I'm not risking my neck for her.'

Berlin had no idea what had transpired between the two men, but as she watched Utkin trudge back to his car, she knew it wasn't good.

'Okay,' said Yuri. 'We go.'

He levelled the gun at her and pointed. He wanted her further away from the garage.

Berlin wondered if he would just shoot her in the back if she made a run for it. But she could barely walk in the deep snow, let alone run. She moved forward slowly.

She couldn't hear Yuri behind her because of the wind and the deep, cold carpet that lay beneath their feet.

She became aware of light playing on the snowflakes. Shadows tumbled as beams swept across the snow.

She glanced over her shoulder and saw Yuri turn.

There was a roar, a dull thud, and he was gone.

Yuri rolled from the bonnet as the Ford slithered to a halt. The bloody windscreen stayed intact for a moment, then shattered and fell in on Utkin. An icy blast engulfed him.

He had had to stop Yuri. He knew that, but he was sick to the stomach. It was an accident. An awful car accident. It happens and no-one would think to take it further.

Now he had to pull himself together.

Despite the fact that he had killed the man he had once called friend.

Even before Utkin's car had come to a complete stop, Berlin began running back through the snow to the spot where Yuri had stood seconds ago. His weapon, the key and the fob lay where he had dropped them. She snatched them up.

Peering into the darkness, she could see the trees illuminated by the headlights of Utkin's car.

Berlin stumbled to the Range Rover and clambered in, glancing into the back seat as she turned on the motor.

Nikki had found a travel rug and was crouched beneath it with Yorkie. She engaged the gears. Her foot hit the accelerator and the Range Rover surged forward.

She braked again.

Anna was still lying in Yuri's boot. If she tried to rescue her now, it would mean giving up Nikki. He was the killer Utkin sought.

The policeman would know an asthmatic woman of Charlie's age was physically incapable of killing a man alone, so someone else was involved.

He must have had Charlie under surveillance, which was how he had come to be hanging around outside her place that first night, when the Range Rover was 'stolen'.

Charlie had kept Nikki well hidden, but the minute Utkin saw him, it would be over.

Utkin gently lifted Yuri's cap. It was a bad move. Yuri groaned and opened his eyes.

'Forgive me, Sasha,' he said.

Utkin put his face close to Yuri's, offering him a final moment of warmth. Poor Yuri. He wasn't evil; just a frightened fool. Like all men with power he was afraid even of those who served him. Fear had made him contemptible.

A motor roared. Startled, Utkin looked up to see two

bright beams bearing down on him. He dived into the snow.

The Range Rover swerved at the last minute and spattered him with freezing spray.

'Stop!' he shouted. He snatched the pistol from his holster as it sped away.

Berlin smacked the steering wheel and cursed herself. She just didn't have the guts. She hoped to Christ Utkin would simply let Anna go. He had no use for her.

As they bounced back onto the highway, she heard a car backfire. It sounded a lot like a gun.

The lights of the garage in the rear-view mirror soon shrank to a point and disappeared. There was no sign of any emergency vehicles on the road, no sirens or flashing lights coming in either direction.

It was possible that no-one had even heard anything. Berlin flexed her fingers and eased her grip on the steering wheel.

Utkin's car probably wouldn't be in any shape to follow them. But he might use Yuri's.

Easing off the accelerator, she slowed to a safe speed. It would take them about three hours to get to the border. The tank was full; they had chocolate.

A laugh erupted from her mouth, which became a sob.

At the edge of the pool of light that rushed along ahead of them there was an endless white plain.

She hummed 'Lara's Theme'. Zayde had taken her to see *Doctor Zhivago* when she was very little. He had cried, she remembered.

He'd patted her hand and told her tears were a sign of strength, not weakness. She didn't believe it then, and she didn't believe it now.

But there was nothing she could do to staunch her own.

86

A lemon haze in the distance: floodlights. The border crossing. Berlin slowed right down.

There was more commercial traffic here than she'd seen on the entire trip. Lorries and vans trundled along, rocking side to side as they negotiated the icy ridges of frozen slush. The Range Rover seemed to be the only domestic vehicle.

Nikki sat beside her. The chocolate had long gone. They were both tired and hungry. The line of traffic closed up. Enormous rigs boxed them in ahead and behind. They crawled forward. She couldn't believe they had got this far. She found it difficult to believe they would get any further.

There were garages on both sides of the road, a couple of restaurants and some nondescript buildings whose roofs were crowded with masts and satellite dishes.

The border control post came into view. There was a car park behind it and Berlin could see men walking back and forth between the buildings, clutching documents.

The traffic came to a standstill.

Two uniformed men were approaching, peering into the lorry cabs as they advanced. One had an enormous German shepherd on a tight leash.

They were checking passports and papers.

Passports and papers that they didn't have. Berlin and Nikki wouldn't even get as far as the border control building. Their descriptions would have been circulated. They would be detained, then disappear into the system.

'This looks like the end of the line,' said Berlin.

She turned the wheel and steered the Range Rover out from between the two lorries. Easing onto the hard shoulder, she drove along it at a leisurely pace, approaching the car park behind the border control post.

At the last moment, but still moving slowly, she spun the wheel hard, drove around the car park and into the empty space behind it. There was no fence.

She put her foot down. The tyres spun, then found traction. The Range Rover shot forward.

They were heading into no-man's-land.

It had always been her destination.

A siren wailed. Border guards ran in all directions. Lorry drivers emerged from their vehicles and the restaurants to gawp.

Berlin kept glancing in the rear-view mirror as the car jolted across the frozen ruts. The sheer audacity of the move had apparently paralysed everyone for a moment.

But now the chaos was unfolding.

She drove to the middle of the field and stopped. She had what she wanted. Witnesses. Dozens of them. On both sides of the border. Shooting them was not an option. Latvia and Russia were uneasy neighbours. Who would claim jurisdiction?

It began to snow.

The guards scrambled to set up a perimeter about two hundred yards away. Berlin knew it was standard operating procedure. They had to stay out of range in case she was a suicide bomber. Binoculars would be trained on them from every angle.

The frantic activity gradually died away.

Now what? They would just wait.

There would be telephone calls, discussions, meetings, arguments; orders sought, issued and ignored. The two sets of border guards, Latvian and Russian, would keep their distance from the Range Rover and each other until someone, somewhere, decided what to do.

No-one wanted an international incident. The buck would be passed up the line.

87

The snow had drifted deep around the Range Rover. Night and day had lost all meaning in the blizzard. Drifts were obscuring the vehicles that encircled them.

Berlin kept to a strict routine: switching on the motor and running the heater for a short time at defined intervals; eventually the tank would run dry. It didn't matter. She'd forgotten what the intervals were supposed to be.

The fog of stale breath, damp wool and dog pee was becoming unbearable. Nikki and Yorkie were subdued, restless, dozing intermittently, their lassitude due to hunger and thirst. Dehydration was a real possibility, despite the frozen water all around them. Berlin didn't dare let them get out of the car.

If hunger didn't drive them out, the cold would.

Who would come forward to arrest them?

Men struggled against the wind to set up portable floodlights, the kind used at crime scenes. They blinked into life, one by one. Berlin couldn't see beyond the halo of light. She could hardly keep her eyes open anyway.

The negotiations, the diplomatic process, was taking much, much longer than she had expected.

It suddenly occurred to her that perhaps there weren't any negotiations. Everyone had simply agreed, by default, to leave them in the field until they disappeared beneath the ice and snow. Frozen, suffocated, silent.

88

It took Berlin a moment to realise that the figure trudging towards them was real. She had begun to slip in and out of a sort of fugue state, aware that she would be heading for the big sleep if she didn't stay awake.

She got out of the car. Nikki, who had slept soundly for hours, did the same, cradling Yorkie beneath his coat. He came and stood beside her.

Berlin could see the advancing figure was carrying a weapon. She raised her arms. No-one would shoot a woman surrendering in these circumstances, surely. Too many bystanders.

Yorkie peeked out and sniffed. His ears went up. He yapped once, then sprang from Nikki's arms and ran. He bounced up and down, then leapt at the man as he came to a halt ten feet away.

Utkin caught the little dog in his arms.

The snow swirled around them. Was she dreaming?

Yorkie yelped and snuffled manically.

Nikki took a step forward. Berlin reached out to stop him, but she was too late. He kept walking towards Utkin.

'Papa,' he said.

89

The family reunion resolved into a snowy tableau before Berlin's eyes. Yorkie lay cradled in Utkin's arms. Nikki had simply left Berlin's side and gone to stand beside his father. They hadn't embraced. The automatic weapon Utkin carried jarred a bit, but otherwise it was somehow seasonal: Happy New Year from Our Family to Yours.

'You have caused me much trouble, Katarina Berlinskaya,' said Utkin.

'I could say the same thing about you,' retorted Berlin.

'Look at this,' said Utkin. He tossed his mobile phone and it fell at her feet. The small screen displayed an unflattering portrait of a corpse. The little commodore.

'Gerasimov's stand-in,' she said.

'I guessed as much,' said Utkin.

'Another of your son's victims,' said Berlin.

'A good child protecting his mother,' said Utkin.

Berlin put her hand in her pocket.

Utkin brought his weapon to his shoulder.

Berlin held up the sweet wrapper from the scene of the murder. She offered it to him.

Utkin relaxed and stepped forward to take it.

'The first was when Nikki was still teenager,' he said.

'Some poor plumber at our apartment who made mistake of arguing with Charlotte. Something trivial. She slapped. He slapped back. Then it happened.'

Utkin touched Nikki's face.

'You blame Charlie,' said Berlin.

'No,' said Utkin. 'I blame myself. But perhaps, as you say, the apple doesn't fall far from tree. Charlotte called me at work. Yuri was my junior partner.'

'You covered up a murder,' said Berlin.

'He was my son,' said Utkin. 'Yuri kept it quiet.'

'He banked it,' said Berlin.

'*Da*,' said Utkin. 'He banked it. When he needed an assassin, he used it. He needed someone who could never betray him. Nikita was perfect. And Charlotte was, well . . .'

'Desperate,' said Berlin. 'He promised her passports. She was very ill. Her lungs.'

She felt compelled to defend Charlie. God only knew why.

Utkin shrugged. 'I didn't know it was that bad,' he said.

'She wanted to take Nikki back to England,' said Berlin.

'And that's where he's going,' said Utkin. 'Russian prison would kill him. You understand. Give me Yuri's gun.'

She handed it over.

Utkin patted her down. He stepped back and looked her in the eye, then raised his arm.

The floodlights died.

Berlin caught a faint but familiar smell.

'I'm sorry, Katarina Berlinskaya,' said Utkin. 'I am afraid I have traded you for my son's future. A man telephoned me and made an offer . . .'

'I'll take it from here,' someone growled.

90

Magnus had taken Peggy Berlin along as his ace-in-the-hole; Teddy Ashbourne couldn't ignore a real, live constituent, even on the second day of the New Year. Hangovers had not yet worn off, but Magnus had worn out his welcome everywhere.

Peggy had seemed unconvinced at first; she was somewhat sceptical of how much clout a backbench Opposition MP might wield. But she took Magnus's point that if she was present Ashbourne would at least listen.

They needed someone on the inside if they were to have any chance of pressing Berlin's case; Magnus knew that all other doors were now closed to them. He ushered Peggy into the office. Sure enough, the beaming Member greeted her warmly. 'Mrs Berlin, is it?' he said, pumping her hand. 'Very pleased to meet you. Happy New Year.'

'Hardly,' said Magnus.

Ashbourne turned to Magnus with less enthusiasm.

'Hello, Magnus,' he said.

Magnus sat with Peggy on one side of Ashbourne's gargantuan desk, which was piled high with books and papers.

Ashbourne sat on the other side with a thin manila

folder occupying the small space that was left in front of him. It all conveyed that Ashbourne was a busy man.

Magnus sighed.

Ashbourne focused on Peggy. A voter.

'So you haven't heard from your daughter since before Christmas?' he enquired, solicitous.

'No,' said Peggy.

Magnus could see the dark circles under her eyes, the evidence of endless nights of worry.

Ashbourne turned to Magnus, who noted the change of tone. 'Ms Berlin has, of course, been named publicly as your source.'

'And to date we haven't heard a thing from the powers that be,' said Magnus. 'Why are they sitting on their hands, Teddy? This dear lady's daughter is missing and . . .'

'Indeed,' said Ashbourne, loftily. 'That's the whole problem. You heard my speech in Parliament, and the prime minister's reply.' He looked pained. 'I've been to the Foreign Office, the Home Office and the Metropolitan Police. They all say the same thing. There's nothing they can do until Ms Berlin returns to London.'

'Why not?' demanded Peggy, surprising Magnus.

'Because she's the only witness to the alleged events at the Park Royal warehouse,' said Ashbourne. 'The premises have been inspected. There's nothing there. There's no evidence whatsoever, no documents, no CCTV, no other witness, to support any of the allegations.'

'What about this Peter Green?' said Magnus. 'You've read my sworn statement.'

'I'm afraid SO15 don't set much store by it, Magnus. On your own admission you didn't actually see what happened at Carmichael's.'

'That's true,' blustered Magnus. 'But . . .'

'There's nothing to put you, or Peter Green, whoever he might be, in the house at that time,' said Ashbourne. 'Or to confirm that he kept you "incarcerated", as you like to put it. There's only your word for it.'

'Why on earth would I lie?' said Magnus.

'It makes a very good story,' said Ashbourne. 'It's the boy who cried wolf, I'm afraid.'

'That's preposterous,' protested Magnus.

Ashbourne opened the manila file and scanned it.

'There's no record of anyone called Peter Green, Magnus,' said the MP. 'Hirst denies all knowledge of him.'

'That's bloody ludicrous. Someone must know who he is,' said Magnus.

'I'm sorry, but there it is. Burghley has nothing on record to confirm his involvement. Its employees have signed the Official Secrets Act and can't even divulge what they had for breakfast. The government has no record of this particular Peter Green even existing.'

'What about Catherine?' said Peggy.

'As I said, Mrs Berlin, nothing can be done until she comes home.'

'But that's just it – she's missing,' said Peggy. It was clear she was having trouble holding back her tears.

Ashbourne stood up and closed his file.

'We understand that there was a problem,' he mumbled. 'With drugs.'

He walked to the door and opened it.

'I'm sorry,' he said.

Peggy felt a little unsteady. A gusty, cold wind whipped her legs as she stood beside Mr Nkonde on the pavement. He offered her his arm. He was still a gentleman, despite what the MP had said. And the MP hadn't been sorry at all. It was written all over his face.

Two policemen were getting out of a car. They put on their caps as they approached. Another policeman, and a policewoman, were striding towards them from the other direction.

Before she knew what was happening one of the policemen had elbowed her out of the way, and he and his colleague had grabbed Mr Nkonde.

'Magnus Nkonde, I am arresting you on suspicion of conspiring to commit misconduct in a public office,' he said.

He kept speaking, and Mr Nkonde started shouting, but Peggy couldn't take in what they were saying. She glanced back to see if the MP could help, but his door was firmly closed. The next moment the policewoman took her tightly by the arm and steered her towards a police car that had pulled up on the pavement. 'Let's get you home,' she said.

Mr Nkonde was struggling with the two policemen. He was still shouting, but the traffic drowned him out. The policewoman put her in the back of the car and jumped in too. She nodded at the driver and the car took off.

*

Alone in her kitchen, Peggy sat at the table with a cup of tea to steady her nerves. She couldn't believe it; her arm was quite bruised. It had all seemed so unnecessary; to think that the British police could behave in that fashion.

But more than anything she was shaken by what the MP had said: Catherine was a drug addict.

Her tea went cold.

91

Utkin and the man who had emerged from the darkness shook hands in a perfunctory fashion: the man Berlin had last seen at Park Royal wearing a supervisor's badge.

He and Utkin were conversing in Russian. Utkin took a package from inside his coat and handed it over.

Berlin glimpsed the evidence bags that contained her passport and buprenorphine.

The supervisor took a passport from his pocket and gave it to Utkin, who inspected it closely, then slipped it in Nikki's pocket. He had brought the little suitcase.

He kissed his son on both cheeks and whispered something in his ear. Nikki took the suitcase and Yorkie from him and went to stand beside the stranger.

'He can't take the dog,' the supervisor said.

'I would advise not to try and stop him,' said Utkin.

The supervisor frowned.

'Did you search her?' he said, indicating Berlin.

'Very likely,' said Utkin. He held up Yuri's gun.

Berlin looked at him. 'Remember your grandfather's tears,' he said, and touched his shoulder.

'Okay,' said the supervisor. 'That's enough. My car's not far, just this side of the border.'

'There will be no problem?' asked Utkin.

'No. We train the border guards. Their jobs depend on us.' He turned to Berlin. 'Let's get going.'

Berlin hesitated, but she had run out of options; she started walking.

The supervisor followed, with Nikki at his side.

Berlin glanced back at Utkin.

The snow fell like a curtain between them.

Instead of taking a straight line across the field to the Latvian border, the supervisor steered them towards the forest. Berlin knew this wasn't the route he had taken on the way in; they had left the faint trail of his footprints.

Nikki had not said another word since he had greeted his father. He kept pace. Following orders.

Gloveless, Berlin kept her hands in her pockets. Sweat soaked into her thermals. The frigid air seared her lungs. The wind dropped as they walked into the dense wood of silver birch. The drifts were fewer, but deeper. Exhausted, she stumbled and fell.

The supervisor stood over her.

Berlin was aware of him glancing around. His eyes had a glazed, spaced-out look. A look she recognised. The smoky smell that hung around him came back to her. Opium.

It would make him careless, unguarded. For a while.

Berlin gestured; she needed a moment to rest.

The supervisor stamped his feet against the cold.

Nikki stood perfectly still.

'It was you that sent me out here when I wouldn't take

your bloody fifty quid,' said Berlin. 'Did you know Gerasimov was already dead?'

The supervisor stared at her. For a moment she thought he was just going to tell her to shut her mouth. But then he shook his head, no. Of course they didn't know.

'He betrayed his wife's operation in London,' said Berlin.

'Yeah, yeah,' said the supervisor. 'We knew all about it.'

Berlin watched him slip into the garrulous state so typical of the stoned. Vague one moment, chatty the next.

'We told British intelligence,' he said. 'But they didn't want to know. Not in the national interest. They just asked us to make sure nothing leaked out. Then you came along.'

He frowned, suddenly edgy. The fairy dust was leaving his brain.

'Who exactly do you work for?' said Berlin.

'The highest bidder,' he said. 'Now get up.'

Berlin struggled to her feet. The snow had soaked into her boots and she could feel it freezing between her toes.

Nikki stood motionless, snow drifting around him, waiting to be told to move again.

Berlin shuffled forward.

The supervisor was taking them deeper into the forest. He beckoned Nikki and they all trudged on. The wind and fatigue made it difficult to talk, but Berlin was determined to keep up the conversation.

'When did you realise I was still alive?'

'When I heard my boss had taken extended leave.'

'Did she work for the Russians?'

The supervisor laughed. 'These intelligence types have more in common with each other than their political masters. And they regard people like us as disposable.'

People like us? Christ. Berlin felt a surge of indignation. 'I know what was delivered to the warehouse,' she said. It was petulant, but she had nothing to lose.

'Yeah?' he said, apparently unconcerned.

'Dead Chechens,' said Berlin.

'Who told you that?'

'Colonel Gerasimova.'

'She lied.'

'What do you mean?' asked Berlin.

'They were still alive,' he said.

Berlin couldn't see his face. The wind moaned and hurled packed snow from the treetops. Branches groaned and snapped under the strain. It sounded like gunfire.

While she had sat there peering at the control room monitor, dicking about with the computer, checking schedules, people were being murdered. In front of her very eyes. In a nondescript warehouse on a bleak industrial estate four days before Christmas.

'How many?' said Berlin.

'Five,' he said.

Blood thundered in her ears. She remembered the tears in Zayde's eyes. He whispered in his gravelly accent, 'Don't worry. They'll pay.' He slid a finger across his throat and gave her a solemn wink. They shared a special, scary secret.

Berlin realised she couldn't feel her feet. She was putting one in front of the other, moving in lockstep with the supervisor, as if they were tied together.

'And they – the government – just let the killers leave the country?' she said.

'*They*,' said the supervisor. He sneered. 'They weren't very keen on the Chechens either.'

'Why not just ship them out?' said Berlin.

'Human rights,' said the supervisor. 'It took them ten years to get rid of Abu Qatada. If you liquidate a few it puts the others off trying.'

'But what was the point if it was a secret?' said Berlin.

'Their comrades knew. The message was clear: we can get you, any time, anywhere. No-one is going to do a damn thing about it.'

'So it was win-win,' said Berlin. 'For the British, the Russians . . .'

'But not for me. I have to clean up the mess.'

He meant her.

It took an enormous effort to keep moving. She glanced at Nikki, plodding along. 'You promised Utkin you'd look after his son,' said Berlin. 'Will you?'

'Why don't you just shut up, Berlin?' he said. 'You're a fucking smart-arse.'

His smile was a snarl, as cold as the black night.

'Smart enough to suss out a prick like you,' she said.

'You know nothing, you stupid bitch, or you wouldn't be here.'

'I know you're a junkie and a killer,' said Berlin.

He stopped and turned to face her.

The wind howled around them. It threw up tiny shards of ice that scored Berlin's face. She watched him, caught in the same maelstrom. He didn't flinch.

'I wondered why those two men just stood there outside the warehouse after they'd finished unloading, having a smoke,' she said. 'They were waiting for you to come back.'

His eyes were black pits.

Berlin took a step, stumbled and went down on one knee in a deep drift.

The supervisor twitched and wiped his face with his hand. She'd managed to piss him off. He seemed about to speak, then reached inside his jacket.

Berlin was still on one knee. She tried to stand, wobbled and held out her hand.

He instinctively grabbed it to steady her.

A shot rang out.

92

For a moment Del didn't recognise the wasted, dishevelled figure that got out of the car. The border guard started waving his arms and shouting at her in Latvian; her vehicle was blocking the traffic.

Berlin took a few awkward steps and collapsed.

Del ran to her as a solidly built young man got out of the passenger seat, clutching a little dog. He stood between Del and Berlin. It was a protective gesture.

Del skirted around him and knelt down. He gently lifted Berlin's head out of the snow. The front of her coat was wet. 'Oh, Christ,' he said.

The young man stood very close, peering down, reading Del's face, as if he was trying to discern his motives.

Berlin opened her eyes. They were clear, but she was far away. Her face and hands were cracked with frostbite.

She gripped Del's arm and tried to lever herself up.

'Stay still,' said Del. 'There's blood everywhere.'

'It's okay, Del,' she croaked. 'It's not mine.'

Fagan lay in the forest, eyes wide, fixed on the treetops. The wind shook a branch, which shed a layer of snow on him. The buprenorphine was in his pocket. It would still be there when spring arrived.

93

Bella opened her front door as Berlin reached the landing. It had taken her a while to hobble up the stairs. She had spent ten days in a Latvian hospital with a drip stuck in her arm. Her feet and hands were still bandaged from the frostbite.

'What happened to you?' asked Bella. She had a parcel tucked under her arm.

'Don't ask,' said Berlin, fumbling to unlock her door.

Bella came over and gave her a hand. 'It's only just started,' she said. 'Bad luck's going to follow you all year. You haven't taken down your Christmas decorations.'

Berlin laughed.

'Here,' said Bella. She handed Berlin a parcel. 'The postman left this for you yesterday. It's good to have you back, love.'

'Thanks, Bella,' she said. 'It's good to be here.'

Berlin retrieved the emergency bottle of Talisker from under the sink and opened it with difficulty. The Yule log was on the table, a tired seasonal centrepiece. Del hadn't sent it. She swept it off the table.

One of the bright red holly berries chinked as it struck the square of tiles that were her kitchen floor.

She stomped on it.

Hirst had forgotten to include a greetings card with their listening device.

A long, hot bath had helped ease the pain in her blackened fingers and toes. A couple of double Scotches hadn't hurt, either. Now that was her only vice: a normal habit.

Her new mobile, courtesy of Burghley, burbled. She picked it up.

'Settling in?' said Del.

'There's no place like home,' said Berlin. 'How are things?'

'Can't complain,' said Del.

The Burghley partners had expressed their gratitude to Del with a new title and a bigger salary. Hush money. Burghley's reputation was intact and, in their business, reputation was everything.

'How's our friend?' said Berlin.

'He seems happy enough. Who knows? They've found a place that's secure. The therapists are going to try to "unlock" him.'

'I hope they've got plenty of sherbet lemons,' said Berlin. 'What about the dog?'

'Still in quarantine,' said Del. 'Have you seen the business pages?'

'Give me a break, Del,' said Berlin.

'Have a look,' he said. 'I'll be in touch soon.'

Berlin put her phone down and opened her new computer, also courtesy of Burghley. They had cleared her credit cards and paid her a handsome bonus, too.

She went to the BBC News site, not *The Sentinel*, to find the item Del meant. There was an article about a woman in Chigwell who claimed the police wouldn't look for her missing husband. A police spokesperson stated that as far as they were concerned he wasn't missing, he just didn't want to be found. There was no indication of foul play.

But the item of interest that Del had mentioned was buried in a column of 'New Company Appointments'.

Hirst Corporation were delighted to announce that Alexander Utkin, a former major in the Moscow Criminal Investigation Department, had been appointed General Manager of their new Russian subsidiary.

They had all been paid off.

She was clean, but felt dirty.

The parcel lay where she had dropped it, forgotten, on the sofa. She took a knife from the kitchen drawer and slit it open.

An old file tumbled out, stuffed with dozens of yellowing pages. A length of string had been carefully knotted around it to keep them secure inside.

She unpicked it.

The symbol emblazoned on the front indicated it was a government file. Some of the documents were typed, some handwritten. It made no difference. She couldn't read a word because it was all in Cyrillic. But she did recognise the small sepia photograph stuck inside the cover.

It was a young Zayde.

The phone rang again.

Berlin picked up. 'Hello,' she said.

'Well?' said Peggy. 'What have you got to say for yourself?'

Bella was right.

94

Berlin watched the moon shimmer and tremble in the wake of a barge. The city seemed different. Something had changed. She scanned the skyline. What was it?

Then she caught her own reflection in the water.

She touched her right shoulder, where she kept a permanent reminder that nothing would ever be the same.

A small blue teardrop.

ACKNOWLEDGEMENTS

To Daria Volokh of Ruslink Russian Language Centre in Melbourne, and Daniel Petrov of Moscow, I can only say a heartfelt 'Spasibo!' All errors are my own. To my editors, Tom Avery of William Heinemann and Arwen Summers of Penguin Australia, many thanks for your patience and perspicacity. Sarah Ballard, Zoe Ross, Georgina Gordon-Smith and Jessica Craig, of United Agents, work hard to keep me afloat. It's much appreciated. Sincere thanks to Ben Ball of Penguin Australia and Jason Arthur of William Heinemann for keeping the faith.

ALSO BY ANNIE HAUXWELL

In Her Blood

The first instalment in the Catherine Berlin series

'A stylishly written and assuredly paced debut that heralds a
promising new series.'
Financial Times

When heroin addict and investigator Catherine Berlin finds the
almost-headless body of her informant, 'Juliet Bravo', she is
unsurprised to discover the death is linked to a local loan shark.
But when Berlin's own unorthodox methods are blamed for the
murder, she realises bigger predators are circling.

Then, after stumbling upon the body of her GP (an unconventional
doctor who would still supply prescription heroin), Berlin begins
to fear for more than her job...

Suspended, incriminated, and then blackmailed into cooperation
by the detective leading the investigation, Catherine Berlin has
seven stolen days of clarity in which to solve the crime – and find
a new supplier.

'I'm hooked on Annie Hauxwell and hanging out for my next fix.'
Radio National Books and Arts Daily

arrow books

A Bitter Taste

The eagerly awaited second installment in the
Catherine Berlin series

*She was ten years old, but knew enough to wipe clean the handle
of the bloody kitchen knife. The night was stifling; the windows
were closed, sealing in the chaos. A table upturned, shattered
crockery. Her distraught mother, bare shoulders raw with welts,
knelt beside her motionless father. The child snatched up her
backpack, and ran...*

London sweats in the height of midsummer, and Catherine Berlin
hides her scars from prying eyes. At the methadone clinic, she
meets an old friend, Sonja Kvist, who begs her to help find her
missing daughter. But the case is not as straightforward as it first
appears, and Catherine soon realises that in order to find the girl,
she must tackle a far greater threat...

arrow books

dead
good

For all of you who find
a crime story irresistible.

Discover the very best crime and thriller books on our dedicated website – hand-picked by our editorial team so you have tailored recommendations to help you choose what to read next.

We'll introduce you to our favourite authors and the brightest new talent. Read exclusive interviews and specially commissioned features on everything from the best classic crime to our top ten TV detectives, join live webchats and speak to authors directly.

Plus our monthly book competition offers you the chance to win the latest crime fiction, and there are DVD box sets and digital devices to be won too.

Sign up for our newsletter at
www.deadgoodbooks.co.uk/signup

Join the conversation on: